My Man, My Boyz

A Novel by
Dwayne Vernon

NORCARJO Publishing
P O Box 47446
District Heights, Md 20753
www.norcarjo.com

Manufactured in the United States of America.

ISBN-978-0-615-14416-0

Editors
Cynthia Diane Lowe (cynthlowe@netscape.net)
Theresa Tellock, (tellock37@uwosh.edu)

Consulting by Life Changing Books
www.lifechangingbooks.net

Acknowledgements

Thank you God, for giving me the talent to write.

Thank you Mom (God rest her soul), Dad and Allyson for always pushing me to do my best.

Thanks to all my family, particularly Nora, Carlton, Joseph, Tonya, Calvin and Jarrod.

Thank you Angelo F. Hart of North Carolina, for telling me to write. Without your encouragement this project would not be.

Thank you to My Aunts, Zelma, Yvonne, Mae Mae, Helen and Cousins Cheryl Herron, Carmen Mbroh, Vera Cherry, Roy Carter, Jr. and Dorshell Clark for your guidance and acceptance.

Thank you to My Boyz - Mike Rogers, Larry Maddox, Robert Beatty, Curtis Cross, Brian H., Darryl M. Smith, Keith Warren and Hector Cruz you guys have always been supportive and had my back.

Thanks to Sharwyn Fryer, LaPhena Westray, Toni Ricks, Angie Davis, Lisa Walker, Lisa Cox and Ledra Dildy. My critics and true friends. Thanks for keeping it real and encouraging at the same time.

Thanks to Mia Harley and Ramona (Mona) Crowder for just being you, genuine, thoughtful and sharing people.

Thank you to Life Changing Books, for all the services that your company provided in helping me take this book to the next level.

Thank you to X-clusive Image Enterprises for all you've done.
www.x-clusiveimage.com

A Special, Special thanks to Donna Sheats, who played the most important role in me accomplishing this task. Reassuring me and rooting me on. You were my rock and I appreciate you thank you very much.

Chapter 1

On a humid Houston night, Tariff finished his dinner. As he sat at his dining room table, he stared at the sterling silver picture frame that hung prominently on the living room wall. He'd always loved his neighborhood of storybook houses and nicely trimmed lawns. Each evening, he sat listening to the mating chirps of crickets and the faint sounds of children being called in for dinner by their parents. Tonight, an overwhelming sense of loneliness churned in his stomach as he stared at the face of the only man he had ever been with; the only man he ever really loved.

The handsomely chiseled face in the photograph was that of Tariff's late boyfriend, James. The two met in high school and their friendship grew into an intimacy that rivaled the happiest of love stories.

James was a six foot two, dark chocolate brother with an athletic build that finely displayed his iron-hard upper body. Even with his loose clothing, you could see the rippling affect of his well-toned physique. His muscular chest and arms always protruded through his shirts as they threatened to shred the fine fabric with one flex. What Tariff liked most about James was his swagger. Not thuggish, but the perfect blend of confidence and masculinity.

As thoughts of James held Tariff frozen in time, his eyes welled up with tears. It was that fateful night two years ago when James was at Wash Express. Always a stickler for polished perfection, James was painstakingly washing his car; something he'd done many times before. "The Express," as it was called, was a spot where the locals would hang out, drink, smoke, and just kill time. Bruthas hit on ladies wearing denim shorts that looked sprayed on, while other guys just hung with their homeboys.

James pulled a dry shammy from the trunk of his Acura and began wiping away the beaded water on his hood and roof. Standing a few feet away was Tonya and her girl Barbara, a pair of ladies as common to The Express as the scented pine trees given away with every wash. Curtis, Carlton, and Chuck, hood rats who also frequented the spot, watched James' careful attention to his ride. Always smooth, James moved like an artist. Each wipe looked like a painter's brush strokes. His flow was soft, subtle, and constant.

"Man, look at how dude is detailin' that ride," Curtis commented to Carlton with mock admiration.

Carlton turned and looked in James' direction, "Man he could prolly drop somethin' on the floor and still eat it without kissin' it up to God." There was an uncomfortable collective laugh between them, before Curtis continued, "Dude is out here e'ry Saturday detailin' his shit like that. Man, Carlton, I ain't never seen no one be such a clean freak on they ride like dude is."

"Yeah, that is a nice car…too bad he gay, though!" Tonya said matter-of-factly. Her need to prove she was in-the-know outweighed the reality that she wasn't part of the guys' conversation.

"Girl, you trippin'! He don't look gay to me," Barbara spoke up. "How would you know anyway Tonya? He ain't ya type. He look like he come from money and all you ever go after are broke ass, wanna-be-balla thugs."

Tonya sucked her teeth. Without missing a beat, she

2

snapped her neck and retorted, "I know 'cause one of my girls tried to get with him and he told her."

"Dude is a faggot? Are you fo' real, Tonya?" Chuck blurted between chuckles.

Before Tonya could respond, Curtis said, "Man, I hate them muthafuckers!" As usual, Curtis gritted his teeth and balled his fist, displaying his angry reflex toward gays. Carlton leaned into Curtis and whispered, "Man, what 'chu say we car jack that niggah!"

"Are you for real, dude?" Curtis commented.

"Yeah, fool, what it do!" Carlton said, in a thick Houston twang. "We need to decide now, 'cause he 'bout to roll."

Tonya and Barbara overheard Curtis and Carlton talking and started to walk away. Barbara mumbled something about how crazy she thought they were. Tonya suddenly felt a guilty pang in the pit of her stomach, thinking maybe she had set off a chain of events with her chatty gossip.

The three hoods then hopped in their car and waited for James to put his shammy in the trunk and drive off. They followed James at a close distance, but were careful to not draw his attention by tailgating. Oblivious to the suspicious unmarked car behind him, James reached for his cell phone and called his baby, Tariff.

"Hey you, I was just going to call you," Tariff said. His voice telegraphed a warm smile. The one thing he looked forward to more than James were James' phone calls.

"Hey, baby, I should be home in about ten minutes. Do you need me to stop and pick up anything?"

"Naw, baby, I think we're all set for dinner. Just hurry home. I love you!" Tariff beamed through the phone. Even ten years into their relationship, their nightly dinners together were never routine.

"I love you, too. See you soon," James said. He hung up the phone and stopped at the light, still unaware of the predators lurking behind him.

Curtis spent the last ten minutes being prepped by his boys. He took one last puff of his blunt and held the pungent smoke in his lungs. It was time to initiate the jack. Curtis jumped from the passenger side as Carlton leaped from behind the wheel, leaving Chuck behind. They did a quick crisscross and flanked both sides of James' Acura.

"GET OUT THE CAR FAGGOT!" Curtis yelled. The shiny silver plated 9mm automatic catching the flicker from the lamp post overhead.

Startled, James turned and looked at Curtis. Fear and confusion filled his eyes.

"Man, I don't want no trouble," James stammered. He raised his hands, his arms trembling as though an arctic cold had suddenly overtaken him. Out of the corner of his eye, James could see a gun pointed at him from the passenger side of his car. While Carlton and Curtis pressed James for his car, Chuck slid into the driver's seat. He was ready to pull off at the first sign of trouble.

"Get out the fuckin' car, you fuckin' faggot! And leave yo wallet on the seat!" Curtis demanded, this time pointing the gun at James' temple. Carlton stayed at the passenger's side door, waiting for James to exit. James slowly slid out of the car. He was terrified of rattling the jackers. As he made his exit, the familiar Busta Rhymes' *I Love my Chick* ring tone went off. He knew it was Tariff calling.

Unconsciously, James reached for his cell phone. Just as he grabbed the phone, Curtis nervously pulled the trigger, firing a deadly shot to James' abdomen. For a second, James thought he'd been punched, but when he touched his stom-

ach he felt the sticky warmth of his blood. James was shot.
He struggled to stand, but collapsed to the pavement. Shock
and fear began to choke him and everything began to turn
white.

"Shit! Shit! Shit! Shit! Why that niggah have to move,
huh? Why he have to move?" Curtis yelled hysterically,
knocking himself in the head with his hand. Chuck sat in the
car, petrified, his head buried in the spokes of the steering
wheel. He kept repeating to himself, *"What did we do?
What did we do?"*

"Man, come on, let's go! You done killed dude we gotta
get the fuck outta here! Come on niggah, let's go!" Carlton
said, pulling Curtis away from the scene and into the waiting getaway car. "Move niggah!" Carlton snapped, pushing
a catatonic Chuck out of the driver's seat. With Curtis' head
spinning a mile a minute and Chuck whispering prayers to
himself, the three drove off, hoping that the horror of the
last five minutes was nothing more than a terrible nightmare.

James heard his cell phone ring for the second time. He
momentarily blocked out the sleepy sensation that was over-
taking him. He struggled to pull himself up on one elbow to
answer the familiar ring.

"Baby, where are you, you should have been here over
10 minutes ago," Tariff said chuckling with mock annoy-
ance.

James heard the words in his head and struggled to make
them leave his mouth. Finally, he faintly heard himself say,
"A couple of blocks away near Elm Avenue, I've been shot!"

Tariff felt the shot of adrenaline and panic hit him.
Before the words had completely settled in his brain, he
yelled, "I'm on my way baby, hold on, don't hang up!"

Tariff sprinted up the street toward where James lay dying. His pace didn't affect his dread-drenched words of support to his soul mate. He didn't want to lose the sound of James' voice. When Tariff reached James, his body dangled between the car door and the ground. He desperately looked around to see one of the neighbors coming around the corner. Tariff yelled for her to call 911 as he slammed his own cell phone to the ground and ran to James' side. Tariff slid down next to James and put his upper body in his lap as he waited for help to come.

"I'm sorry to spoil our anniversary, baby," James uttered with short breaths, his eyes almost completely closed.

The sound of James apologizing shattered Tariff's heart. "You didn't spoil anything baby. We're goin' to have plenty more to celebrate," Tariff said, tears streaming down his cheeks. James could feel the life force slipping out of his wounded body. James suddenly started to see a warm soft light, and the sound of Tariff's voice grew muffled and faint. He fought to look at Tariff, but his vision became blurry and all he could think about was whatever was waiting for him on the other side.

"Listen, Tariff," James dribbled out, "I want you to know that I have always loved you and I always will. Baby…" James paused before continuing, "if I don't make it I want you to know I will still be with you. As he felt his heart drumming to a slower beat, he finally said, "But I want you to love again, okay?"

Tariff shook his head from side to side in disagreement, not wanting to hear what James was saying to him. "Don't talk like that James, just hold on for a little longer. It's going to be alright. You're not going anywhere." Realizing that time was rushing by, Tariff looked up frantically, eyes darting from corner to corner, wishing to see flashing lights and hear siren sounds of hope, but there were none. The cool and eerie silence told the story. As Tariff looked back down at James, he had closed his eyes. They would never open again. Rocking James in his arms, Tariff cried and kissed James' lips.

The sound of the phone ringing brought Tariff back to the present. He felt the tears leaving his chin and, wiping them away, he walked to the phone somberly answering, "Hello."

"Hey, man, what's up? You sound a little down. Did you have another one of those flashbacks?" Mike asked from the other end.

"I'm ok, what's up with you?" Tariff tried very hard not to let his best friend, Mike, truly hear the pain he was feeling come across on the phone.

Mike picked up on it right away. "Man, you sure you okay?"

"Yeah, everything's cool. I hear congratulations are in order," Tariff said, attempting to pep himself up.

"Yeah, you know it! I got that promotion I was waiting for. In fact, that's why I'm calling. The other guys and I are meeting tonight for a celebratory drink and I figured if you weren't busy, you might wanna come out for a bit."

"You know I'll be there. I just need to take a shower and get myself together," Tariff responded, looking over at the clock to see what time it was. "I'll be there around 9:30. Is that cool?"

"Cool. We'll see you then."

Just before Tariff hung up the phone, Mike said, "It will get better, I promise you…and I love you, man. I'll always be here for you, cool?"

"Thanks, man, I appreciate that and I love you too, bruh!" Mike and Tariff said their goodbyes and Tariff headed upstairs to get ready. He stopped and looked over at his reflection in the closet door mirrors. He marveled at his six-foot frame, his 195 pounds of smooth, dark-chocolate tone. He was one not to work out consistently, and looking at his physique, you could see most of it was genetics. The broadness of his shoulders and the six pack abs that looked as though they were drawn on his stomach made him feel a little better about himself. He couldn't help but look at his small but round ass, and perfectly formed legs for a man of his size. He was a well put together brutha with a lot to offer when the time was right. If that time were to ever come again.

Chapter 2

In the locker room, used towels were everywhere, hanging off benches and lying on the floor. The room had a strong scent of masculinity. The aroma of different colognes, as well as the scent of Ben Gay and Icy Hot hung in the air. Football equipment lay strewn about in front of the lockers. Players sat on the benches trying to get a quick rest before getting dressed and going on their way. Sounds of showers running and loud conversations echoed throughout the locker room.

Reese had just gotten out of the shower. He had been at practice most of the day. While getting dressed, he began talking with a couple of his teammates, Antoine and Keith, who were also on the practice squad. All of them were looking forward to the day when the coach would call them into his office to tell them they would be signed to the team. Reese had gotten hurt in his senior year of college. It was the last game of the season and Reese had just run the ball for a first down. As he was tackled, one of his teammates was pushed and landed on both of Reese's knees, causing one knee to twist into an abnormal position. Reese had to be carted off the field, unable to walk. His NFL career had come to an abrupt end in a split second. Unable to make the draft, he went through a depression. But never gave up on his dream of being in the NFL, so he continued to work with a conditioning and strengthening coach. Mike, Reese's lover of six years, always encouraged him not to give up. Reese sometimes wished he had Mike's confidence. Mike always lived by the glass being half full theory. Reese was afraid that no team would take a chance on him. He felt coaches would think he was too old and wouldn't make it, but he pushed himself everyday to the limit, determined to prove them all wrong. His conditioning coach was able to get him onto the practice squad of the team. They both felt that if coaches could see him practicing he would have a better shot of making it. Reese knew this was his one and only shot. As Reese looked at the clock on the wall, he saw that he needed to get dressed quickly so he could get out of there and meet the guys for Mike's celebration. Reese was startled by his coach's voice.

"Reese, could you come into my office after you get dressed?"

"Sure, Coach, I'll be right in," Reese said, as he watched the coach disappear behind his door, his mind began to wander. Could this be the break he'd been practicing so hard for or was this the end of his dream? Reese tried to keep optimistic thoughts in his head. Shaking the conflicting thoughts away, Reese grabbed his jacket from the locker. As he slid an arm through, a small box tumbled out of his pocket. He picked it up and opened it. It was the rings he had bought for him and Mike about a week ago. It was two rings made of silver, neither Mike nor Reese liked gold. They felt gold was played out. Under the dim lights in the locker room, you could still see the shiny reflections coming from the rings.

This was a special night for Mike, and Reese wanted to make it even more special. He took one last look at the rings before closing the box and putting it back into his pocket. As he walked to the coach's office, he patted the pocket where the small box sat for luck. He took a deep breath and knocked on the door.

Coach Thomas' chatter ceased. He yelled for Reese to enter. As Reese opened the door, he saw Antoine shaking the coach's hand. Reese and Antoine both eyed each other and as Antoine walked by, he smiled and winked at Reese. Reese didn't know what to make of Antoine's gesture. In Antoine's own little way he was trying to let Reese know not to worry.

"So Reese," the coach started to speak, "how do you think practice has been going?" Reese thought for a second, tried to clear all the thoughts jumping around in his head and focused on the question the coach just asked him.

"Well Coach, I think I've been doing pretty good in practice. As you can see, my knees are fine and I've gotten my speed back. Since I've started working out, I have more strength in my legs and it's harder for players to tackle me."

The coach smiled and said, "I agree. You are in pretty good shape. You surprised a lot of us here. Now, back to why I called you here today…It appears our starting running back has a fractured bone in his foot. It looks like he's going to be out for the next three to four months, maybe more. It all depends on the x-rays. So what I've decided to do is to sign you onto the team as our starting running back."

Starting running back? Did I just hear that right? Reese couldn't believe what the coach had said. He tried hard not to jump out of his seat. The coach went on speaking, but Reese was still trying to comprehend what he had just heard.

"So, do you think you're ready for this?" the coach asked.

Reese sat up straight and responded to the coach with much confidence, "Yeah, Coach, I can handle it. I won't let

11

you down."

Coach responded with a smile, "I know you won't. I'm having the contract drawn up as we speak, and in the next day or two we will go over the specs of it all."

Standing with a broad grin on his face, Reese thanked the coach. As Reese walked out of the door, he spotted Antoine sitting on a bench, stuffing his gym bag. Antoine immediately stood up when he noticed Reese approaching.

"Well?" Antoine asked eagerly, "did you get signed?" Reese smiled, and couldn't contain his excitement.

"Yeah, I did."

"Well, what about you?" Reese asked.

Antoine smiled back, "Yeah, man, I did too. I will be the starting line backer now that Bruce signed with another team." As they both jumped up and down they slapped each other a high five, acting like children. As the guys in the locker room watched, they knew exactly what the two were celebrating. Reese paused for a second and put both his hands on Antoine's shoulder.

"Look man," Reese said, "we have to show the Coach that he made the right decision."

Antoine shook his head in agreement and said, "Lets go out and celebrate."

Reese nodded his head, "Man, I would love to, but I have a previous engagement." They congratulated each other one last time and Reese walked out to his car. After Reese shut the door, he sat for a moment, soaking up the recent news. He grabbed the steering wheel, and put his head between his hands. He couldn't believe that everything he worked so hard for was about to come true. Overwhelmed by the fear of not doing well and not knowing what to expect, he just thought of what Mike would tell him.

Reese's cell phone rang, shaking him from his thoughts. He immediately reached into his coat and, not finding it, patted himself down. By the time he found the phone, the call had already gone to voice mail. He looked at the caller ID and saw it was Mike. He smiled happily and called him back.

"Hey sweetheart," Mike said as he answered.

"'Sup baby boy," Reese replied as he absentmindedly ran his fingers through his curly hair.

"I talked to all the guys and everyone will be at the club tonight," Mike said.

"I should be there in an hour or so," Reese replied. Mike slyly asked. "So what will you be wearing?"

Reese responded coyly, "Those black jeans that you love seeing me in so much."

"Can't wait to see you," Mike said smiling through the phone.

"Ditto."

They said their goodbyes, their usual I love you's, and hung up. After Mike hung up, Reese sat still, deep in thought, his hands tapping the steering wheel as if it were a drum. After a few minutes, he decided he would wait and tell Mike, after the celebration, about his meeting with the coach. He wanted this night to be about Mike, because he was so proud of him, but one thing he did know was that he would get there before everyone else and give Mike the ring. As Reese started his car and proceeded to drive off, he knew that finally, his life was headed in the right direction.

Chapter 3

An hour or so later, Mike sat at a table with his back to the door, waiting for the guys to arrive. Reese walked in carrying his five feet, ten inch, true running back's physique. He weighed in at a solid 210 pounds and his size was evenly distributed between his bulging arms and thick muscular legs. From the corner of his almond shape eyes, he could see a group of queens who sat in a booth pointing at him, watching his every move. As he scanned the club looking for Mike, he chuckled to see some of the queens kicking their legs up as if they were challenging each other. He turned the heads of all the men in the club. Finally, he saw Mike and walked up behind him, kissing him on the neck, "'Sup, baby boy?"

Mike, who was five feet, eleven inches, slim and dark skinned, could almost pass for Morris Chestnut. He had the same sexy smile and pretty white teeth.

"'Sup you! You finally made it! How was your day?" Mike asked as he flashed that Colgate smile.

"It was good, but my day has just gotten better now that I've seen you." Mike blushed and beamed a huge smile, looking at his mate of 6 years.

Reese smiled, "Yeah everything was good, real good."
"I'm glad to hear that, and I know one of these days that coach of yours is going to see just how good my man is and bring him on to the team. I know they see something 'cause they signed you to the practice squad. I have faith in you, baby," Mike said, reassuring his man and being his opti-

mistic self.

Reese wanted to tell Mike about his practice today and his conversation with his coach, but decided against it until he signed the contract and things were final. He didn't want to get Mike's hopes up and he had to make sure he wasn't still dreaming himself.

Reese looked at Mike, "I'm glad we're the first ones here. I wanted to talk to you about something." Mike's smile quickly diminished. He didn't know what it was that had Reese looking so serious.

"What's up, sweetheart?" Mike asked, hesitantly.

"I just wanted you to know that I am so proud of you. You have always set your goals and stayed focused to get them accomplished. Look at you, you're now the Head Manager of one of the top IT departments in the country. They couldn't have made a better decision."

Mike sighed with relief, then smiled again, even bigger than before.

Moving closer to Mike, Reese reached into his coat pocket and pulled out the velvet box. "I've loved you since the day we met at that dinner party. Who would have thought that six years later, you would have made these the best six years of my life. No one can come close to loving you like I do. You've always stood behind me and you've always been there to catch me when I fell. What more on this earth could anyone ask for? You have become my fresh air in this polluted world."

Listening intently to Reese, Mike's big brown eyes started to well up with tears that were threatening to fall.

"I give you this ring and commit myself to you for the rest of my life. If it were legal to marry you, I would, but this is as close to it as we're going to get. This ring is a sign of my commitment to love you and to always be there for you, as you have been for me. These rings are a match because I want the world to know that I am committed to the love of my life," Reese continued.

The well of tears became a waterfall running down Mike's cheeks, blurring his vision.

"Those are the only tears that I ever want to bring to your eyes…tears of joy. I love you, baby boy."

Choking back tears, Mike managed to say, "I love you too!" The two shared an intimate kiss just as the rest of the group started to arrive. Jay, Demetrious, and Tyrell all looked at each other then at Mike and Reese, trying to figure out what they had just interrupted between the two.

Tyrell, in typical fashion, was the first to say something. "What up, dawgs?"

Demetrious added his little bit. "What did we just interrupt here?" Everyone laughed, knowing they had just caught a tender moment, but didn't know what it was about.

"So where's Tariff?" Demetrious asked as he looked around the club.

"He should be here any minute now, I hope," Mike said in between sniffles.

Just before Tariff walked up, Jay piped in, "So D, are you two dating or something…What's going on?"

With a big smile on his face, he said, "Naw, we're just close friends."

Just then, Tariff walked in and everyone turned and looked at him with big smiles on their faces.

"'Sup guys?" Tariff asked with raised brows, coming in on the tail end. The group greeted Tariff warmly and started the celebration for Mike's promotion.

A good while later, the whole group laughed and drank

martinis and cosmos as Tariff cleared his throat to get everyone's attention. He lifted his glass in a toast to Mike.

"To our best friend, Mike, I couldn't think of a more deserving person than you. May God continue to bless you with your desires. He's already given you a good job and a good man. May he continue to keep your blessings flowing."

The whole group joined in cheers of "Here! Here! Here!" Demetrious and Tariff stole a glance at each other and smiled. Tariff liked Demetrious' smooth, almost flawless skin, not a pimple or blemish in sight. Demetrious' skin was pecan brown. His eyes looked almost Asian. Demetrious' hair, was a little straighter than most black men. He was tall and lanky, and always maintained a well toned body.

After all the toasting, Mike started to walk toward the bathroom and Tariff caught up to him. Once inside the bathroom, Mike showed Tariff the ring.

"Man, what is this?" Tariff asked in surprise.

"Reese committed himself to me tonight," Mike beamed.

"You are so lucky, man. Never take him for granted. Here today, but may be gone tomorrow," Tariff said, remembering what happened to James.

"Trust me, I know a good man when I see one. I'm in it for the long haul. The same thing is going to come to you when you least expect it."

"I hope so," Tariff said, not sure if he really believed it.

When Mike and Tariff returned from the bathroom, the guys were putting on their coats and saying their goodnights. Tariff spoke up before Mike. "Man, y'all calling it a night already?"

Jay responded, "I'm meeting my boy, Daunte for breakfast tomorrow. He has something he wants to talk to me about."

The group bellowed a chorus with "Awws."
Demetrious added, "So is this a new man you ain't telling us about?"

Tariff co-signed with a nod, as he gave Jay a friendly push.

"Yeah Jay, What's that about?" Tyrell chimed in. "Look guys," Tyrell continued, "he got the freshly trimmed five o'clock shadow going on and the diamond sparkling in his ear.

"Noooo! Noooo! Actually, he's one of my straight friends. He doesn't know about me."

"Yeah okay, if that is the case. Just be careful of those straight guys," Tyrell offered a word of caution, "for some reason they think that because you're gay, you want them. They don't think gay men and straight men can just be friends. They think we always have an ulterior motive."

"You're right about that," Jay said. "I'll talk to you guys later, be careful getting home. Jay replied going into his protective mode. "Yo, Mike, congratulations again. I love you, boy!"

They all hugged Jay before he walked toward the door.

"Hey, Tariff, can I get a ride with you man? I left my car at home and took a taxi here straight from work," Demetrious asked, grabbing Tariff's arm before he headed out the door.

"Sure, man, no problem." They headed out together toward Tariff's car that was parked on the other side of the parking lot.

"I appreciate the ride, Tariff," Demetrious said.

"I told you it wasn't a problem. I go past your house on

my way home anyway."

"Man, this was a long day, but Mike's doing so well, I wouldn't have missed this night for the world," Demetrious added, making conversation on the drive home.

"I know what you mean," Tariff said through a wide open yawn.

"Man, you look tired. Tell you what, why don't you just crash at my crib and then drive home in the morning?" Demetrious offered.

"I don't want to put you out."

"It won't be a problem. Besides, I'll feel better knowing you're safe and not driving half asleep."

"Cool." Just as the word left Tariff's mouth, he pulled up into Demetrious' driveway. He didn't live that far from the club. They both lazily got out of the car and took what seemed like the never ending walk to Demetrious' door. Demetrious pulled out his keys and turned the lock before crossing the threshold of his home. He reached in and flicked on the light beside the door. Tariff followed right behind him into the living room. They both plopped heavily down onto the chocolate leather sleeper sofa and started to chit chat about the events of the day, and what they had planned for the next day.

Tariff told Demetrious that he was having lunch with Mimi tomorrow. "Oh yeah, she was at the shop for a minute or two today and didn't even mention it," Demetrious said.

"She comes by the barbershop pretty frequently, doesn't she?"

"Yeah, she's my diversion," Demetrious replied. "The guys at the shop are always trying to get into everybody's business. So, to make sure there's no friction on the job, she stops by and acts as if she's my girlfriend. I even have a picture of the two of us on my stand."

"Man, is it worth going through all of that?" Tariff asked.

"I don't know, but you know straight bruthas have too many insecurities and the minute they find out that you're gay, they looked at everything you do as a come on to them. I only have a couple of months left before I go to a new shop, so it's just until then. Besides, I think Mimi's boyfriend is getting the wrong idea about us."

"Well, you can't really blame him, can you? Mimi needs to tell him so there's no misunderstanding." Tariff suddenly changed the subject and looked at a picture on Demetrious' coffee table. "You have a nice looking family. That's a new picture I see. Are you guys close?"

"Yeah, we're pretty close. We just took that picture a few weeks ago. My dad keeps asking me when I'm going to get married and have kids and I keep telling him I'm not ready. I wish he would just drop it."

"Why don't you just tell him the truth?" Tariff questioned again, challenging Demetrious' coming out.

"I wish it were just that simple. My father is so old school, I'm afraid if I tell him, I'll lose my family."

"I feel you man. It took my family a while to get over it, but the bottom line is it's not about them. This is my life and I have to live it my way. Their only job is to love me and accept me as I am. If they couldn't or wouldn't do that, then that would be something they had to deal with. But they eventually came around."

A few quiet moments passed. All they could hear was the ticking of the clock that sat on the end table next to the sofa. Feeling a sudden rush of attraction, Demetrious moved clos-er to Tariff on the sofa and grabbed his hand. Tariff was caught off guard, but at the same time he didn't mind, because it felt good, and he was starting to like Demetrious a lot. Demetrious started to stroke the side of Tariff's face. They both just sat there, looking into each other's eyes. Demetrious leaned in and gave Tariff a long passionate kiss. Suddenly Demetrious pulled back and whispered in Tariff's ear, "I guess we should get ready for bed?"

Not saying a word, Demetrious went upstairs to pull back the covers on his bed and pick up his room a little bit before Tariff came up. Tariff sat quietly on the sofa, confused, feeling as if he were cheating on his late love. Demetrious gave his room a once over before he headed back downstairs to get Tariff. As he came down the stairs, Demetrious noticed that Tariff wasn't on the sofa where he left him. He walked around the end of the sofa and noticed that Tariff had fallen asleep. He pulled the blanket off the back of the sofa, kissed him on his forehead, and whispered, "Good night," although Tariff couldn't hear him. He turned and went back upstairs to his room and removed his clothes. Demetrious climbed into bed and almost instantly drifted off to sleep.

Tariff entered Demetrious' room with no clothes on and slid into bed next to Demetrious. Demetrious pulled him close, gently kissing him, taking his bottom lip into his mouth. Slightly biting Demetrious' lips, Tariff responded with more passionate kisses, erections growing on both ends, full and hard, Demetrious flipped Tariff, made his way on top, and then licked the nape of his neck, then down his body. With every touch of Demetrious' tongue, Tariff let out a soft moan, then another, his moans growing louder with each lick. Tariff repositioned himself and made his way down to Demetrious' waiting and erect manhood, slowly taking him into his mouth, eventually putting in every inch.

Demetrious struggled to get away from the feel and warmth of Tariff's mouth, but Tariff pulled him back down, to satisfy him even more. Demetrious moved Tariff to the middle of the bed and somehow managed to release his manhood long enough to turn him over again. He licked Tariff's back, down the center, then lifted Tariff's ass in the air. In a quick gesture, Demetrious grabbed a condom from the nightstand and slowly slid it down his hard shaft. He nudged Tariff's legs apart so he could get into a good position. Tariff relaxed as Demetrious took his finger and slid it inside of him to apply the lube. Demetrious felt the warmth as he entered at a slow and cautious pace to ensure that his man was being satisfied. Eventually, all nine inches of hard chocolate was inside. The deeper he went, the more Tariff moved with him. Their love making filled the room, just as Demetrious yelled out, "Baby, I'm coming! I'm about to..." The alarm clock went off and Demetrious woke from his dream with sweat running down his chest and his penis hard as a rock, throbbing.

He got out of bed and walked downstairs only to find that Tariff had already left and gone home, but not without leaving a note:

Thanks for letting me crash here. I slept pretty good. I came up to your room, but you were sleeping so peacefully I didn't want to wake you. I'll see you at dinner tonight. Thanks again,

Tariff

Demetrious sat back and looked up to the ceiling, then closed his eyes and started to smile, thinking about the dream he'd just had, about Tariff, before his alarm went off and spoiled his soon to come true fantasy.

Chapter 4

At about 8:00 in the morning, Jay sat at a breakfast table in a restaurant not far from where he lived. He liked this particular restaurant because it was never really crowded. It was a small diner that made the best breakfast. As Jay looked around, he noticed the older black man that was there every time he came. This man always sat at the same table drinking coffee and reading the paper. This particular morning, Jay also noticed that there were more people in the place than usual. The smell of bacon filled the air and the sound of the spatula as it hit the grill. The waiters and wait-ress rushed from table to table, making sure they didn't keep their customers waiting too long. Jay grabbed his head as he heard a few dishes being dropped in the kitchen. Jay was waiting for Daunte to show. Jay's dark aviator shades hid his bloodshot eyes as he slowly sipped on his a coffee. Trying to get over the previous night of drinking. As he leaned back, Jay caught his reflection in the metal napkin holder and groaned. Jay was normally a clean cut guy, but this par-ticular morning, who would have known?

"Damn man, looks like you tied one on last night!" Daunte said, walking up to Jay.

"Yeah, do you think you could whisper?" he said with a pleading smile. "I was out drinking with the fellas and cele-brated a little too hard."

"I can tell," he said loudly. "Yo, why you never invite me out wit you and your boyz?" Daunte asked.

"Jesus," Jay whispered cradling his temples, "I will next

time. What did you need to talk to me about?" Jay asked, changing the subject.

"Damn, dude, you in a hurry or something?" Daunte asked, surprised by Jay's abrupt question.

"Sorry man, I'm just a little under it, that's all."

Jay pulled off his shades to show Daunte his eyes. He didn't want him to think there was anything wrong.

"Well, dude, it's like this. It's my girl…I think she dippin' out on me!"

"Whoa, why you think that?" Jay asked.

"She's always on the phone with this guy she claims is just an old close friend, but yet I ain't never met him. I don't know, she tells me not to be jealous 'cause it's not what I think."

"Don't you believe her? I mean, why would she lie to you? You have to trust her. How long have you been together?" Jay rambled, question after question.

As if he didn't hear Jay, Daunte continued, "About a year from now, I plan to marry this girl. I don't know if I told you, but she was married once before, but she doesn't ever talk about it. She did say she'd tell me about it one day. When I met her she had just moved here from Charlotte. 'Making a fresh start of things' is what she called it."

Jay looked down into his coffee cup and then back at Daunte, who had suddenly stopped rambling and was now focused on something behind him. He sat still with a wild expression on his face. Staring past Jay, Daunte had his eyes locked on the scene over Jay's shoulder.

"Those two guys over there were holding hands," Daunte said in disbelief. "I hate gay people, dude!" Daunte spit, "They all are going to hell."

"Say what?" Jay replied in disbelief as he leaned back in

his chair.

Daunte repeated himself, "I said they going to hell!"

Holding in his anger, Jay responded, "Why would you say that?"

"'Cause sleeping with the same sex is wrong. The Bible says so!"

"Well, in the Bible, it also says it's a sin to lie, curse your parents, sleep with a woman out of wedlock or while she's on her period. I'm sure you've done one of the above, if not all." Jay quickly responded, his wit catching Daunte off guard.

"Dude, that's something totally different."

"How is that different?" *I know he's not serious,* Jay thought.

"It just is. There are different types of sin. Some are worse than others. The Bible says it, Jay. *Man should not lay with man as he does with woman...* it's an abomination. An abomination, dude!" Danute continued. "I don't know what you thinking, but don't no where else does it say abomination, you feel me?"

Past irritated and feeling himself ready to throw what remained of his coffee in Daunte's hypocritical face, Jay said, "You know what really gets me about people and their interpretation of the Bible? They're always trying to make homosexuality a bigger sin than every other sin. I was brought up to believe that no one sin is greater than the other and before people start judging and making comments like that, they should make sure they got their own shit together. Man, I got to go. I'll talk to you later." With that said, Jay tossed some money on the table for his coffee, grabbed his shades and coat, and walked out the door.

Looking puzzled, Daunte leaned back in his seat, not

knowing what to think about what just happened between him and Jay. He continued staring angrily at the happy couple, a hatred brewing in his chest that was about to boil over.

Chapter 5

As Tariff headed into the Amazon Grill to meet Mimi for
lunch, he heard her from the parking garage. The Amazon
Grill was one of their favorite spots. They were known in
the area for their seafood. The restaurant was on the 20th
floor, which was also the top floor. The place was nick-
named "Heaven," a credit to the view. The tables were
draped with white table clothes. In the center of the table
were candles that were lit and sat inside a small bouquet of
blue and white flowers. Sounds of light jazz flowed through
the restaurant. The room had a very intimate setting.

"Hey Mimi, how are you?" Tariff said between a hug
and kiss.

"I'm fine, baby. Tariff why do you call me Mimi when
my name is Mia? My sister is the only person that calls me
Mimi well except for you and Demetrious of course."

"Tariff smiled, no reason I've just gotten use to calling
you that."

Mia stood about 5'8 inches, but to see her in heels anyone would think she was closer to 5'10" tall. She was thin,
but thick in all the right places. Her Issey Miyake perfume
lingered in Tariff's nostrils as he stood smiling at her. She
was dressed conservatively, but sexy, as usual. Mimi's complexion was creamy, smooth caramel. She didn't have to
wear much make-up, because people always told her she
looked like a supermodel. Mimi's hair was long enough for
her to wear up or down. At work she always wore it pulled
back and in a bun. She felt that it made her look more in

charge especially since men didn't take pretty women seriously in the work place. Tariff couldn't help but think how beautiful, almost regal she looked.

"That must have been some phone call you were on when I walked up. I saw that smirk on your face."

"Go 'head," Tariff blushed. "That was just a message from Demetrious. We're having dinner together later, so he was just calling to confirm the time."

"So what's going on there?" Mimi teased.

"What do you mean?" Tariff asked, stepping aside so she could enter the elevator. The elevator was full. Mimi grabbed Tariff's arm to steady herself. After a few stops, they finally reached the restaurant. The hostess greeted them and led them to their table. Once the hostess walked away, Mimi set her purse down and looked at Tariff.

"Ok, now, don't answer me with a question, give up the dirt," Mimi insisted.

Tariff let out a brief sigh. "Demetrious is a nice guy and all, we've been kind of hanging out for about four months or so. That's about it." Tilting her head and smiling, Mimi looked at Tariff.

"Well, you know what they say, it hits you when you least expect it. Next thing you know, you guys will be in love. I think that would be good for both of you," Mimi said.

"God I love her," he thought, *she's such a mother hen.* "You're a trip! So what's going on in your life? How are things with the boyfriend going?" Tariff asked, happy to change the subject.

"Actually, things are going pretty well." Mimi paused and smiled at him before she continued. "He wants to marry me."

"Aww, Mimi, baby, that's wassup! I would think you'd be ecstatic, but you sound like you're not completely sure. What's going on?" He hoped there was nothing serious.

"No, I do and nothing's going on. You know I was married before and I sort of lost trust in men," Mimi replied, looking suddenly distant.

"I understand, but you can't punish the entire male species for what one man did. What exactly happened that made you so distrustful?"

"It's just too much to get into, but I will some day. The only problem we have is that he doesn't trust me. He thinks that I'm cheating on him," Mimi said, as she abruptly opened her menu.

"What would make him think something like that?"

"I think it's my friendship with Demetrious. I tried to explain to him that D and I are only friends and it's not that type of relationship."

"Have you explained to him that Demetrious is gay and you're just helping him cover that up while he works at the barbershop?" Tariff demanded, between sips of his water.

"Oh, hell no! You don't know Daunte like I do. He has this underlying dislike for gay men. Well, now that I think about it, it's not underlying at all. He hates gay people, period! I don't understand why, but I guess I do owe him an explanation."

"That would be good, because you know a situation like that could get all twisted and cause more problems than necessary."

"So, Tariff, what's with you and Demetrious? Don't think for a minute that I forgot," Mimi asked, as she played with her earring.

"Leave it alone, Mimi! There's no story to tell," Tariff

said one last time before they ordered their lunch. Mimi watched as he ate, thinking why does he always separate his food?

Finally Mimi asked, "Does Demetrious separate your food when he fixes you a plate?"

Tariff smiled at her with his eyes crinkling, "Are you going there again?"

Mimi pleaded, "I'll leave it for now. Next time we're together I want details."

"You're so generous," Tariff said sarcastically.

When the two finished their lunch, the waiter came over with the check. Tariff grabbed it and smiled, "You paid for the last lunch. I got this one." Mimi slipped her credit card back in her purse and sipped what remained of her martini. They both get up to leave. Tariff walked Mimi to her car, kissed her on the cheek. Quickly they hugged and said their good-byes.

*   *   *

The last couple of weeks Jay had been working on a big project for his office. Lately it was work, the gym and back home, but no matter how busy Jay got, he always found time to call his boyz and check to make sure they were okay. Jay began to look over some spreadsheets he had been working on. Jay's love for numbers, made him a perfect accountant. He loved his job and was good at what he did. Jay was 31 years old, but looked much younger, and he used this to his advantage. He was always in the gym. Some called him a gym rat. He loved the compliments he got so that pushed him to work out even harder. Jay's complexion was on the light side, his hair was cut fairly short, sporting the waves. He hated being a called "pretty boy." He preferred to be called handsome.

Jay always wanted harmony amongst his friends and family, but since he couldn't get that from his family, he sought it more from his friends. Jay's eyes made their way to the pile of messages sitting on his desk. He saw a couple of messages from Mike and he saw a reminder he had written to himself to call Tyrell. He was a little worried about Ty, a nickname they sometimes called him. Ty had been missing in action since Mike's little celebration. Even before then, Ty had been somewhat reclusive and that was not normal for him. Jay decided since he had a minute he needed to call his boy and find out what was the real deal.

"'Sup, Ty? Where you been hiding? We've barely heard from you since Mike's celebration," Jay asked.

As he rubbed his square chin Tyrell said, "Man, I've just been really busy here at work."

"Mmmm," Jay murmured, slightly twisting his lips. "Who is he? What's his name? Where did you meet him?"

"Who is who?" Tyrell questioned, his voice slightly cracking.

"The guy that's keeping you from your friends, punk! You know what I mean."

"Go 'head with that, man, it's not like that. We've just been hanging out. You know how that is. He seems pretty cool, but it's nothing serious," Tyrell said, looking at the pile of work on his desk and preparing for the inquisition.

"So what's the real story? How did you guys meet? You know, the particulars," Jay relentlessly quizzed.

"Okay, dude Damn! You should've been a detective the

way you interrogate! He works downstairs in our copy center. I think he's been here about 10 months."

"Okay, keep going!" Jay said, fully immersed in Tyrell's details.

"I saw him for the first time about 7 months ago. We have some new job training program that gives opportunities to those who wouldn't typically get hired. You know, the ones with not much experience.

"So you gawking over some dude at your job?" Come on, Ty, you know you don't shit where you eat. That's bad business! It could blow up in your face if you two get together and it doesn't work out. Besides, you haven't mentioned this guy to any of us at all."

Nervously Tyrell stated as he scratched his perfectly tapered cut head. "Yeah, I know, but, like I said, it's nothing that serious and the only time I'll run into him is when I'm leaving from work." Tyrell regretted his lies, but felt it was necessary.

Jay's other line buzzed. "Hold on that's my other line… Hello, Jay speaking, how can I help you?"

Mike's voice boomed from the other end, "'Sup, bruh?"

"What's up, boy, what's happening on that end?" Jay asked.

"Nothing much, you know how we do. Look, check this out! Reese and I have some news we'd like to share with the gang. So, if you're free Saturday night, we'd like for you to come by so we can chat. I've already talked to Tariff and Demetrious."

"Sure, I can make it, but what's it all about?" Jay interrupted.

"Sorry man, you just have to wait 'til you get here on Saturday," Mike giggled.

"Can't you at least give a brutha a hint?"

"Of course! The hint is Reese and I have some info to share with you guys and I'm not telling you anything else," Mike teased.

Knowing Mike couldn't keep a secret, Jay laughed. "Mike, you crack me up."

"Well, I need to go so I can hit Tyrell up and let him know," Mike said.

"He's holding on the other line. Want me to fill him in?" Jay replied.

"Yeah, that's cool. That man's been missing in action. Must be a new man in his life. You know how we do when we meet a new man." Mike laughed to himself thinking back on when he met Reese.

Jay responded, "Yeah, I know. We've all done a ducking act one time or another."

"Just tell him I expect to see him there Saturday, cool?"

"Alright man. Later." Jay clicked back over to Tyrell. "Sorry 'bout that, You still there?"

"Yeah, niggah, I'm here! Another ten seconds and I was about to introduce you to Mr. Click," Tyrell jokingly snapped.

"Don't do me like that. That was Mike. He and Reese are having us all over on Saturday night. They have some news to share."

"What's that all about?" Tyrell asked.

"I'm not sure. I tried to get him to give me a hint, but he wouldn't give up a thing."

Tyrell laughed, "Man, you know Mike usually can't keep a secret. Must be big."

"Must be," Jay replied.

"I hate to cut you short, man, but its lunch time. I'm

about to run out and grab a bite, but I'll see you guys on Saturday." Tyrell said, rushing Jay off the phone.

"Alright. I'll see you then and you can finish telling me about your new friend, cool?"

"Bet!" Tyrell responded. He hung up the phone and left his office.

Taking the elevator to the lobby, Tyrell walked out the double glass doors trying to decide where to get his lunch. A rich, familiar baritone voice broke his thoughts.

"Yo, I been calling you for a minute. Where you headed?"

"What's up, Chuck, how is your day going?" Tyrell replied, a slight smile forming on his face. Chucks presence was a welcomed one.

"Everything is good man, I'm just about to go and work out during my lunch break. "Where you headed?"

"I'm not sure. Probably down to the café on the corner to grab a quick bite."

"We still on for tonight? You know, a drink, maybe a movie or something?" Tyrell asked.

"Yeah, that'd be cool, but I gotta be home by 10:00."

"Man, what's up with that, you always have to be home by 10:00. You married or got a curfew or something?" Chuck snickered at Tyrell's comment.

"Naw, man my day starts early and I just like to get in bed at a decent hour. It's just my routine."

"Oh, okay, I feel ya! Nothing wrong with a steady routine."

"Well, let me get going so I can get back. Just meet me in the garage after work and we'll take it from there," Tyrell said.

"No problem. See you then." Chuck smiled and winked

at Tyrell. "Enjoy your lunch." As Tyrell walked away he thought about his first meeting with Chuck...

About four months ago Tyrell had taken some documents down to the copy center where Chuck worked. Normally, this was his assistant's job, but she was out that particular day and he needed copies for an afternoon meeting. Tyrell caught the elevator down to the copy center. As he approached the counter, the echo of the copy machines running told him they may be really busy. He grabbed a request form to complete. Tyrell had never been down there and he was unsure of the process. Chuck, who had been working behind the counter, looked up and saw a confused Tyrell scratching his head, Chuck walked up to the window and asked Tyrell if he needed any help.

Tyrell smiled, "Oh, so this is where you work, I always see you on the elevator at the end of the day, but I never knew where you were coming from."

Chuck smiled, "Yeah, this is where they keep me."

"'Sup, man." Extending his hand, Tyrell introduced himself. I work on the 5th floor in accounting."

"Nice to meet you, Tyrell. I'm Chuck. What can I help you with?"

Tyrell handed him some documents, "I need to get this job done. It's urgent. Can you squeeze me in?"

Chuck glanced at the document request, noticing the office name.

He looked at Tyrell and asked, "Where's Simone?"

"My assistant is out sick today," Tyrell said raising his eyebrows. "On the day I really need her!"

"Well, I hope she feels better and, yeah, I think I can complete this for you in about an hour. It's not too busy here today." Chuck responded.

Tyrell expressed his surprise, "An hour! Man, that's earlier than I expected! I really appreciate this. I'll have to treat you to lunch or something for helping a brutha out. Damn, Tyrell thought, " what a treat that would be for me, sexy as you look!"

Chuck responded, "Man, I'm always ready to eat!" He laughed catching himself in his attraction for this man.

"Great! I'll see you in an hour."

When Tyrell returned, a couple of hours later, Chuck had his project all done. Tyrell smiled, "You're a lifesaver!"

Chuck smiled, flashing his dimples, "But don't forget about that lunch!"

Tyrell grinned and said, "Anytime," as he pulled out a pen and wrote down his office extension and cell number.

"Man, call me when you ready to go," Tyrell stated as he handed Chuck his number. They looked at each other for a brief second, enjoying the attraction that was too new to name. With a smile, Tyrell turned and walked away.

Tyrell snapped out of his deep thoughts just as he entered the café to get his lunch.

Later in the day, Chuck finished his work in the copy center. He looked up at the clock and saw that it was already five. He gathered up the remainder of his work and decided to finish first thing in the morning.

He straightened up his work area, hung his smock on the back of the door and headed out, taking the elevator down to the garage where he saw Tyrell waiting by his car. Tyrell spotted Chuck and motioned for him to come over.

"I'll see you guys on Saturday. Love you, bruh!" Tyrell said, ending the phone conversation he was having as Chuck got in the car.

"You got another niggah on the side I should know

about?" Chuck inquired. He couldn't believe how comfortable he had gotten with Tyrell. They had been talking and going out since the day they met seven months ago at the copy center. Chuck always hung out with the more thuggish bruthas because he felt that it hid the fact that he was attracted to other men. Tyrell seemed so easy to talk to. Through him, Chuck was seeing a whole new side to being gay. Everything fell into place so easily, but Chuck was still a little scared because everything seemed too good to be true. Chuck grew to be more comfortable with his sexuality and less concerned with his voluntary "don't ask, don't tell" lifestyle.

Tyrell got into the car, looked over at Chuck and saw he was daydreaming. He called Chuck's name and Chuck looked over.

"What are you thinking about?" Tyrell asked.

Chuck didn't respond.

Tyrell smiled and said, "Oh yeah, to answer your question that was my boy, Tariff. We've been friends for years."

"Define *friend*, if you will," Chuck asked.

"What do you mean?"

"Do you mean *friend* that you use to date and now you're *just friends,* or do you mean *friend* as in *buddy with benefits,* or just real good friends?"

Tyrell was turned off by Chuck's questions, but brushed it off and answered, "As in, that's my dawg…no benefits. Why you asking, anyway? You're not jealous or anything are you? What, you trying to be my man or something?" *Say yes! Say yes!* Tyrell thought.

"Man, go ahead with that," Chuck said, enjoying the thought.

After several minutes of awkward silence, Tyrell pulled

into his driveway.

"Damn those newspaper people," Tyrell says, walking up to his front door.

"They keep delivering my paper after I leave. I'll cancel this shit if they keep it up." After fiddling with his keys, he unlocked the door and walked in, followed by Chuck. Tyrell picked the mail off the floor and placed it on the breakfast table in the corner.

"You want a drink?" he offered Chuck. "I'm going to throw a couple of steaks on the grill." Tyrell walked inside the door and hit his alarm code to turn it off. Tyrell always made sure that his house was clean because he never knew when he might have guests. His walls were the color of a butter cookie. He had a couple pieces of nice black art pieces displayed in the foyer. Tyrell knew that since this area was the first thing people saw, it had to be impressive. They both walked down the foyer, and went into the living room. Tyrell didn't like a lot of furniture. He felt the less the furniture the more spacious the place looked. Tyrell always liked to entertain in his basement. The 48-inch flat screen on his wall made the room feel like a theater. All the movies he collected were stocked neatly on shelves in alphabetical order. A nicely stocked bar with all types of liquor framed the wall opposite the television.

Chuck admired how Tyrell's bachelor pad was set up.

"Make yourself at home. You know where everything is. I'm going to run upstairs and get out of this suit. Give me a second."

"Alright, no problem," Chuck replied.

Chuck instantly made himself comfortable and made he and Tyrell a drink. He walked around the dining room and spotted a picture he hadn't seen before on the buffet table near the window. As he checked it out, Tyrell returned from changing his clothes. "So, you know any of those people in the picture?" Tyrell joked.

"That was quick. Nope, I just know you!" Chuck said, smiling at Tyrell with a seductive grin. "So are these friends or your brothers?"

"These are my friends," Tyrell responded, taking the picture from Chuck to point out everyone. "This is my boy, Tariff, the one I was talking to when you got in the car. This is my boy, Mike and his friend Reese, and the other two are Demetrious and Jay."

"Nice looking group of brothers. I wish I had friends like this. I only hung with the friends I used to because, with them, I could hide my sexuality, but all along, those guys were trouble for me," Chuck said.

"Well, it's like my mother always told me…show me the company you keep and I'll tell you who you are," Tyrell said somberly.

"I hear ya man. Can I tell you something?" Chuck asked, suddenly becoming serious.

Hearing Chuck's tone, Tyrell became nervous *What is he about to say?* Tyrell thought anxiously. Then he let go of his fear and said, "Sure, dude. What's on ya mind?"

Chuck was quiet for a second and then said. "It's like this, I like you, I like you a lot and…I promised myself that if I started to fall for anyone, I would be totally honest. I don't ever want a relationship based on lies and secrets."

Looking perplexed, Tyrell just stood silently and listened.

"I got out of prison about ten months ago." Tyrell thought to himself, *that would explain why he has the jailhouse body and those two tattoos.* One of the tattoos was on his abs. It spelled out **FOR LIFE** in Gothic letters and the other covered his whole back. It was an outline of a cross.

"I got the job at the firm through this work release program." Chuck continued, "I'm in a halfway house now. That's why I always have to be home by 10:00. I have six more years of probation to do, and then I'm done with my sentence."

"You're joking right?" Tyrell asked.

"I wish I were, man," Chuck whispered, dropping his head. "I so regret what I got myself into. Those friends I was telling you about, well, they tried to rob a guy and he got killed. I didn't expect it to go that far, but it did. I ended up turning state's evidence against them. So I only got eight years spent two in prison and the rest were converted to probation. They let me out on good behavior. Otherwise, I would still be locked up."

"What happened to the other guys?" Tyrell asked.

"Let's just say they will be in prison for a long time to come. Turned out they had committed a lot more crimes than I was aware of."

"Wow, I mean, I don't know what to say," Tyrell said, unable to find any words.

Chuck looked up and straight into Tyrell's eyes, "Please don't judge me. That part of my life was not me. All I ask is for a chance to show you and the world that a brotha can learn from his mistakes and do better. All I want is a second chance, but all people see is my past, it doesn't matter what I do now in the present. Folks think that I'm going to end up back in prison, but I won't." Chuck paused and waited for Tyrell to respond.

"So...do you wanna to take me home now that you know?"

Tyrell was overcome with admiration, respect and love. He smiled and thought *This could really be the man for me.*

Chuck asked, "What is that crazy grin about?"

"Why are you so ready to go? Man, we have steaks to eat," Tyrell said as he playfully threw a piece of ice at him.

Chuck smiled, "Yeah, we have steaks to eat."

Chapter 6

Daunte walked through the door and immediately hollered for Mia. When he didn't get an answer, he walked down the hallway. There were African paintings all along the walls. Both Daunte and Mia loved African art. Most of the furniture had a similar theme. The room was somewhat dark, even with the two dim lamps and the incense that burned had a strong musk smell. The sound of the shower running alerted him as to Mia's whereabouts. He walked into the kitchen, and grabbed a beer and took a big gulp. Just as he brought the beer down from his mouth, Mia appeared in front of him wearing only a robe.

"Hey, boo, I didn't hear you come in," Mia said.

"Hey sweetheart, I heard you in the shower so I came in the kitchen to grab me a beer."

Mia walked over to him and gave him a tight hug and a big kiss. She massaged his shoulders, noticing how tense he was.

"So, you had one of those days, huh?"

"Yeah, one of those days is right. Now, all I wanna do is relax, watch some TV, and spend some time with my girl." His voice dropped to a seductive whisper.

"Sounds good to me." Mia kissed Daunte's lips in a brief, but passionate embrace.

"I called you today, but you were out of the office."

"You must have called me while I was out to lunch."

"How was lunch? Who did you go to lunch with?" Daunte immediately questioned. His insecurity began to show. His seductive whisper quickly faded away.

"Nobody. Just one of my good friends."

"Male or female?"

"Male, what's with all the questions?" Mia quipped, feeling a bit irritated and uneasy, "Does it matter? Come on baby, let's not go there again."

"Go where, Mia?"

"Boo, we're only friends. I've told you that a thousand times already."

"Then why haven't I met this guy? I've met all your female friends."

"You'll meet him soon. I promise."

"Mia, you've been saying that for a while now."

"Okay how about..." A frantic knock on the door cut their conversation short.

"Daunte, it's Ms. Johnson from downstairs," the voice from behind the door yelled. Daunte opened the door.

"What's wrong, Ms. Johnson?"

"My toilet is overflowing and water is running everywhere. Can you come down and take care of it right now?"

"I'll be right there, let me grab my tool belt. Just turn the water off using the knobs behind the toilet." Ms. Johnson nodded her head and headed back down stairs to do as Daunte said.

"There goes our evening," Mia mumbled in the air.

"I know. I'm sorry, baby," Daunte apologized, hearing her mutters. "This part-time maintenance man job for the building pays good money. It's helping us to save for our wedding and honeymoon."

"Alright, well don't be too long and I'll see you when you get back. I love you, Daunte."

"I love you, too." Daunte headed for the door to take

care of Ms. Johnson's leaking toilet.

Mia walked into the kitchen after Daunte left and poured herself a glass of wine. As much as she hated the fact that Daunte had this part-time job, she knew he was right. She just became a little selfish when it came to spending time with her man. Mia had the sultry sounds of Phyllis Hyman playing in the background. Mia had an old soul and loved to listen to music from back in the day. She felt that they didn't really sing about love today, that the songs of today were too degrading to women.

As Mia's mind wandered, she replayed the conversation that she and Daunte had when he first walked in the door. As much as she argued with Daunte, she knew he was right. She thought about how she would feel if Daunte hung out with a woman that she didn't know. Could she be just as patient, trusting, and understanding? How would Daunte feel if he knew that Demetrious and Tariff were both gay? Mia thought, *I'm going to talk to Danute when he returns, so he will understand.* Mia finished off her wine and turned off the music. She walked into the bedroom and got out of her robe and slipped into her sexy lingerie. The wine started to go to her head and, as she lay down to wait for Daunte, she fell asleep, never hearing Daunte walk in.

As Daunte returned to his apartment from fixing Ms. Johnson's toilet, he noticed that the place was completely dark and quiet. The only noises he could hear were the sounds of the refrigerator motor and the drip of the faucet. The light from the television seeped under the bedroom door. Daunte walked over to the faucet, turning it on and off, hoping to stop the drip. He reached into the fridge and grabbed another beer and a piece of cold chicken. As he placed the chicken on a small plate and put it inside the microwave, he drank his beer and watched the chicken go round and round on the carousel. He started to think about the conversation he and Mia had before he went to Ms. Johnson's apartment. Deep down, Daunte knew he could trust Mia and he loved her deeply. Picking up the beer he took another gulp, and looked in the direction of the bedroom, shaking his head and smiling. He thought, *why am I allowing myself to get all worked up, probably over nothing?* He finished what was left of the beer and chicken and headed to the bedroom. As he walked in, he saw Mia lying across the bed, fast asleep. He sat down on the bed and watched Mia sleep for a few seconds.

Mia woke up, "Hey, baby," she said with a yawn, "what time is it?"

Daunte looked at the clock on the night stand. "It's almost midnight."

Trying to stay awake, she asked, "Were you able to fix Ms. Johnson's toilet?"

"Come on now, baby," Daunte says, "you got to ask? Of course I fixed it! You know your man can fix anything."

Mia let out a faint laugh, "Yeah, what was I thinking about?"

Daunte kicked off his shoes and, lying across the bed, he put Mia's head onto his chest.

"Baby," Daunte said, "I love you so much. I'm going to try and not to be so jealous." Daunte tapped Mia, but heard a small snore which told him she had fallen back asleep. He looked around the room, and squeezed Mia a little, then dozed off to sleep himself, still wearing his work clothes.

*   *   *

Mike lay across the bed in a pair of boxers when Reese walked in from his Saturday afternoon football practice. "Hey, sweetie, how was practice?"

"They tried to kill me out there! Your man is tired," Reese responded.

"Don't forget the guys are coming over tonight," Mike reminded him.

"I remember. You haven't told them anything have you?"

"Baby, would I ruin your surprise?"

"Hmmm, …yeah, you would if given the chance." Reese let out a hearty laugh, knowing how his man couldn't keep a secret.

"It was hard, but I did manage not to slip and say anything. Although Jay tried to pry a hint out of me."

"Yeah, it is hard," Reese said playfully, as he grabbed his throbbing penis.

"Well, I guess it's my job to get it back down," Mike said with a devilish grin across his face. Reese walked over to Mike. Mike pulled him down on top of him and kissed him passionately. Mike then slowly moved to start nibbling Reese's earlobe, at the same time putting Reese on his back on the bed. Mike nibbled at his nipples, making his way down to Reese's chest to his rock hard abs while still stroking Reese's manhood through his boxers. A few soft moans escaped as Mike continued his journey to send Reese into ecstasy. Soon they were both out of their boxers completely naked. Reese grabbed a hold of Mike and flipped him into the position he once occupied. He repeated all of what Mike had done to him. They went at it, as if they hadn't seen each other in months. Just this morning, they had made love before they both left the house for the day. Reese turned Mike over onto his stomach and with his tongue, traced the letter Y on his back. First the left shoulder, to the middle of his back, and then to the right side, making the letter V. He moved back to the point of the V and, from there he moved down the crease of Mike's back completing his letter Y. He stopped as he reached the top of his ass, continuing until he reached his destination. There, he really began to give his lover pleasure. The two of them went at it for some time taking turns pleasing each other before they both finally fell into each others arms and to sleep.

Reese and Mike were awakened by the television. Mike had set it to remind him of a show he wanted to watch. "Baby, get up we need to get dressed and ready before the guys get here."

Reese didn't bother to open his eyes.

"Okay, baby, go ahead and take your shower and wake me when you get out," Reese muttered with closed eyes. "Then I'll take mine. Just let me sleep a few more minutes."

"Okay, I know you're probably still tired from practice." Mike kissed Reese on the cheek and walked into the bathroom. Mike took his time in the shower, letting every drop from the pulsating showerhead hit every inch of his body. Still half asleep, he stood under the massaging water trying to wash away the sleep so he'd be ready when the guys arrived. Standing there, watching his silhouette, Reese decided to join him.

"Got enough room in there for me?" Reese purred playfully.

"Sure there is," Mike said with a smile, "but I thought you were still sleeping."

"Obviously not anymore," Reese responded in a deep sexy voice. "Now move over-- I'm coming in!"

"Be my guest," Mike said, stepping back to allow Reese in.

They showered thoroughly, taking their time to clean each other from head to toe. After fifteen minutes of steam and soap, they rinsed, towel dried, and got dressed. Mike decided to go to the kitchen to fix a few snacks before the gang showed, but was interrupted by the door bell.

"What's up, stranger? Long time no see," Mike warmly greeted Tyrell.

"Go 'head with that man."

"How's everything going, Ty?" Mike said.

"Everything is everything! And you?" Tyrell said as he walked into the foyer. "Where's Reese?"

"He's upstairs still getting dressed. You know how Reese is," Mike joked.

"And just how is Reese?" Reese questioned, startling Mike from behind.

"There's my main man, what's up, Tyrell?" Still giving Mike the playful evil eye. Reese gave Tyrell a brotherly hug.

"It's all good in the hood, as they say," Tyrell answered.

"You want a beer or something while we wait for everybody?" Reese asked.

"It's kinda early for a beer…but what the hell, it's the weekend. Yeah, a beer would be cool." Reese walked to the kitchen to grab a Heineken when the doorbell rang again.

"I guess we know who that is," Mike said, as he jogged lightly toward the door. "Speak of the devils…"

Jay, Demetrious, and Tariff walked through the door one by one, bags in hand.

Reese emerged from the kitchen with beers for every-one.

"Tyrell said it's too early, but dammit, its seven o'clock somewhere in the world. Drink up fellas!" Reese said with a big smile on his face.

They spent the next ten minutes going back and forth with basic small talk. An occasional unified laugh would break their banter until the question was finally asked.

"Okay, to hell with the drinks and the chit chat what's this meeting all about?" Demetrious asked.

Reese puts down his beer and began. "There are two things or three things rather I wanted to talk to you guys about. First, my baby and I are committed to each other for the long haul and he's stuck with me just like you guys have…"

The room was filled with a clap of laughter once again. Jay interjected, "That's not news, we knew it would happen one day," Demetrious walked over and pushed Jay.

"Alright you knuckle heads. Anyway…" Reese contin-ued, "Secondly, you guys know that I got hurt back in my senior year in college and couldn't play football that year. As you all know, I've been working with a training and con-ditioning coach and playing on the practice squad. Well, to make a long story short, they took me off the practice squad and I finally got signed to the team. It looks like I will be starting. They signed me to a two million dollar contract and they included other incentives and bonuses that I will receive based on my performance."

Demetrious jumped up first to hug Reese with congratu-lations. The rest followed and began to hug Mike as well, knowing that Reese had committed himself to him and to his NFL contract. Reese finished by saying, "Thirdly, when

I met Mike, all of you guys treated me just like I was already part of the group. You embraced me and you guys were always encouraging me. So, I'd like to thank all of you by doing something special."

"How special?" Tyrell jokingly asked.

"As a way of showing my sincere thanks and grati- tude...I'd like to take all of you on a four day, three night trip to South Beach, Miami. All expenses will be paid by me, of course." Everyone jumped up from the sofa and cheered in celebration of the last bit of news Reese shared.

"Alright, hell yeah!" Jay exclaimed.

"Thanks bruh, this is really cool of you!" Demetrious chimed in.

"South Beach here we come! Watch out Florida," Tyrell yelled out.

"So, when is this trip?" Jay asked.

"Soon, real soon. I know y'all gotta let your massa's know you be leaving the plantation for a while, but I'll tell you when," Reese said.

They all stood around and hashed out the plans of their trip until late that night. They finally said their goodbyes around 10:30. When the last of the guys left, Mike closed the door behind them and walked into the kitchen where Reese was rinsing the dishes and putting them in the dish- washer.

"I am so fortunate to have a good man like you," Mike said, walking up behind Reese, putting his arms around his waist. "You know you didn't have to do this Miami trip, but I'm quite sure those guys appreciate it."

"Those guys are like family. I love them just as much as you do. I've been blessed with a good man, home, and good friends. If I died today, I would be a happy man. I thank

God for all that I am and have and I thank you as well for sharing all of this with me."

"Well put those dishes down so we can go upstairs and have our own celebration," Mike encouraged, grinning from ear to ear.

"I guess the dishes can wait," Reese said, dropping the dish towel on the counter. I'll race you." They both ran toward the stairs.

*   *   *

The sound of Kenny G's instrumental CD played in the car. Demetrious loved instrumental jazz and Kenny G was one of his favorite artists. Tariff leaned back in his seat, getting caught up in the sounds of the sax. As Demetrious drove one hand on the steering wheel, the other in his lap, a long breathless moment passed.

Finally, Demetrious spoke, "That's real nice of Reese to treat us all to a trip to South Beach."

"It is really nice of him," Tariff agreed.

"Now we just need to get him to get us tickets to the games," Demetrious said. They both had to laugh at that.

"Now that would be off da hook," Tariff replied. "So are you coming in? Or are you going to head home?" Tariff asked. Demetrious had parked his car at Tariff's house so they could ride together.

Demetrious was quiet for a moment. Then he looked over at Tariff, mischief in his eyes. "That depends…"

"Depends on what?" Tariff asked.

"Depends on whether or not that is an invitation to spend the night?" Demetrious slyly responded.

Tariff was silent for a brief second before he finally spoke. "Yes, it is!" Tariff gave in.

With that said, Demetrious opened the car door and got out. They walked into Tariff's house, both eagerly anticipating what the night would bring. As they walked in the door, Tariff looked back.

"Let me turn on some music. You want anything to drink?" Tariff offered.

"Water would be cool. I can't keep drinking that beer. Got to watch the stomach, especially now since we're going to South Beach."

"Last I saw, the stomach looked fine to me. So did the rest of your body," Tariff complimented.

Demetrious smiled. "You think?"

"I know..."

Tariff turned on the radio and Luther Vandross' *So Amazing* quietly flowed from the surround sound. Demetrious walked over to Tariff, his hand out as a formal invitation, "Dance with me."

"You mean now?" Tariff asked as he blushed.

"Of course I mean now! Boy, don't act like you're bashful." Demetrious grabbed Tariff's hand and pulled him in. They slow danced for what seemed like an eternity, enjoying the comfort of each other arms. To the rhythm of the R&B melody, they slowly caressed each other, tenderly massaging each other's back. Demetrious found Tariff's lips and kissed him gently. They shared a kiss for a moment and then Tariff's body tensed up when he looked at the picture of James on the fireplace mantle.

Tariff's sudden tension made Demetrious take a step back. Tariff was staring at something behind him and Demetrious turned around to see the picture of James. Not wanting to compete with a photo, Demetrious stopped dancing, kissed Tariff on the cheek, and said, "I think I'd better leave now."

"Why?" Tariff inquired.

"Because, even though you're here, your mind and heart are still somewhere else." Tariff looked away from Demetrious and gazed at the picture of James for a brief moment. Demetrious turned Tariff's face back to his.

"Hey, its okay!" Demetrious said. Demetrious had always been the one that the guys saw as understanding and easy to talk to. No wonder everyone looked to him when they needed advice.

"You'll know when you're ready and, right now, you're not ready. It's best if I say 'good night'." With that, Demetrious turned and headed for the door. Tariff stood in the middle of the living room floor looking at Demetrious' back as he walked away to leave. As soon as Demetrious closed the door, Tariff walked to the door and opened it. He watched as Demetrious got in his car to drive away. Before Demetrious started his car, he ran his hand down his face and turned to look at Tariff standing in the doorway. They shared a brief stare and Demetrious started his car and drove away.

Tariff closed the door when he could no longer see Demetrious' car. He walked back into the living room and starred at James' picture.

In his head he could hear James speaking his last words *"If I don't make it, I'll still be with you, but I want you to love again."*

"I'm trying baby, I'm really trying," Tariff spoke to the picture. He put the picture back on the mantle, turned off the stereo and the lights and walked up the stairs to his bedroom, alone.

Chapter 7

The YMCA was the place where Daunte and Jay worked out and played basketball frequently. All 10 courts were taken. Sound of balls bouncing on the hardwood floors echoed throughout the gym and tennis shoe bottoms made the normal scuffing noises. Some courts had the guys playing shirts against skins. Some were showing flat stomachs with defined abs, others had big beer bellies that they were trying to work off. They all had sweat rolling down their heads and chests, sweat that left traces around the necks and underarms of those players that were still wearing shirts.

Jay and Daunte ran a friendly game of one on one. After Jay took possession of the ball for the umpteenth time, Daunte stopped and took a breath.

"Yo man, what was that all about the other day? Why did you get so upset and storm out?"

"You know how dramatic I can be at times." What Jay really wanted to say was, *you pissed me off with your anti-gay ass,* but he didn't. He just let it go.

"Do I?" Daunte asked raising his eye brows.

"What's that suppose to mean?"

"Just forget it. Anyway, I tried to have a conversation with my girl the other night, but we got interrupted."

"Well, how was it going before you got interrupted?" Jay asked, as he wiped the sweat from his face.

"In so many words, she told me I needed to trust her, so, I'm going to give it a rest for now."

"Only give it a rest if you feel comfortable with giving it

a rest. 'Cause if you're not satisfied, it's going to eat away at you." Jay explained.

"You're right, I'll think about it. Anyway, let's hit the showers so we can get out of here," Daunte said as he started to gather his things.

"That sounds like a plan to me." They headed to the locker room, horsing around as they went.

Jay and Daunte had just finished their showers and stood at their lockers wrapped in towels. Daunte sat on the bench and started to lotion his body. Daunte had always taken pride in his body, even though it was average, it was good enough to keep his woman happy and to turn a head or two. Daunte had very dark brown skin, he always kept his coal black hair neatly trimmed, with no facial hair. He had the baby face going on. Daunte was a very well-groomed man that alone turned women on. Daunte stood at five feet-ten inches tall and was borderline chunky, but carried it very well.

"Man, that was a good workout," Jay said as he slowly rolled his shoulders, showing that he was worn out. It got me kind of tired too; I could go home and go to sleep."

Daunte laughed, "Man, you always talking about going home and going to sleep, but today it sounds like a good idea. So when are you and your lady going to come over so we can all double date. I know my girl, Mia, she likes that kind of shit. Man I'd really like for you to meet her and I definitely would like to meet your girl."

Jay thought to himself, *He really doesn't have a clue about me.* Daunte isn't ready to hear the truth.
So Jay played it cool and said, "You're right, man, I haven't met your girl." Daunte stood up and dropped his towel to start to lotion the lower part of his body. He faced Jay to lis-

ten to what he was saying. Jay had to force himself not to look and check out the package. Either way, no matter what, Jay was not attracted to Daunte in that way, but the way Daunte always talked about laying the pipe to his girl, Jay was a little curious to see what he was working with. Daunte always wore big tee-shirts and would put them on first, but this particular day he didn't. Daunte always looked people in the eye when he spoke. Jay was impressed with that because he felt that showed a person's confidence, but now was not the time for Daunte to look into his eyes. Jay needed a quick diversion, so he could check out the candy cane.

Jay finally asked, "Hey, Daunte, I forgot my deodorant do you have any?"

Daunte, responded, "Yeah, man, I have some right here." He turned his head to look in his bag. Jay's eyes immediately went down below. Jay was shocked at what he saw and thought to himself, *"Damn! My boy is packing!"* By the time Daunte looked up, Jay had already surveyed the merchandise. Without missing a beat, Jay went right back to his conversation about them double dating. Jay wasn't sure how to address his question, but still felt now was not the time for him to inform Daunte of his sexual preference.

So he finally responded by just saying, "We will plan something soon."

Daunte thought for a second, "So bruh, why don't you want me to meet this lady?"

Jay didn't like lying about this and wanted to be honest, but he felt Daunte was just not ready. Jay changed the subject to when they would be coming back to work out and what body part they would be working on. Daunte followed suit. They finally got dressed and walked out. As they

61

walked out, they both saw this girl that had been hot on Daunte's trail since he started working out there. She stood there talking to her girlfriends. She was about 5"8 inches tall, wearing a spandex halter top and spandex shorts, with abs that looked like Janet Jackson's. She had a tom boyish cut, but still looked feminine. You could tell her girlfriends' bodies weren't as toned as hers. One stood there with the same thing she had on but, she showed the stretch marks of child birth and her tummy bulged slightly over the waist of her shorts. The other girl that stood there was the tallest of the three and was dressed in sweats. You didn't need an imagination or x-ray vision to figure out what was going on under those sweats.

She could use some time on the tread mill, Jay thought.

Daunte wanted to avoid her and her friends, but couldn't so he asked Jay, "Man, don't leave me! Help me get away from her!"

Jay laughed, "Man I got you, but why don't you just tell her you're not interested?"

"I did, but she doesn't care, she just wants to ride my dick, dawg. If you ask me she's making a fool of herself trying to throw her drawers at me. Anyway, I love Mia too much to mess around on her. You know there are a few of us good bruthas out here. Believe it or not, some of these women can be just as treacherous as the men," Daunte stated.

"I hear you on that man," Jay agreed. She didn't see Daunte and ended up walking in another direction with her girlfriends.

Jay watched her walk away, and turned to Daunte, "Man, looks like you don't need to be saved." He and Daunte both laughed, their laughter was interrupted by Daunte's cell phone. He looked at his phone and smiled when he saw it was Mia.

He answered, "Hey hold on for one sec." Daunte gave Jay some dap. Jay left Daunte to his phone call and walked out.

* * *

Chuck stood in front of Tyrell's about to knock on the door. He knocked softly, then waited for him to answer. Not hearing any movement, he knocked a little louder. Tyrell finally opened the door, wearing a pair of shorts and nothing else. "What's up, man? I didn't disturb you, did I?" Chuck asked as he longingly eyed Tyrell's body.

"Naw, I was expecting you, remember?" Tyrell said as he threw Chuck a quick wink. "I see you made it with no problems." Chuck walked in still looking lustfully at Tyrell as he stepped away from the door.

"I was just in the basement watching some TV. You want something to drink before we head down?"

"Sure, what you got to drink?"

"Let's see, I've got beer, orange juice and, some Kool-Aid…" Chuck laughed at his last drink option. He hadn't drunk Kool-Aid since he was a child. He thought it was rather sexy and cute that Tyrell still drank it as an adult.

"I'll have a beer." Tyrell grabbed a couple of beers out the fridge and handed one to Chuck. As they were descending down the stairs to the basement. Chuck asked, "How did the meeting go the other night with your boyz?"

"Aww man, it went well!" Tyrell said, excitedly. "My boy Reese got an NFL contract, so, to celebrate, he's taking all of us on an all-expense paid trip to South Beach."

"Damn, that's some gift! I've heard about South Beach. You guys should have a good time there."

"Well, you could have a good time too, if you went."

"Is that an invite?" Chuck said with a big grin on his face. "You ready for me to meet the boyz? Things between us must be getting serious if you want me to meet your boyz already," Chuck said, leaning in and giving Tyrell a big Cheshire cat grin. Tyrell grabbed a pillow from the sofa and threw it at Chuck.

"How much would a trip like that cost anyway?" Chuck inquired.

"Actually, all you have to do is get the plane ticket. Reese is taking care of everything else. Can you swing a ticket? I can help you if you need me to."

"Naw dawg, but I appreciate that. I've been putting some money away and saving for this project I'm working on. I think I can swing a ticket. That's the least I can do."

"What project is this, if you don't mind me asking?" Tyrell was glad to see that Chuck had goals, was responsible and self-sufficient.

"I don't want to jinx it, but, you'll find out in due time." Chuck replied.

Tyrell picked up another pillow and hit Chuck on the arm with it.

"Secrets already, huh?"

"Yeah, but it's a good one. Anyway, about the trip, just let me clear it with my probation officer and get permission to go, 'cause when you're on probation, you are restricted from doing a lot of things, especially traveling. My probation officer and I are cool, so I'll see and let you know. But whether I go or not, I'm happy for you and your friends."

"Oh, so you have to get permission to travel?" Tyrell asked.

Chuck looked down, embarrassed, "Yeah it's one of the stipulations of my probation. I'm not trying to get into any more trouble. I want to do everything by the book. I think we can get a travel pass, as long as we give them enough time to process it."

"Hey, look, man, look at me!" Tyrell softly pleaded, "You do what you need to do! Keep ya head up, it's okay! It's good to see a brutha trying to turn his life around." Tyrell gave him a big smile and a wink then lifted his chin up to look at him.

Chuck looked up into Tyrell's warm, sincere eyes and took a sip from his beer.

"The trip is in the next few weeks, so go ahead and get started on it," Tyrell added.

"I will first thing tomorrow morning. So what movie are we going to watch?"

Tyrell stood up and dropped his shorts and then said, "Who has time for watching a movie."

Chuck smiled and looked Tyrell up and down like he had at the door. He took another sip of his beer while admiring Tyrell's naked body. "Man, I like your style," he said, then dropped the beer and grabbed Tyrell in a hungry kiss.

Chapter 8

Mike sat in his office drumming his pencil up and down on his desk. As he looked out his door he could see the secretaries, bullshitting around as usual. He could see their computer screens, some were reading profiles on Myspace.com and others looking at clothes. A couple of the ladies were engrossed in conversations, drinking coffee, as if they were on break. *Good thing smoking is no longer allowed in the building,* he thought, *then things would really be lax.* But as long as his secretary did her work and kept him out of the bosses office he didn't care. The sounds of the office became a distraction, so Mike got up and closed his office door. The ringing of the phone was a welcome interruption. "Hello, Mike speaking. How can I help you?"

"What's up, man?" Tyrell blared from the other end.

"What's up, Tyrell," Mike said with a slight sigh. He didn't mind being interrupted, but knew his conversations with Tyrell could potentially go on forever, further keeping him from doing any work. "So, you finally came up from under that man to give a brother a call, huh?"

"Go ahead wit dat man. So are you ready for the trip?"

"As ready as I can be, but, if I don't get through this pile of work on my desk soon, I won't be going anywhere."

"I feel ya there man."

"Man, I was thinking. It's real cool of Reese to do this trip for us, man. He didn't have to, you know? But, that was good looking out on his part."

"Oh, no doubt, I agree! So how are you going to adjust

to being the wife of a football star?"

"Man, don't go there! I ain't nobody's wife, but, then again, with all that money I'll be whatever he wants me to be."

"I'm with you on that. Anyway, I was going to bring my boy with me to Miami you think it will be okay with Reese?"

Mike laughed, "Hmmm, things must be serious. Sure, it's cool! You'll have your own room, so I don't think it will be a problem at all."

"Cool, I'm going to get off this phone and call him to make sure he's got his schedule cleared so he can pick up his ticket."

"That'll work. Oh yeah, I almost forgot, we're all staying at Tariff's house the night before the flight, since he lives closer to the airport."

"That's cool. So how are things with him and Demetrious?" Tyrell inquired.

As much as Mike wanted to get back and finish his work, he couldn't help but do what he loved to do best, gossip. "Man, they're trying to work it out. D's hanging in there and being patient. Man, you know D, he has more patience than all of us. You know since James was killed, Tariff hasn't let himself fall in love with anybody. That wall has been up for a long time now and it seems like D is trying to break it down. They are two good people who deserve each other. I think they will find their way and maybe, just maybe, this trip to Miami is just what the doctor ordered. You feel me?"

"I feel ya! I do miss our boy, James. It's still hard sometimes to believe that he's gone," Tyrell said somberly.

"I know what you mean. Like, just the other day Reese and I were watching *The Best Man* and the scene came on where the stripper Candy came out and we started singing it to ourselves. We bust out laughing because we remembered that crazy dance that James would always do when that song came on. You remember? Mike continued. He'd start gyrating like a freak with his hands over his head..." Mike broke into laughter at the thought.

"Oh, hell yeah," Tyrell laughed along with Mike. "For a black man he had no rhythm at all..."

They laughed together for a little while until Mike finally said, "Well, we'll have plenty of time to laugh and reminisce. I have to sort through this massive mound on my desk. I'll talk to you later boy, ok? Love you!"

"Alright, man. Love you, too. Later!" Tyrell said.

As they hang up Tyrell's cell phone vibrated.

"Hello"

"Hey Ty, its Chuck."

"Man, I know your voice. What's up? I was just talking about you to my boy, Mike."

"About what? What's up?"

"Not much I was just asking him what he thought about you coming with us on the trip. He said it would be cool since we'd all have our own rooms."

"Cool, well, I talked to my probation officer and he said it would be alright as long as I continued to do my nightly check in by phone," Chuck said trying to contain his excitement.

"Damn, he's the man! That will work."

Chuck laughed, "Yeah he is, I didn't think it would be a problem, I had to fill out some forms, but now I'm all set. I just have to stay out of trouble while I'm there. There are more specifics, but you get the gist of it.

Tyrell responded, "Don't worry. I'll make sure you stay

out of trouble."

"So, I'm going to go ahead and purchase my ticket."

"Cool, man, talk to you later. Oh by the way, we're all going over to my boy Tariff's house the night before, since he lives closer to the airport."

"Where does he live?"

"Not to far from the car wash near Elm Avenue."

"Oh, OK… I know where that area is. When I was younger I use to hang out not too far from there."

"Either way I'll just pick you up and we can ride over in my car," Tyrell said. "Okay, baby, sounds good."

"Talk to you later, got to get back to this print job."

*   *   *

After a couple of weeks of finishing up office work, buying beach clothes, hitting the gym hard, and packing, the guys headed over to Tariff's house to go on their trip to Miami. Mike and Reese were the first ones to show up at Tariff's with their colossal luggage. Reese leaned on the doorbell with his elbow, unable to free any hands due to his bags.

"Damn, dude, I'm coming," Tariff yelled from the inside. "You better be dying out there to be leaning on my bell like that." Tariff opened the door like he was pissed off and then broke into a smile. "Damn, is y'all moving or something? Y'all have enough bags to last a month." Mike and Reese both burst out laughing when they actually took a look at how many bags they were holding. "Come on in, guys, take a load off."

"What's up partner?" Mike finally spoke after setting the bags down in the foyer.

Reese chimed in, "What's up, boy?"

"All is well on this end. Jay just called, he should be here any minute." Tariff paused before closing the door, "Actually, there he is now."

Jay pulled into the driveway and hopped out excitedly. He ran up to the doorway and said, "All I'm going to say is 'what happens in Miami, stays in Miami." They all laughed. Tariff closed the door behind them and began showing the guys their sleeping quarters for the night. "Ok, so, Jay, you got the couch, Mike and Reese, you have the guest room, and Tyrell and Chuck got the office. Any questions?"

"Yeah," Jay said, "What you got to drink?"

"Lush," Mike whispered.

"I heard that!" Jay yelled back, heading to the kitchen to get his vacation started early.

"You know where the alcohol is, man!" Tariff said. "And bring me one, too!"

Jay grabbed a couple of beers from the refrigerator and tossed one to Tariff. Tariff caught the beer and cracked it open without hesitation. He took a sip as Mike and Reese headed upstairs with their bags as the doorbell rang again.

"I know who that is," Tariff said, as he sat his drink down and sprinted to the door. He opened the door with a great big smile on his face. Something he'd done lately whenever he saw Demetrious. "What's up, man? What you know, good?"

"I'm cool, just a little tired," Demetrious added. "I see the cars out front. Am I the last one here?"

"Naw, Tyrell and Chuck haven't gotten here yet. Jay's in the kitchen and Mike and Reese are upstairs."

Demetrious gave Tariff a quick kiss and then stepped inside to holler at the others. Mike and Reese came from upstairs to greet Demetrious.

"What's up, fellas? I see we're almost all here."

"Dawg, put those bags up and come down and grab a drink," Reese said to Demetrious.

"Where am I sleeping?" Demetrious asked with a playful grin.

"Just put them in my room. That's where you'll be sleeping tonight. All the other rooms are taken." Tariff had a giant ear to ear smile on his face as he relayed the sleeping arrangements.

"That works for me. I'll be back in a few minutes, guys." Demetrious walked upstairs to Tariff's room with a devilish grin on his face. He was excited that he was getting closer to Tariff, but had yet to break through the fortress that Tariff had built around himself. Demetrious came from upstairs after putting his stuff away, looked at Tariff and smiled again.

"So, where's Tyrell and this new found friend of his?" Demetrious asked. "Has anyone heard from them yet?"

"No, let me call him on his cell," Mike said. He put the phone on speaker and they all listened quietly, grinning at the same time.

Tyrell looked at his caller ID and then glanced over at Chuck who was admiring the scenery as they drove down the street.

"Hello, Mike," Tyrell answered, "I know you're calling to check on a brutha! We should be there in about three minutes. Is everyone there yet?" Everyone in the background began to laugh, giving Tyrell his answer.

"We'll see ya'll in a few!" he grinned into the receiver.

Clamping the phone shut, and looked over at Chuck again. "What's wrong, dude? Why you so quiet?"

Chuck let out a light sigh, "No reason, just thinking, you know…"

"About…?"

"Nothing in particular…just thinking." Chuck was obviously day dreaming. He stared out the window for a few more seconds before finally speaking again. "Your boy must live up in the cut, huh?"

"Why you ask that?"

"No reason, I was just wondering, 'cause I've never seen this part of the city before."

"Well, unless you've lived out here you probably wouldn't know this part was back here. We'll be there in a few minutes going this way. Looks like everyone is there but us."

"I'm looking forward to meeting them." Chuck shifted in the passenger seat to sit upright. He'd been leaning against the door and glaring out the window. His right arm was starting to fall asleep.

"You alright, man? You have nothing to be nervous about. These guys are real cool," Tyrell said, noticing Chuck fidgeting.

"Oh, yeah, I'm cool dude. Nothing to worry about," Chuck said unconvincingly.

"Come on, this is me you're talking to."

"Well, maybe I'm just a little nervous."

"Don't worry, they don't bite. Just be yourself and you'll be okay."

"Alright. Hey, thanks again for inviting me along."

"I wouldn't have it any other way. Just take this time and enjoy yourself."

Five minutes later, Tyrell and Chuck pulled up into Tariff's driveway. Tyrell turned off the ignition, looked over at Chuck, and gave him a wink.

"You ready?" Tyrell asked.

"Yeah, I'm ready. You make it seem like I'm about to walk into something I may not want to."

Tyrell opened his door and stepped out as he said, "Not at all, I'm telling you, my friends are cool!" He pushed the trunk release button on the side of his door and popped the trunk. Chuck had packed light, just one bag and a jacket. Tyrell on the other hand, like his friends, had multiple bags.

"I guess I still have the prison mentality," Chuck awkwardly joked.

"What do you mean?"

Chuck gestured to his bags, "I'm not use to having a lot...you never know when you gotta pick up and go!"

"Oh, man," Tyrell laughed, "I can never decide what to wear so I end up bringing everything. Come on, let's go in." They grabbed their bags out of the car and walked up to Tariff's door. After one ring, Tariff answered.

"Yo, Ty, what's up? This must be Chuck."

"Hey, man, how's it going?" Chuck nervously stuck out his hand to shake Tariff's. "I've heard a lot about you Chuck. Nice to finally meet you!" Tariff said, trying to make Chuck feel comfortable.

"I've heard a lot about you, too. Nice to finally meet you." Small beads of sweat started lining Chuck's forehead.

"Well, come on in. I'll show you where you're sleeping and then we can go meet the rest of the guys." Tyrell and Chuck walked through the living room and briefly spoke to the others before they headed upstairs. "I'll make a more formal introduction when we come back down."

They put their bags down and headed back downstairs to hang with the fellas. Tyrell introduced Chuck to everyone "Yo, fellas, this is Chuck. Chuck this is everyone." They greeted Chuck in unison.

"What you guys drinking?" Tariff asked.

"You know me, beer is fine," Tyrell spoke.

"Chuck, you?" Tariff gestured to Chuck.

"Oh, yeah, beer is fine, too," Chuck stumbled. His nerves were starting to be too much for him.

"Damn, Chuck is fine, I wonder if he's got a brother?" Jay joked to Reese. Reese gave him a playful tug. As Jay fell back, he knocked the picture of James down flat.

"So Chuck, have you been to Miami before?" Tariff asked, as they sat down in the living room with the rest.

"Naw, man, I've been so busy I haven't had time to do much of anything. This is the first trip I've taken in a long while. So this is a welcome break."

"Tariff, where's the car? I didn't see it in the driveway?" Jay interrupted.

"In the garage. I had to make room for all y'all."

"Is it as clean as always?" Reese questioned.

"And you know this. I don't even know why you asked me that," Tariff said with pride.

As time passed, Chuck got more and more comfortable with the guys. Before he got locked up, Chuck used to bartend part-time to bring in a little bit of change. So he offered to make the guys a different variety of drinks. He worked with whatever alcohol Tariff had on his bar, which was a lot. Tyrell was impressed with the fact that Chuck knew so much because all he could make was rum and coke and that didn't even come out right. Chuck made a couple of French Martinis and the guys really liked that. Once the conversation of football came up, Chuck once again was in his element.

Every chance Chuck got, he spent it watching a football game. He didn't care who was playing, he just wanted to watch it. As the evening went on the guys all settled down and started watching a few movies that Tariff had in his library. The guys were trying to decide what to watch and they finally agreed on *Beauty Shop*. Finally, Mike stood up and said, "I think Reese and I should head to bed." He stretched his arms and yawned to further the effect. "Reese has already had a long day so I need to get him to bed." They all turned away from the movie long enough to wish Mike and Reese a good night and immediately turned back to the movie.

Mike and Reese walked into the bedroom. They called it the orange room because Tariff had painted the walls and the ceiling pumpkin orange. The drapes, comforter, and everything else, was black. The room had what you would call a sexual flavor.

Mike turned to Reese, as he closed the door behind them, "I'm so excited about this trip tomorrow. Thanks again."

"Anything for my baby boy!" Reese said with a smile, which quickly turned into a yawn. Reese walked over to Mike and planted a quick kiss on his cheek as the two fell on the bed.

After a silent moment or two, Mike said, "Chuck seems to be a nice guy. Seems like he's a little shy though, but I guess that would be natural, meeting us for the first time."

"Give him time," Reese said, "after a few days around you guys, trust me he will start to open up. I know I did after I was with them for a minute."

"Now all that needs to happen is for Jay to find him somebody." Mike managed to say between yawns. He continued, "Jay is a nice guy. He'll find someone in due time." Too tired to get up and out their clothes, Mike and Reese told each other good night. Reese gave him a quick peck on the lips.

"Good night to you too, baby boy, and thank you again," Reese said.

"Thank you for what?" Mike asked, with a tired and puzzled look at the same time.

"For allowing me to come into your life." Reese squeezed him tightly and slowly closed his eyes. Mike just smiled and fell off to sleep.

Demetrious and Tariff settled themselves in bed after straightening up down stairs. Demetrious looked up at the ceiling when Tariff came out of the bathroom after brushing his teeth. "What are you thinking about? You look like you're in real deep thought," Tariff asked.

"Naw, I'm just a little tired."

"Yeah, it has been a long day for all of us."

"Man, you know I miss James, too, but I think that he would be okay with us being together. I know he would want you to love again."

Tariff eased into bed and pulled Demetrious closer too him, "Just be a little patient with me." Tariff kissed Demetrious on the back of his neck and snuggled in closer to him, quickly falling asleep.

Demetrious couldn't fall asleep right away. His thoughts were nagging at him so he offered up a prayer to the Almighty: *Lord please bless all my friends and me. Keep us from harm's way. Protect us and keep us safe in Miami. Help us get there and back safely. Thank you for giving me the patience to help Tariff through this time. I love this man with all my heart and I know that someday that love will be returned without reservations. AMEN.* Demetrious turned to Tariff, watching him sleep, and kissed him softly on the lips, then whispered in his ear, "I'm here to stay and soon your heart will feel at home." After giving up his silent prayer to God, Demetrious closed his eyes and fell off to sleep.

Now in their room, Tyrell and Chuck prepared for their own rest. They both stripped down to their boxers and Chuck put on a pair of pajama bottoms. They climbed into bed, with Chuck sitting up at the top and Tyrell lying down at the bottom.

"I think my boys like you," Tyrell began. "Looks like you made a good impression."

"You've got a cool bunch of friends. You can see that there is a lot of love between you guys. I wish I had that kind of love."

"Man, those guys will grow to love you just like they do me. They'll see just how special and loving you can be."

With a big smile on his face, Chuck said, "So you think I'm special, huh? And you love me?"

"Yeah, I guess I really do. You are a good man, in spite of your past. You seem a little surprised."

"A little. I felt it, but I just never heard you say it."

"So you knew then?"

"I had an idea but sometimes you need that confirmation. You know what I mean?"

"I guess I do." With a seductive look, Chuck wiggled his finger in a motion for Tyrell to come to the end of the bed where he was. They shared a kiss and Tyrell moved his head onto Chuck's shoulder.

"You know, I didn't think anyone would ever give me a second chance. I thought people would always look at my past and see this bad person. Thank you for looking at me as I am now. I promise I won't let you down or disappoint you in anyway."

"You will, but that's what life is all about. There's a chance that I will let you down or disappoint you, too, but that's what makes a relationship special. We do things unintentionally to each other, but then, we make up for it later." Chuck lightly plucked Tyrell on his forehead, "I see now. Let's get some sleep." Chuck reached over and turned off the light beside him. Tyrell turned on his side and Chuck spooned in behind him.

"Tyrell?"

"Yeah?"

"I love you, too."

"I know."

"How did you know?"

"I felt it. Now go to sleep." With their arms inner-twined they drifted off to sleep.

Jay found that he was the only one left downstairs to finish watching the movie. As he watched the guys leave and go upstairs to there bedrooms, he started to think to himself, *one day I will have someone too,* but for now the closeness and the love he had for his friends was enough.

Jay felt the familiar vibration of his cell phone on his waist and looked down to see the name that appeared across the caller ID. The very sight of the name and digits now flashing from his midsection annoyed him. He snatched the phone from his belt and threw it to the end of the sofa.

"What the fuck?" Jay said to himself. As he turned the volume up on the TV, Jay could still hear the muffled vibrating once again.

To stop the continual purring of his cell, Jay reached over and flipped open the phone, "What do you want? I thought I told you never to call me again!" Jay yelled.

"Wait Jay, I need to talk to you," the caller said.

"We said all we needed to say, months ago. What could you possibly have to say to me that would change anything? I can't believe you're calling me after all this time."

"I'm outside your door. Can I come in, or can you come out, so we can talk? It'll only take fifteen minutes."

A satisfied and cold grin crossed Jay's face as he replied, "Well, you're out of luck bruh, because I'm at Tariff's house right now." *Dammit,* Jay thought to himself, *Why did I tell this niggah that?*

Whether out of reflex or genuine concern, Will asked, "What's up with that? Why are you there?"

"You lost the right to ask me questions like that a long time ago," Jay retorted.

"I'm on my way there. I just want fifteen minutes of your time and then, I promise, I'll leave."

Jay rolled his eyes, "Fine man. And fifteen is all you get."

"I'll call you when I'm out front," Will said.

"Fine," Jay replied, hanging up the phone without even saying goodbye. Jay began pacing. He could feel beads of sweat beginning to form on his brow.

"Why is this motherfucker calling me and what's so important that he has to talk to me tonight?" Jay asked himself. *Damn, should I wake up the guys?* He started to question himself even more. He began to feel the trickle of sweat run from his brow down the side of his nose. Jay was getting so worked up he nearly missed his cell phone vibrating. *Ugh*...Jay thought, *he must be out front.*

"Hello," Jay said.

"Hey Jay, I'm here. Can I come in?"

"Hell no, I'll come out," Jay muttered.

As Jay grabbed for the door knob, he looked up the stairs, shook his head and walked out, leaving the door unlocked. Jay walked to Will's car, parked at the curb in front of the house.

"Man, you might as well get out of the car, because I'm not getting in," Jay said. His arms crossed in front of him, he shifted from one foot to the other.

"Fine, man."

"So, Will, what is so urgent that you needed to talk to me tonight?"

"You're looking good Jay," Will stated.

"Thank you, but I know you didn't come all this way to flirt, so what do you want?"

"I miss you Jay, and I want us to try and work things out."

Jay stepped back and let out a sarcastic laugh, "You have got to be kidding! After all you have done to me? Well, looks like you don't need fifteen minutes after all."

Will motioned toward Jay, but Jay backed up, his balled fist down by his side.

"Jay, I know I was wrong and I have apologized to you over and over again," Will said.

Jay looked down and then looked back at Will. His icy glare began the statement even before he even began to speak. "My boys would stomp a mud hole in your ass if I told them what you did to me. Hell, I'd be right there with them!"

"But Jay…"

"Man, don't interrupt me! The first time you pushed me, Will, I let it go. Call it stupid, but I forgave you. You told me you would never do it again. Then two months later you got upset over some stupid shit and what did you do?"

"I didn't..."

"No Will, what did you do?"

"Jay, I know I was wrong."

"Will, I don't want to hear all that, I asked you a question. What did you do!?"

Will knew he wouldn't be able to avoid Jay's question. The veins on Jay's neck throbbed, but even in his anger he stopped short. Any response would probably have him waking up everyone in the neighborhood.

"I know... I ripped your shirt off you and the chain you had around your neck, and I closed the door in the basement, so you couldn't leave out."

"You need to get some help," Jay sputtered. "You need to get your temper under control before you hurt somebody. I can't be around you. It's your lucky night. I haven't told my boys, but if you come around me again or even talk to one of them, I will tell them the whole story."

"Jay, I still love you man."

"Will, you bring new meaning to the phrase 'loving someone to death' and I just can't be a part of that. I just pray you can recognize that love doesn't have to hurt - especially not intentionally."

"Come on, Jay," Will struggled to talk over Jay, to no avail.

"For the record, I knew you checked my cell phone at night while I slept, but I didn't care because I had nothing to hide from you. You accused me of so many things and all the time you were just obsessing about the shit you were doing behind my back."

"What are you talking about Jay?" Will looked around nervously.

"Let me explain this to you Will, so you can understand. I wondered why you were always going through my cell phone. So one night after you had a few drinks and passed out. I went through yours."

"So?"

"Yeah, so I was right, because I saw text messages from not only one guy but two guys, and let's say they weren't messages asking about final scores on any NBA games or what time the next church service was being held. So now I ask you, who was cheating on whom?"

"Jay, those guys didn't mean anything to me."

"Whatever, Will. Let me break it down for you. I don't want you or your 'love' anymore!"

"We can get counseling, man," Will replied.

"Change that 'we' to 'I' and you're on your way to recovery."

Will motioned toward Jay, but Jay backed up even further.

"Man, if you want to finish this conversation, I suggest you step back and keep your distance."

"But Jay…"

"But Jay nothing. I have to go in and get some sleep, I have an early day tomorrow, and besides, your fifteen minutes were up minutes ago. Good night!" Jay said as he turned to walk away. Will leaped forward and grabbed Jay's arm. His grip was firm, but as Jay quickly snatched away, a look of disgust came across his face.

"That's what I am talking about, Will. When the words fail you, that's all you know. You haven't changed. Good night and goodbye. It's over!" Jay said as he hurried to the front door.

"I'm sorry Jay," Will called out, disappointed in himself.

Just as Jay stepped in the house and locked the door behind himself, Will got into his car, sat there for a minute thinking he had made matters worse. He eventually drove off. Jay watched the car until he couldn't see it anymore. Jay walked from the foyer to the living room before he heard a voice call from upstairs.

"Jay, are you okay?"

Jay looked up and saw Demetrious at the top of the stairs. He was rubbing his eyes as though he was startled by some strange noise.

"What's up D? What are you doing up?"

"Man, I was thirsty and came down to get something to drink, but I thought I heard your voice outside the house."

"Oh, Okay, Jay replied.

"Are you okay?" Demetrious asked.

"Yeah man, I'm ok. I couldn't sleep so I just went outside to get some air."

"Oh ok, you just look a little frazzled."

"Naw man, I guess I'm starting to get tired," Jay said.

"Alright, man. Get some sleep, we have an early day."

"I will. Good night," Jay said with relief.

Chapter 9

The guys arrived in Miami in full star class style! The flight was so smooth and relaxing, that all the guys had just begun to enjoy the flight, when just that quickly, it was over. The flight attendant announced over the intercom, "Welcome to Miami. The time is now 10:30. Please enjoy your stay. If you're laying over here in Miami and continuing with us, we will be departing in about fourty-five minutes. Again, welcome to Miami and we looked forward to having you fly with us again soon."

The guys gathered up their bags and exited the airport to the limo Reese had waiting for them. They piled in and headed for the hotel. The sun shone brightly, in the cloudless sky. Blue waters greeted the shore and the palm trees moved with the slight breeze that blew as they pulled up to the hotel. The checked in and headed for their rooms. Once situated, they gathered in the hotel restaurant for breakfast. They all decided to stick with the continental breakfast of bagels, muffins, fruit juice and coffee. Everyone wanted to be ready for the beach.

"What's the plan for tonight?" Jay blurted out.

"Man, we haven't even decided what were going to do today," Demetrious commented with a chuckle.

"So what are we going to do," Jay said as he rolled his eyes at Demetrious with a grin on his face.

"How 'bout we walk off this little breakfast and then hit the beach and maybe do some shopping?" Reese suggested. "Sounds like a plan. They all chimed in and nodded their heads.

"Now that we got that out the way, so what's the plan for tonight?" Jay said insistently, as he tried to stop himself from laughing.

A clap of laughter broke out from the group. "Okay, Jay, do you have any suggestions?" Tyrell asked.

"OK, now that y'all finally got around to asking me," Jay said with a smirk on his face." There's this club called Hearts. I think we should go check it out."

"That would be cool. What do you guys think?" Tyrell asked.

"Sorry guys," Reese spoke up, "now that my NFL career will be kicking off, I think I need to skip that." Reese knew that for now he had to keep his sexual orientation on the low. "You know how homophobic people can be. Not that I am a big star or that people know me, but once the season starts, someone may come out and say they saw me. I didn't even think about that when we met for Mike's celebration. I just have to be low key," Reese told everyone. "Besides, I want to take my baby on the town tonight and do something special with him. So how about you all hit the club and we'll meet you for an early morning breakfast?"

"Knowing how you all are, that should be around 3:00 a.m.," Mike said knowingly.

Demetrious was the first to co-sign Reese's suggestion, "That sounds like a plan. While we're out today, we can find out what restaurant is open until that time of morning."

"You just remember who you're with when we hit the club." Tariff felt he had to remind Demetrious that they were there together and for him not to get any ideas about roaming off. Demetrious smiled, he liked the sound of that coming from Tariff. *Maybe he's coming around,* he thought to himself.

Tyrell turned to look at Chuck to get his reaction to the conversation. "Trust me, you don't have to worry. I'm with you all the way." Chuck said as he gave Tyrell a big smile and squeezed his thigh under the table. They quickly paid the check and walked around for a bit before hitting the beach. As soon as they found a spot on the beach, Reese, Mike, and Jay dropped their bags, pulled off their clothing and made a mad dash for the water.

There were people all over the beach. There were guys that walked the shore with their girls holding hands. Sailboats off the shore in the middle of the ocean cruised along. Bodies were buried in the sand. Kids dunked each other in the water. The air was heavy with sound of laughter. There were men and women giving you body, while others needed to cover up. Some people sprawled out on blankets trying to get that tan.

Tyrell, Chuck, Demetrious, and Tariff sat in the lounge chairs that lined the beach. Tyrell grabbed Chuck by the hand, "Baby, lets go get in the water!"

"That's okay, dawg, I don't know how to swim!" Chuck responded jerking away.

"Don't worry I'll protect you!" Tyrell said sticking out his chest.

"Maybe later. I'm going to chill right here and enjoy my drink," Chuck said as he held up his glass.

Tyrell turned to Tariff and Demetrious, "What about you two?"

"Alright, man, I'll go," Demetrious said, getting out of the chair.

"I'm with Chuck," Tariff said with a slight chuckle. I'm just going to sit here and finish my drink. I'll get in a little later." Tariff wasn't ready to hit the water. This was a good time for Tariff to get to know Chuck a little better. Tyrell and Demetrious headed into the water with the others, leaving Chuck and Tariff behind.

"So, Chuck, how you liking Miami so far?" Tariff asked as he sipped on his drink.

"Man, this is alright. I love this weather! The blue skies and white sand, man, it's picture perfect."

"Yeah, even though we haven't been here long, I can tell it is a nice place. You know, this is the happiest I've seen Tyrell in a while," Tariff said, as he watched the guys as they played in the water. "I can really see you make him happy."

"Man, I'm trying. He makes me happy as well. From the first time I met him, I felt something." Chuck said smiling happily, as he thought back to the day Tyrell walked into the copy center.

"I'm happy to hear that."

"Tyrell is the only guy that I've really cared for this much."

"I know how you feel. I feel that way about Demetrious. The first guy I loved like that was killed a couple of years ago."

"Man, I am so sorry to hear that," Chuck said. "That had to be hard."

"It is hard, but you know, things are getting better." Tariff turned away for a moment to watch Demetrious flip Jay in the water.

"Man look at those two, they are nuts. Jay took his death real hard," Tariff continued, "if it wasn't for Demetrious, I don't know what we would have done about Jay. He went into a deep depression, but Demetrious was able to bring him around. Jay is the youngest of the group, but he acts like our father. Since my last lover's death, he has become very protective."

"If you don't mind me asking, what happened to your first friend?"

Tariff started to tell Chuck, but stopped as he noticed Demetrious and Tyrell starting to head in their direction.

"Man, we can finish this conversation some other time. The guys are on their way back up and I don't want to ruin their trip."

"You guys should have gotten in the water. It feels good out there," Demetrious said as he looked for a towel, "What are you guys talking about?"

"Nothing much. Just getting to know Chuck." Tariff gave Chuck a wink and then looked back at Demetrious.

"How was the water, babe?" Chuck asked as he threw Tyrell a towel.

"The water was cold as hell, but it felt good." Tyrell caught the towel and sat down on the opposite end of the same lounge chair were Chuck sat. Mike, Reese, and Jay returned to the group. The guys lay out on the beach and chatted for an hour or so.

Finally, Mike made a suggestion, "How 'bout we grab some lunch and do some more site seeing?"

"Well, I met this guy that's sitting over there and he knows a couple of great places to go eat," Jay said. "Actually he may join us. Let me go over and get a number from him and we can get out of here." Everyone agreed and Jay ran over to the guy. When he returned, they all gathered up their stuff and headed for the hotel to shower and change.

The guys got back to their hotel rooms, the early flight,

swimming and walking around had pretty much tired them out. After they showered they all had slept right through lunch. Jay woke up in his room, the drapes were opened, he stared out at the bright sun, and pretty blue sky. *This is heaven,* he thought. He sat up and looked over and saw his room phone was blinking. He had a message. Jay picked up his phone and, after calling for his messages and found he had missed a couple of calls from Ricky. He erased the messages and called Ricky.

Ricky answered, "Hello," with his deep Barry White voice. It immediately brought a smile to Jay's face.

"Hey Ricky, it's me Jay. I'm sorry I guess I slept right through lunch. I must have been tired, 'cause I didn't even hear the phone ring."

Ricky responded, "I kind of figured you guys must have fallen asleep."

Jay, says, "I'm about to call the guys and see what they are up to. I know everyone has got be hungry about now. I hope you will join us, or did you already eat?"

"No man, to be honest after I called you, I took a shower and fell asleep myself." They both had to laugh. Jay's laughter came at the thought of Ricky wrapped in a towel.

"Sounds good to me," Ricky said. Hit me up when you guys are ready to leave your hotel. I'm going to get dressed."

"OK man, that will work."

A short time later, all of the guys met in front of Ricky's hotel waiting for him to join them for dinner. After a couple of minutes, Jay spotted Ricky coming toward them. Ricky wore a cream colored linen set that complimented his honey brown complexion. Jay introduced everyone to Ricky and they began to walk down the strip. As they walked down the strip toward the restaurant, Ricky smiled and extended his hand comfortably as Jay made the introductions.

"So Ricky, how long are you here for?" Jay asked.

"For about four more days. What about you?"

"The same. We got here today."

"I just got here today as well. I needed a vacation from work."

"Yeah, I know how you feel. What type of work do you do?" Jay asked, as he watched people as they walked by.

"I'm an attorney with this law firm in Charlotte, but I'm thinking about relocating. I just haven't decided where yet. So what about you, what do you do?"

"Back home, I'm a certified accountant."

"Where's home?" Ricky asked as he put on his shades.

"I hail from the good ol' boy state of Texas. I'm from Houston." Jay put a countrified tone in his voice.
Ricky laughed, "You're funny man. I've never been to Houston."

"Well, maybe you should come and check it out."

"Well, maybe I should… oh, the restaurant is right up the street. We're about five more minutes away," Ricky said.

"What's on your agenda for tonight?" Jay asked.

"Well, we're going to have dinner and then my boys, Reese and Mike, are going to go spend some time alone. You know how lovers are!"

"No, how are they?" Ricky asked.

"So, does that mean there's no one special for you back in Charlotte?"

"Nope! No one, but my bird!" *But one day* Ricky thought.

Jay let out a little laugh.

"And who's waiting for you?" Ricky asked.

"Not a soul. Not a soul."

"You know I have to ask this question right?"

"What question is that?" Jay asked as he looked behind at the guys.

"Why is a fine specimen of a man like you single?"

Jay thought about Will. "I was in a relationship, but turned out he wasn't the right one for me. Maybe I will tell you about it one day. I guess now I'm just waiting for the right one to come along. So, why are you single?"

Ricky, thought to himself *DAMN! He's fine.* They were so involved in their own conversation, they forgot about the rest of the guys that walked behind them.

"Actually, I'm divorced. I was married for a year and half and I've been divorced for about a year now." Jay got a pondering look on his face, his mind going a mile a minute. The expression on his face cued the next answer from Ricky.

"I know what you're probably thinking."

"What is that?" Jay said with a raised eyebrow.

"That I was one of those 'Down Low' brothers that cheated on his wife."

"Well, were you?" Jay responded too late to stop himself.

"Man, I actually loved my wife. I thought we would be together forever, but I couldn't fight those desires I had. So I told her about them. You know the funny thing is, I had only been with a man once before I got married. All the time I thought it was an experiment, but it was just who I am and I couldn't fight it anymore."

"That's deep. How did your wife take it?" Jay asked.

"It was hard for her at first. She wanted us to get counseling, but deep down inside, I knew counseling wouldn't help. So we agreed to go our separate ways. Even though she was upset, she respected the fact that I never cheated on her."

"Is she still in Charlotte?" Jay asked as he looked around.

"No, she ended up moving to make a fresh start. I think she moved somewhere in the Midwest. I did hear she met someone and she's very happy."

"Good for her," Jay replied with a nod and smile on his face.

"I only wish the best for her."

They finally reached the restaurant after almost walking past the place. They all walked in. The hostess asked them how many were in their party. They gave their answer in unison again like a choir, then they all broke out in laughter.

They looked over the menu and decided to order a bunch of appetizers and share them rather than get individual meals. Reese and Mike were planning to have a quiet dinner alone when they left the others so they wanted to leave some room for that.

They were just chilling, getting to know Ricky, when Reese stood up, "I hate to break up the party, but we have plans, right, baby?"

"Yep, we sure do! Why don't we all meet back in front of this place around 3:00 a.m. Does that work for everyone?"

Everyone agreed and decided since they were leaving, it was time to hit Club Hearts and see what was popping. Reese got the check and paid for the meal. They all protested, but he insisted and no one wanted to go against that. They all got up and headed for the door. All the guys except Mike and Reese headed for the club. Reaching the club in record time, they stood in line, waiting to go inside. While standing in front of the club, Chuck looked at Tyrell and said, "You know I've never been to a gay club before."

"Really? They're okay, but none of us really frequent them. We all hate the cigarette smoke so we go when we want a good drink and the gang has something to celebrate. Just don't get in here and lose your mind looking at all these men." He gave Chuck a sheepish grin and put his arm around his shoulder.

Chuck patted Ty on the ass and smiled, "I got mine!" They finally got through the line and entered the club and headed straight for the bar to order some drinks. When they found a table, Jay and Ricky headed for the dance floor.

"Looks like Jay has found his weekend play toy!" Demetrious said to no one in particular.

Tariff co-signed, "And he's not bad to look at either." Ricky had a baby face, he was in his early thirties but looked to be in his mid-twenties. His hair was cut extremely short. He stood about 6'2" tall. His clothes were tailored, revealing an athletic body. The atmosphere was jumping and the place was live.

"This club is off the hook," Jay yelled over the loud music.

"Yeah, it is," Ricky said as he smiled at Jay with his LL Cool Jay lips. Everywhere you looked you saw men, and only a couple of women. Lots of guys stood around with their shirts off showing off their bodies. Jay and Ricky stayed on the dance floor for some time flirting with each other in their only little sly way.

They were all having such a good time. A while later, Jay and Ricky made their way to the table with the rest of the group. You could hear peals of laughter coming from their table. The night flew by and before they knew it, it was already time for them to meet Mike and Reese. Tariff looked at his watch, "Damn guys, its 2:45! We need to get out of here so we can meet up with the love birds."

"Time sure flies when you're having fun," Tyrell said jokingly, while finishing off the last of his apple martini. They made their way to the exit and headed down the street, back to the spot where they all agreed to meet. It was a festive night, people were partying all over the place. The more they walked, the more they saw. Homeless people sat on the walkways, asking people for change. One guy standing over a garbage can throwing up was so drunk that he had to hold his arms on the side of the can to keep himself up right. Sidewalks were so crowded that it was almost impossible for everyone to walk together. But the weather was great with clear skies and a slight breeze carrying the scents of the night.

After they walked a few blocks, the guys saw Mike and Reese up ahead. They also saw two men they didn't know. One that stood in front of Mike and Reese and the other behind them.

"Who are those two guys Mike and Reese are talking to?" Tyrell was first to ask.

"Probably just some other couple they met or someone looking for directions," Demetrious replied. Chuck's attention shifted immediately, his street sense kicked in. He picked up the pace in his stride. He had a bad feeling about the two strangers. Chuck reached Mike and Reese before the rest of the guys and he immediately moved Mike and Reese behind him and put himself in a position to face the two strangers.

"Is there a problem here?" Chuck snapped. Just as he took a step toward the man, he saw the quick flash of a knife being pulled from his pocket. Trying to step back, Chuck stumbled, allowing the man an opening to jab the knife violently into his stomach. Without a second thought, both men took off running. Tyrell and the guys saw the two strangers running away and became more confused about what had just happened. Meanwhile, Chuck grabbed his stomach and then looked at his hand, which was now covered with his own blood. The realization that he had just been stabbed started to sink in. He grabbed his side immediately thinking that would stop the pain. Chuck started to fall backward, Reese caught him before he hit the ground, not realizing what Chuck already knew. Reese noticed the blood on Chuck's hand and shirt.

"What the fuck!" Reese shouted out.

"Shit, it hurts," Chuck managed to get out as his breathing became shallow.

Reese looked at Chuck's face and saw his color changing. As he held him, Chuck began to tremble.

Tyrell ran over and leaned over Chuck. "Chuck, man, What's wrong? What's wrong? Oh my God!"

Reese looked at Tyrell, "I think he's been stabbed."

"Stabbed!" Tyrell yelled out.

"Somebody call 911!" Reese shouted. By this time, people started to gather around, to see what had happened.

A male voice from the crowd, yelled, "I already have, help is on the way."

As Ricky ran over, he pulled off his shirt and handed it to Reese, "Put this on his wound and apply pressure to help stop the bleeding."

Chuck moaned in pain and Reese was having a hard time trying to stop the bleeding. Chuck, still conscious, looked at Tyrell.

"Don't worry, I'll be okay," Chuck said as he grasped for a breath. Chuck's mind started to race. He felt weak, fear started to kick in. All Chuck knew is that he didn't want to die.

"Stand back, people," Ricky said to the crowd as he looked at Reese and told him to continue to put pressure on the wound. While Reese applied pressure, Ricky checked for a pulse and he noticed that Chuck had stopped breathing. He started mouth to mouth, and in the background he could hear the approaching sirens, as well as a voice from the crowd that yelled, "The ambulance is here!" The crowd began to murmur, "Is he dead? Is he dead?" The EMTs made their way to Ricky and Reese.

"He's not breathing and he's been stabbed," Reese said to them as they took over.

"We can take it from here," the EMT said as he frantically worked on Chuck. Reese and Ricky's hands were both drenched with Chuck's blood. Reese tried to wipe the blood off using his shirt. As Reese looked over and saw them continuing to work on Chuck, the reality of what happened had started to sink in. Reese started to punch into the air, as he filled up with anger. Mike ran over to Reese and tried to grab his arms.

"Come on, baby, come on, baby, everything will be fine," Mike said, not really knowing even if it would be.

"What the hell just happened here?" Tariff asked, trying to fight the memories of James.

Mike started to explain through his anger, "The two guys walked up to us and asked us for directions. We tried to tell them we weren't from here. One of them showed us a gun in his waistband and wanted us to follow them. Then, out of nowhere, Chuck stepped in front of us and one of the guys pulled out a knife and stabbed him." Interrupting Mike's explanation to Tariff, Tyrell blurted out, "We need to get to the hospital!"

The EMTs got Chuck breathing again, but his pulse was still weak. They got him stabilized and then moved him on to a stretcher. The EMTs started to roll Chuck toward the ambulance with Tyrell right by his side.

"I'm going with him!" Tyrell managed to say between sniffles.

"What hospital are you taking him to?" Mike asked the EMT.

"Florida General." Mike relayed the information to the others. Mike ran back over to the ambulance to let Tyrell know that they would catch a cab and meet him there.

"Don't worry, Ty, he's going to be alright, man." Mike was trying his best to reassure Tyrell, but deep down he was scared.

"He has to be, man, he just has to be," Tyrell kept saying to himself.

Tyrell sat there in the ambulance watching them hook the intravenous tube up to Chuck. He watched Chuck as he lay with the oxygen mask on, barely breathing. As he watched, Tyrell prayed. Finally, the ambulance pulled up to the hospital and the doors swung open. Nurses rushed to his man's side. As they took Chuck off the ambulance and wheeled him in, they asked Tyrell to wait in the waiting area. Ten minutes later, the gang all showed up. When they got inside they spotted Tyrell sitting in the waiting room in a complete daze. He didn't see the guys come in. Demetrious yelled his name, Tyrell didn't respond. Demetrious called him again and Tyrell looked up. As Demetrious sat next to Tyrell, he put his arms around him for comfort.

"How is he man?" Demetrious asked.

"I don't know. No one has come to talk to me yet.

"Damn, man, how did this happen?" Demetrious yelled, pushing back his chair.

"I'm going over to the nurse's station to see what I can find out."

"I'll go with you. Wait up." Jay was right on Demetrious' heels. They approached the nurse sitting behind the counter.

"Excuse me nurse," Jay said. The old gray haired nurse looked up and took off her glasses which hung on a chain.

"Yes, may I help you gentlemen?"

"We're trying to check on a patient who was just brought in with a stab wound to the stomach," Demetrious asked. The nurse asked for his name, looked at the charts and found the only victim brought in with that type of injury.

"Yes here he is. The doctor is in with him now. He should be out shortly to talk to you."

Jay, thought for a second, "Can you tell us anything?"

The nurse stood up, "I'm sorry, sir. I wish I could, but you will just have to wait in the waiting room."

Two police officers come through the swinging doors of the emergency room. The husky white officer asked loudly, "Were you with the gentlemen that was just stabbed?" Ricky stood up. "Yes sir, you need to talk to Mike and Reese," he said, pointing to them. Mike and Reese gave a quick synopsis of what happened and managed to give the officer a description of the guys that attacked Chuck. The officer collected all the needed information, gave Mike his card, and walked out just as quickly as he walked in. Mike turned and hugged Reese tightly.

"Man, what the hell just happened here?"

Trying his best to comfort Mike, Reese squeezed him tighter, "Baby, it's going to be okay. Chuck is going to be just fine."

"You know he just saved our lives."

Demetrious and Jay returned to Tyrell's side to let him know that the doctor was in with Chuck and he would be out shortly to give them an update on his condition.

"In the meantime, I'll find a cafeteria and get us some coffee. It looks like it's going to be a while," Ricky suggested. Reese decided to go with him to give him a hand. Tyrell was pacing back and forth in the waiting room. When Ricky and Reese left, he finally sat down in a chair and put his head in his hands. Jay and Tariff immediately went to his side.

"Look, man, don't worry. He will be alright." Tariff was hugging him to his shoulder.

Jay chimed in, "Yeah, Chuck is strong. He's going to make it. You'll see."

Lifting himself from Tariff's shoulder, he looked from one to the other, "You think so? You guys are such good friends." They stood up and hugged each other.

Their embrace was soon interrupted by the doctor's voice, "Excuse me gentleman."

Tyrell, with an anxious look on his face asked, "Doctor, is he going to be okay?"

The doctor cleared his throat and looked directly at Tyrell, "He's lost a lot of blood and luckily the knife didn't puncture any vital organs, but I do want to keep him overnight for observation. My assistant is still in there closing his wound with stitches. We've given him a sedative and a pain killer so he can rest comfortably through the night."

"Thank you, doctor," Tyrell said with some sign of relief

on his face. When can I see him?"

"Give me about thirty minutes and then I'll have the nurse come get you."

"Thank you again, Doc." The doctor walked away, leaving them in the waiting room, just as Reese and Ricky walked back in carrying the coffee.

"So, what's up? How's he doing?" Reese was asking Mike as he handed him a cup of coffee.

"The doctor says he's going to be fine, they're just going to keep him overnight just as a precaution."

Reese lets out a sigh of relief, "Man that's great."

"Yes, it is," Reese said.

"You guys might as well go back to the hotel and get some sleep. I'm going to stay here for the night."

Tyrell was making it known to them all that he had no plans of leaving. "Well, we can stay too!" Jay said.

"I appreciate that, man, but you guys go ahead and get some sleep, its been a crazy and wild night and I know you guys have to be exhausted."

As he looked at Ricky's and Reese's blood stained clothes he loses his train of thought for a second, "I'll be okay and I'll call you guys in the morning." Tyrell was adamant about them leaving. He felt that there was no sense in everyone staying.

"Man, are you sure?" Mike expressed his concerns about leaving him there alone.

"Yeah, I'm sure. There's no need for all of you to be here, besides I know how to call if I need you." Tyrell was putting on a brave front by flashing Mike a fake smile.

They all decided to listen to Tyrell and leave, giving him a great big hug and reassuring him that they were only a phone call away. As all of them walked out of the hospital,

Jay looked back not wanting to leaving his friend behind. Tariff put his arm around Jay's shoulder, "Don't worry. Tyrell will be okay. If anything happens, he will call us." As they walked out, they caught a taxi across from the emergency entrance and headed back to the hotel.

Tyrell sat there waiting and waiting. Thirty minutes seemed like an eternity. Finally, after a forty-five minute wait, the nurse came out to the waiting area and asked Tyrell to follow her. He nodded his head and she escorted him to Chuck's room. When he went inside of his room, Chuck was fast asleep. Tyrell just stood beside his bed and stared at him while he slept.

He bent down and whispered, "Don't you ever scare me like that again." He kissed him on the forehead, grabbed the extra blanket off the end of his bed, and headed to a chair in the corner of the room. He took a quick look around the room and then laid his head back and fell asleep.

Chapter 10

The next morning, Chuck woke up disoriented. He squinted to see where he was as he tried to sit up. The pain in his stomach caused him to moan a little. "Baby, don't try to move," Tyrell said out of concern.

"Where am I? What happened?"

"You're in the hospital. You were stabbed last night. Do you remember anything?"

Chuck rubbed his head, as he tried to remember, "All I can recall is Mike and Reese standing and talking to two dudes." Tyrell sat down beside his bed and recounted the whole story to him.

"You've been here all night?" Chuck asked.

"Right over there," Tyrell said, as he pointed to the hard plastic chair in the corner of the room near the closet.

The doctor walked in and greeted them both. "Good morning, gentlemen. I'm Dr. Johnson." Turning to Chuck, he asked, "How is our patient feeling?"

"Okay," he responded, gently touching the gauze over his wound, "but I'm a little sore."

The doctor removed Chuck's chart from the end of the bed, pulled out his glasses, and placed them on his pointed nose. After a quick glance at the chart, Doctor Johnson pulled back the sheet to examine Chuck's wound.

"Everything looks good. You have quite a few stitches so you're going to be a little sore for the next couple of days, but you will be fine, you can go home this afternoon. Once you get home, go straight to bed and get a good night's sleep. I'll prescribe some antibiotics to fight off any infection and a pain killer for any discomfort. Just know that you're a lucky man." The doctor shook their hands and left the room to continue his rounds.

Tyrell kissed Chuck lovingly on his cheek and stood up, "Let me go call the guys and let them know what the doctor said."

Tyrell found a courtesy phone and dialed Mike and Reese's room.

"Hello," Reese answered.

"Hey man!" Tyrell said as he watched the nurses going back and forth.

"'Sup Ty, how is our boy doing? Are you okay?" Reese asked, not giving Tyrell a chance to answer.

"Chuck is fine, man. The doctor said he can come home today, so we should be there this afternoon sometime."

"Aw, man that's great. We'll see you guys back here."

"Alright man, let the other guys know for me please," Tyrell replied.

"Cool, no doubt. So Ty, how you doing man, you okay?"

"I'm okay man, just a little sore from sleeping in that damn hospital chair," Tyrell said as he stretched.

"Give our love to Chuck, man."

"I will. Thanks."

"We love you, Ty," Reese said before he hung up.

Tyrell smiled, "I love y'all too, man."

Tyrell hung up the phone and walked back to Chuck's room. He sat down in the chair outside of the room and replayed the last 24 hours over and over in his head. Lord, he thought, *thank you.* At that moment Tyrell realized just how much he loved his man. Tyrell got up and walked back in Chuck's room. Chuck was fast asleep so he sat in the familiar chair from last night and watched Chuck sleep.

*   *   *

Ricky sat in the lobby of Jay's hotel with a cup of coffee. He faced the bank of elevators. The hotel was decorated with Victorian furniture as well as abstract art. The unusual blend was pleasing to the eye. The blue smocked landscaping staff busily watered the many plants. The hotel was crowded with people rushing in and out. The two bell men were dressed in their dark grey uniforms. Ricky's attention was focused on a lady near the bellman stand who was trying to put her screaming daughter into a stroller. Out of nowhere, Jay walked up and tapped him on the shoulder.

"Have you been waiting long?" Jay asked.

"Oh no, I just got here. How's your boy doing? Is he okay?"

"He's going to be fine. They're releasing him this afternoon."

"Man, that was some scary shit last night," Ricky commented as he took a sip of his coffee.

"Yeah, it was, wasn't it?" Jay said, as he plopped down next to Ricky and leaned back.

"Well just thank God that he's going to be alright."

"You came through like a champ," Jay mentioned as he patted Ricky on the back.

"Awh, man, go head. I didn't do anything that anybody else wouldn't have done." He quickly changed the subject, "So what are your plans for the day?"

"Well, I just came from Tyrell and Chuck's room. The

guys and I filled it with flowers and balloons so when Chuck gets in from the hospital, we'll all be there to give him a hero's welcome."

"That's really nice of you guys to do that for him."

"What would be nicer is if you could make it too," Jay said as he looked into Ricky's deep brown eyes.

"Thanks for asking me, I would like nothing better than to be there."

Jay and Ricky stole a moment to take a stroll along the beach, to get to know one another. Jay got a call from Mike, who called to let him know that Chuck and Tyrell were on their way to the hotel.

Later that evening, Chuck and Tyrell pulled up in front of the hotel and Tyrell helped Chuck ease out of the taxi.

"I'm fine, man," Chuck said, as his male pride kicked in.

"I know you are, man, but for now, just humor me," Tyrell said holding out his hand.

"Shhhhhhhhh! I can hear the doors opening on the elevator," Demetrious said trying to get everyone to be quiet. The guys heard Tyrell as he stuck his key card in the door. "Surprise!" He and Chuck were definitely surprised as they walked into a room filled with flowers and balloons.

"Man, you guys didn't have to do this. Thanks!" Chuck said with a big grin on his face.

"No. Thank you!" Mike said, as he walked over and gingerly gave Chuck a hug.

"Man, if you hadn't intervened, no telling what might have happened," Reese said, gratefully. They talked and laughed for sometime until the guys noticed Chuck yawning.

Tariff turned to Chuck, "Well, we're going to get out of here and let you get some sleep."

Jay agreed, "We don't want to wear you out. So we'll talk to you guys later."

"I am a little beat," Chuck said. "Thanks again, guys. I really appreciate everything." One by one they said their good byes and headed for the door.

Later that night, Tariff, Jay, Demetrious, Mike, Reese, and Ricky sat at Blue Waters a restaurant on Ocean Drive. The restaurant had seats on the side walk and the patio. Lots of the visitors and locals alike frequented the restaurant because it had a gay-friendly atmosphere. The guys sat, ate some dinner, and people watched. The strip was very crowded that night. Parties were going on at most of the bars up and down the strip.

"Man, ain't it amazing how most of these brothas' passing by, holding their girls' hands, are staring at us just as much as at the girls are," Jay said, making his own observation.

Ricky noticed the same thing, "What gets me is how sneaky they try to be about it."

Demetrious, not fazed by it, turned to the group, "Man, that's all the time. So we got three nights left here in Miami. What should we do?"

Ricky made a suggestion, "Well, there's a play in town. We can try and catch an evening show the day after tomorrow. That way your boy, Chuck, won't have to walk and move around a lot and he won't wear himself out."

Tariff, looking inquisitive, asked, "What's the name of the play?"

"It's an E. Lynn Harris' stage play called *Not a Day Goes By,*" Ricky said.

Reese looked over at Mike, "I heard of that. I tried to get tickets for us but it was always sold out."

"I heard of it too. It actually got great reviews," Tariff spoke up.

"Cool, I'll pick up the tickets tomorrow," Ricky said taking a bite of his burger.

"I'd like to make a toast to good friends *and* to good friends!" Jay said as he winked at the guys and lifted his glass.

Tariff added in, "And a hero's toast to Chuck for his bravery."

They all clinked glasses, as Reese called over the waiter, "Another round for everyone?"

After a while, the guys decided to take a walk along the beach to enjoy the warm Miami night. As they prepared to leave, Mike looked across the way and turned to Reese, with trepidation in his eyes "Sweetheart, there go those guys that tried to rob us last night."

Reese looked around, "Where? I don't see them."

Grabbing Reese's shoulder, Mike turned and pointed, "Over there." Reese caught sight of them and without another word Reese immediately headed in their direction, the others followed.

Mike caught Reese by the arm, "Sweetheart, come on. Don't go over there. We don't need you or anyone else getting hurt."

"What do you think we should do?" Demetrious asked.

Jay, tapping his fist together said, "I say we go over there and kick some asses."

"Sounds like a plan to me!" Reese co-signed.

Reese turned to Mike, "Baby boy, run over to the bar and call the police."

Mike gave Reese a quick peck, "Just be careful." Then he sprinted to the bar.

Reese turned back in the direction of the two guys and he and the boyz headed over to confront them, "Yo, dawg you remember me?" Reese said angrily.

The guy that actually stabbed Chuck looked Reese up and down, "Naw, champ should I?" By this time the other guys had made a full circle around the two so they couldn't get away.

Not getting the response he wanted, Jay stepped up, pushed Reese out the way, and pointed a finger in the guys face. "You and your boy here are the muthafuckers that stabbed our boy last night!"

"Y'all guys got the wrong ones," the guy replied.

Out of the corner of his eye, Tariff noticed one of the two guys reaching under his shirt. He snatched the guy's hand and without a second thought, he gave him a right hook across the face, knocking him to the ground with a thud. Jay and Reese grabbed the other guy. Jay was just about to connect with his face when Mike showed up with two police officers in tow.

The two cops apprehended the two assailants as well as Tariff. They slapped handcuffs on all three. Demetrious, stepped to the cop for handcuffing Tariff, but Reese held him back.

Reese explained to the two officers, "These are the two guys that tried to rob us last night, in fact one of our friends took a knife trying to protect us from this one here," as Reese pointed the assailant out. The cops pulled out the two guys ID's and ran their names through their computers. The information came back that the two were wanted for a series of robberies in the area. Once the cops got all the information straight, they released Tariff from the handcuffs.

The two officers took the two guys off in a squad car.

The guys decided to forget about the walk on the beach and headed back to the hotel.

Demetrious grabbed Tariff by the arm, "Man, what just happened back there?"

"What do you mean?" Tariff asked as he pulled away.

"Why did you punch that guy?" Demetrious demanded, as he looked Tariff straight in the eye.

"Somebody needed to teach those punks a lesson. I needed to let them know they just can't go around stabbing and robbing people and shit. If you dish it, be able to take it," Tariff replied as anger flashed across his face.

"You were thinking about James weren't you?" Demetrious asked as he looked off.

Tariff had a solemn look on his face, "Man if I could have only been there…"

"I think we've all said that to ourselves at one time or another. We all loved James so much and to think about what he went through that day breaks my heart." Demetrious hugged Tariff as they walked, "Come on, baby, it will be okay. Let's go back and give Tyrell and Chuck the good news about those thugs," Demetrious suggested.

"How about we tell them in the morning?" Tariff commented smiling.

"You're right, they're probably asleep anyway."

Just a few yards behind them Jay and Ricky were caught up in what had just happened. "I have never seen my boy Tariff react that way."

"Really?" Ricky said in disbelief.

"Believe it or not, he's the calm one of the group. His first lover was killed a couple of years ago. These guys were trying to car jack him and it went bad."

"Damn, man, that's some sad shit," Ricky said, reacting

to Jay's news.

"Tariff has had a hard time trying to get over it, but I can tell, it's still hard for him sometimes, just like it has been for all of us."

"So did they catch who did it?"

"They did, but from what I understand, one of them got out some months ago, I'm not really sure about all the specifics. It turns out this brutha turned states evidence against the others and he got out on good behavior or some shit."

"So how does Tariff feel about that?" Ricky asked.

"I don't know. The guys and I try not to bring it up. We all still suffer from the shock of James getting killed. I don't think any of us has truly gotten over it. We just take each day as it comes. Some days are better than others, you know what I mean?"

"I know what you mean, but you know, I just don't get these bruthas out here. Why do they feel they got to rob and kill each other? And for what? A few pennies. Don't they know that if they got a damn job they would have money instead of going around carjacking and killing people that are just trying to make an honest living?" The conversation between Jay and Ricky was getting intense, but it was real life.

"Naw, what gets me is when they find out you're gay, they want to punk you. But little do they know, the only difference between them and us is who we sleep with. I have this buddy back home named Daunte. We're really good friends, but I know once he finds out about me, our friendship will change. Truth be told, I don't want to sleep with him no more than he wants to sleep with me."

"Well, if he can't accept you for who you are, then he's

no friend. If a person doesn't bring positive energy to your life then you need to get rid of them."

"If he sees gay guys, he calls them 'faggots'," Jay said.

Ricky was now feeling philosophical, "I wonder, does your boy know that the way we black men feel when the white man calls us niggers, is no different than the way a gay man feels when they call him a faggot? They are so quick to say they hate gay people but it's possible that some of their best friends, brothers, uncles, aunties, sisters, even fathers and mothers are gay. What happens when they find out do they stop loving them and began to hate them."

"Sounds to me like they are more mixed up then we are." Jay felt himself getting angrier by the moment, so he changed the subject.

"So, Ricky, why haven't you tried to get me into bed yet?"

"The truth?"

"Nothing but!" Jay said.

"I think you're a cool brutha. The type I could see myself chilling with. It's hard to find a brutha out here that's got his shit together, you know what I mean?"

"I definitely know what you mean," Jay replied.

"I'd like to continue seeing you. I'd like to visit you in Houston and see where this could go." The thought of that brought a smile to Ricky's face.

Jay, gave him one of those Kodak smiles and, said, "So you want to get to know little ol' me?" trying to sound like one of those southern bells.

Ricky started to grin at how silly Jay was acting, "I would, how do you feel about that?"

"I like that, but what happens when things get serious? Don't forget you're in Charlotte and I'm in Houston."

"I am considering relocating anyway. Maybe I can add Houston to my list of cities to check out." They reached Ricky's hotel first. Jay and Ricky, stood in front of his hotel. The other guys stopped to wait for Jay.

"I guess this is good night," Ricky said as he stared deep into Jay's eyes, with a slight smile on his face.

"I guess it is, unless you would like for me to come up with you?"

"You must have been reading my mind," Ricky said as he smiled even more.

Jay turned to Demetrious, Tariff, Mike, and Reese and gave them a wink, and told them he would see them at the hotel in the morning.

Chapter 11

The next two days the guys hung out on the beach and did some shopping. Tyrell spend that time taking care of Chuck. On the third day later that evening, Tyrell and Chuck were in their room getting ready for the play when the phone rang. Tyrell answered it, "Hello, we're almost ready. We'll be down in about five minutes."

Tyrell hung up the phone. "That was the guys. They're all waiting for us in the lobby." Chuck grabbed his jacket off the back of the chair and headed for the door.

Tyrell was concerned. He wasn't sure if Chuck should be going out so early. "Are you sure you want to do this, Chuck?" Tyrell asked as he watched Chuck head for the door.

"I'm fine man, I'll be okay. My stomach does still hurt a little, but I can handle it."

There you go again, that male pride is kicking in. Tyrell thought. "You know it would be okay if we stayed in. I know the guys will understand."

"Ty, I've been in that bed all day, that's what's killing me," Chuck said as he pointed to the bed.

Tyrell walked over to Chuck. "Look promise me if you feel any pain you won't try to hide it from me. Promise me you will let me know."

"Okay, don't worry. I promise you, if I feel any pain you will be the first to know, scouts honor," Chuck said, raising his hand as if he were a boy scout.

Tyrell laughed as they walked out the room and headed

to the elevator. Tyrell eyed Chuck as he stood next to him in the elevator. Chuck caught Tyrell staring.

"Baby, I told you I'll be okay. Don't be such a worry wart," Chuck said with a big smile on his face.

As the elevator doors opened, the gang all stood there in a half circle. Both Chuck and Tyrell's eyes became fixated on the wheelchair that Reese stood behind. Chuck the first to speak as he pointed at the chair.

"Who is that for?"

Reese walked from behind the chair. "Chuck, we all agreed that the chair would be a good idea for you. Man, you have just been stabbed. So we wanted to take precautions."

"Right," Jay chimed in. "We knew that if you re-injured yourself, Tyrell would kill each and everyone of us." Tyrell started to feel warm all over.

This is why I love these guys so much, Tyrell thought.

"I appreciate the thought guys, but I can't ride in this chair," Chuck said.

"Chuck, let me put it this way. If you don't ride in this chair, then none of us are going to go to the play and we will all be out of money. So the decision is yours. What is it going to be?" Demetrious asked.

Chuck turned his head and looked at all the guys knowing they meant what they said. He walked over to the wheelchair and sat down.

"Wise decision, man. Now let's get out of here," Jay said.

When the play was over, the guys stood outside of the theater. Tariff noticed a quaint restaurant across the street.

"Is anybody hungry?" Tariff asked.

"I'm always hungry," Demetrious said. Everyone else

agreed.

"Why don't we grab something from the restaurant over there?" Tariff suggested. As they walked over, they noticed that the sign said *open mic.*

"Let's go in and get a few laughs at these people performing," Jay said.

As they walked in, a tall thin young man dressed in black pants and a white shirt and black bow tie walked over, "Good evening gents. How is everyone doing tonight? How many in your group?"

"Good evening to you too," Mike spoke up as the guys watched a young lady reading poetry on the stage. "There are six of us."

"Thank you, sir, please follow me."

As they walked to their seats, they noticed how small the restaurant was inside. Only about 25 tables faced a small stage. The drapes that hung around the stage were red, the same color as the table clothes. A shiny black piano on the side of the stage was being played by a gentleman probably in his mid to late thirties which was evident by the gray streaks in his hair. He was dressed the same as the host that greeted the guys at the door. The host seated them a little close to the stage so Chuck's wheelchair wouldn't be in anyone's way. "Your waitress will be with you in a minute. Enjoy your evening."

As the group ate and watched the different performers, Chuck wandered on whether or not he should test the waters and perform. The MC got on the mic and asked if there were any more performers. Chuck got up out of the chair walked slowly toward the stage. He took the mic from the MC. The group turned and looked at Tyrell. All he could do was shrug his shoulders. The whole room clapped and welcomed him on the stage. Jay stood up and started to whistle. Chuck stepped to the front of the stage, "I'd like to sing this song to someone very special. "

He stepped back and whispered something to the gentleman that sat at the piano.

Chuck began to sing and the whole room fell silent. Tyrell and the guys sat there, completely stunned. His voice was crisp and clear and he had a range that was out of this world. The guys knew by Chuck's facial expression when he was in pain, but he still belted out that song. The guys continued to watch him in awe. He sang a song by Tony Terry, *When I'm With You.* It was one of Chuck's favorites. The ladies started to scream. When he finished the song and left the stage, the audience cheered and cried for more. The audience wanted another performance. Had he been at his best, he probably would have done another song, but he walked back to the table instead. People were shaking his hand and patting him on the back. It was so crazy and unreal, the reception he was getting from everyone. The guys were clapping, Jay continued to whistle.

"Man, if I heard that on the radio, I would have gone right out and bought the CD," Reese said as he patted Chuck on the back and shook his hand at the same time.

Tyrell was just in complete shock, "Baby, you didn't tell me that you could sing like that."

"You remember that project I told you I was saving for." Chuck tried to get Tyrell to remember.

"I remember."

"Well, this is that project. I'm saving so I can complete a demo tape. You think they would like me?"

"Like you? Man, they are going to love you!"

Tariff now offered his kudos to Chuck, "You have some

set of pipes on you, man."

Demetrious still couldn't get over Chuck's performance, "I am beside myself. Dawg, you tore it up! Damn man!"

Chuck was all aglow and beaming from ear to ear at the reception he was getting.

"Thanks guys! I'm glad y'all liked it." The group listened to a couple more acts and then left. The waiter brought over the check, the guys paid and as soon as Chuck was about to leave the people again clapped and shook his hand on his way out.

"Baby, looks like you got a fan club." Tyrell bent over to whisper in Chuck's ear.

As the guys walked down the street Tyrell and Chuck lagged slightly back from the rest of the group. As Tyrell pushed Chuck in the chair, he could see that Chuck was tired. "We can stop here and catch a taxi."

"That's fine man, whatever you want," Chuck said trying to get Tyrell to relax.

"Baby, why didn't you tell me you could blow like that? I never heard you open your mouth to even hum, let alone sing."

"I stopped singing when I got locked up, even when I got out I really didn't sing much at all. My life was a mess and I had nothing to sing about. Then you came along and changed all that. You became my inspiration and I got my passion back."

Chuck flashed Tyrell a big smile. "I felt your love in every word and how you sang, I was so blown away." Tariff and Demetrious overheard Chuck and Tyrell's whole conversation, so when they talked about the part about Chuck being locked up, Tariff and Demetrious turned to one another and mouthed the words LOCKED UP silently to each other. Chuck and Tyrell continued with their conversation, unaware of what Tariff and Demetrious now knew. The guys flagged down a taxi and finally they reached the hotel. Tyrell could see that Chuck's face started to flinch. Chuck tried his best to hide his discomfort. "Well guys, I'm going to take Chuck up to the room and get him in bed."

"Alright fellows, talk to y'all a little later. I really enjoyed the play. Thanks again," Chuck replied.

Jay stayed at the hotel long enough to grab a change of clothes and his toiletries and then headed back over to Ricky's hotel. Tariff and Demetrious reached their room and started to talk about the conversation they had just heard.

"I can't believe Chuck was locked up," Tariff said with raised eyebrows.

"I'm just as shocked as you are." Demetrious sighed, dropped his head and rubbed the back of his neck as he shook his head from side to side. Demetrious continued, "I wonder what he did and why Tyrell didn't tell any of us."

As Tariff slipped out of his pants he said, "You know he must have a good reason."

"Well, he knows we're not the judgmental type. Do you think any of the other guys know?" Demetrious questioned.

"I doubt it. My guess is we're the only ones. They will tell us in due time."

"Well, either way, Chuck is a pretty nice guy and he did put his own life in danger to save Mike and Reese."

"Yep, you're right," Tariff said as he pulled back the blankets on the bed. Both climbed into bed and snuggled up with each other before falling asleep.

Ricky and Jay hung out in Ricky's hotel room. Ricky finished packing his suitcase. Ricky wanted to spend the little time they had left together.

"I guess this is our last night together for a while." Jay said as he walked out onto the balcony. As he looked up into the sky, he thought about how beautiful the full moon looked, its beams of light reflecting along the water as it hit the shore. The accompanying warm breeze made everything perfect.

"These days went by pretty quick," Ricky said softly as he walked up behind Jay and put his arms around his waist. They stood there enjoying the night, each one not wanting the night to end.

Ricky whispered in Jay's ear, "You know this night was made especially for us."

Jay leaned back his head on Ricky's chest and said.

"You know I haven't felt this safe and secure in such a long time."

"Why is it that all the good guys you meet live in other cities?" Ricky wondered, "I would love to come to Houston in a few weeks if that's okay with you."

"Of course it's okay with me." Jay smiled at the thought. Ricky turned him around and looked in his eyes, "I just want to hold you again our last night here."

Jay got lost in Ricky's bedroom eyes, "I can't wait to make love to you." Jay gave Ricky a big seductive smile. Ricky, who was much taller than Jay, leaned down and planted a kiss on Jay's lips. As the kiss ended, Jay turned back to look out into the ocean, Ricky put his arms back around Jay's waist. As they both looked back out to the water they swayed from side to side. The sound of the waves hitting the shore was their music.

"You're a special man, Jay," Ricky whispered in his ear.

The next morning everyone was at the airport. Jay said goodbye to Ricky while the others checked in their bags.

The guys finished and made their way over to where Jay and Ricky stood.

"Man, you need to make your way to Houston. I'm sure Jay would love that," Demetrious spoke as he put his arm around Jay. Demetrious knew Jay was a little down and he always knew how to get him to smile.

"Well, we're working on that already," Ricky said as he smiled at Jay. "I'll be down that way in a few weeks. Hopefully, I'll see all of you guys then and we can hang out and do something. And Chuck, you take care of that stomach, man."

"I will surely do that." Chuck winced a little as the words left his mouth.

"Oh, and Chuck, I'm going to be looking for that new CD of yours soon."

"COMING SOON to a store near you." Chuck used one of those commentator voices. Everyone gave Ricky one last brotherly hug and then headed to their separate gates. Ricky and Jay glanced back at each other. Ricky shot Jay that sexy smile and wink. Jay smiled, winked back, and jogged up to catch the rest of the guys.

"You okay, knucklehead?" Demetrious asked Jay as he grabbed Jay's head putting him in the headlock.

"Yeah," Jay laughed. "I'm fine man, thanks."

The guys landed back in Houston, where a limo waited to take them back to Tariff's house so everyone could pick up their cars and go home.

Tariff walked into his foyer and dropped his bags down. "One of the best things about traveling is coming back. God, I'm glad to be back to the comforts of home."

Demetrious came in the door behind him, "It is good to get back. I need to get going. I need to get myself ready for work tomorrow."

"Would you like to stay for dinner?" Demetrious smiled at the invitation and he was happy that Tariff had started to open up.

"I guess I could do that." Tariff gave him a hug, "Man, why don't you just spend the night."

"Hey, don't I have some clothes upstairs?"

"Man of course you do," They embraced for a second and then headed into the kitchen to start dinner.

*   *   *

A while later, Tyrell and Chuck pulled up to Tyrell's house. He and Chuck unloaded the bags from the car and headed into the house. Chuck decided to stay at Tyrell's since he really didn't have to check into the halfway house until the next day. Tyrell carried all the bags into the house because of Chuck's injury. As they entered the house, the phone rang. Tyrell scrambled to set the bags down and catch the phone before it stopped ringing. He reached the phone, "Hello, hello, who is this?" Tyrell slammed down the phone.

"What was that all about?" Chuck said as he closed the door behind him.

"It's probably just some kids playing on the phone."

"Look at the caller ID." Chuck suggested.

"It's marked private. Oh well, let's get you settled in. I know you have to be a little tired."

"I am kind of tired."

Tyrell took the bags upstairs and got Chuck settled into bed. He turned the TV on for Chuck and headed downstairs to grab a snack for both of them to munch on. After watching TV until about midnight, Tyrell noticed that Chuck had fallen asleep. Tyrell turned off the TV and drifted off to sleep. Around 2:30 a.m. the phone rang again.

When the room completely dark, Tyrell looked over at the clock, but his vision wasn't focused yet. He picked up the phone and answered sleepily, "Hello, hello. Who is this? Who is this?"

Chuck jumped a little, "What's going on? Who is it baby?"

"It was another one of those phone calls where no one said anything, they were just breathing."

"Again?" Chuck said still a little drowsy from the pain killer he took before bed.

"Yeah, again."

"I don't like this. Do you know who it could be?" Chuck asked as he tried to stay awake.

"I don't have a clue."

"Maybe it's an old boyfriend," Chuck said starting to doze off.

"It could be, but I doubt it. I'm not going to worry about it." They settled back in to go back to sleep. Chuck, with his free arm across Tyrell's chest, drifted back to sleep. Tyrell was wide awake looking up at the ceiling, trying to figure out who it could be that was calling. Minutes later, Tyrell's eyes closed.

Chapter 12

Jay was awakened by the ringing of the phone. "Hello?"

Daunte's voice boomed through the phone, "What's up man? How was Miami?"

"What's up, Daunte?" Jay managed to shake his sleepy voice, "Man, it was cool. I just got back yesterday evening."

"Good to hear, are you hitting the gym today?" Daunte asked.

"Most definitely. I took the day off, so I'll be there around five. I'm about to get some more sleep so I can have some energy for it," Jay said trying to rush Daunte off the phone.

"Alright, man, I'll catch you later." Jay hung up the phone, grabbed his pillow, putting it over his head, trying to block out the brightness in his room. The phone rang again. Now a little on the grumpy side, he answered a little harsh, "Hello?"

"Dang, man, did I wake you?"

Jay didn't catch the voice, "Who is this?" Jay said as he rolled his eyes.

Ricky playfully answered, "Oh, how soon we forget!"

"Ricky?" Now Jay had lost his grumpy attitude and sat straight up in bed.

"The one and only! Is there any other?"

"What's up man? I see you made it back to Charlotte in one piece."

"Yeah, I did. I'm here at the office playing catch up," Ricky said as he thought about their last night in Miami.

"I feel you. I took the day off and I'm glad I did."

"I just called to tell you that I can't wait to see you again. You've been on my mind since I got back," Ricky said.

"See, that's what I like to hear. You took the words right out of my mouth. I was thinking about you too." A smile crept across both their faces. Damn, Jay looked at himself and saw his manhood was hardening just from the sound of Ricky's voice.

"Hello Jay, Jay…" Ricky called.

"My bad man, I kinda got distracted a little. I'm back now."

"Cool. I just wanted you to know that I'm going to take a look at some law firms out where you are."

"That would be fine, man"

"I got to get ready for a briefing. I wanted to hear your voice while I had a free moment. So I'll hit you up later."

"Alright then, don't work too hard." Jay hung up the phone, he tried to go back to sleep, but visions of Miami and Ricky kept creeping into his thoughts.

*   *   *

Demetrious had his last customer in the chair before his lunch.

"What's up guys?" Mimi asked.

"Hey Mimi," the barbers greeted her, as she sashayed over to Demetrious' booth and gave him a kiss on the cheek.

"So Mimi, when you going to drop that bama and give me a chance," one of the barbers said.

"When I do, baby, you will be the first to know," Mimi

said with a chuckle.

"Hey, baby, I came to see if you wanted to get some lunch."

"Sure, this is my last customer till 3:00 p.m. and I'm just about done. Have a seat." Mimi picked through the many magazines on the stand. She picked up the Sister to Sister magazine, her favorite. After about twenty minutes later, Demetrious and Mimi walked out of the barbershop and headed to lunch.

"So how was the trip?" Mimi asked.

"The trip was off the hook. We had our share of drama but overall it was good."

"I tried calling Tariff to see if he wanted to join us, but his secretary said he was in a meeting and would be most of the afternoon."

"That man stays busy." Demetrious laughed brushing the pieces of hair off his clothes.

They reached the little cafe not to far from the shop. They walked in and grabbed a table in the corner. Mimi sat back and looked at Demetrious as she played with her earring.

Here it comes. Demetrious thought. *I'm about to be drilled. She's playing with that earring.*

"So how are things working out between you two?" Mimi asked.

Demetrious started to laughed, "We're making headwaves. I do think Tariff is still really grieving hard over James."

"Why are you laughing at me, D?" Mimi asked as she leaned back in her chair.

"Did anyone ever tell you that when you're about to ask questions you start playing with your earring."

"Someone may have mentioned it. I can't remember right now," Mimi answered sarcastically. "Now you can answer my question. How does that make you feel?"

"Sometimes it hurts, but Tariff is a good man and I have to remember that he and James were together for some years. James was his high school sweetheart. It's not easy to get over something like that."

"Well, you hang in there and just be patient," Mimi said as she reached over and put her hand on top of Demetrious' hand.

Demetrious changed the subject, "You know Mimi, we don't have to keep up this charade anymore. You know, you pretending to be my lady and all."

"Really? What's with the change?"

"If Tariff and I are going to be together, I have to be comfortable with myself. How can I expect to make him happy when I'm to busy trying to hide from everyone."

"You should never let anyone make you feel bad about who you are."

"I thank you for all you've have done for me. It's meant a lot. Plus, it will ease the strain on you and your man."

Mimi smiled, "Thank you baby. I know you guys will be alright and so will my man and I."

"Baby, love yourself and love your man. Everything else will fall into place for you."

"Well, in a month or so, I'm going to a new shop and it will be a fresh start."

"I know all about fresh starts." Looking off in the distance, Mimi started to think about her first husband.

"Mimi, you okay? I lost you for a second there."

"Yeah, I'm fine."

The waiter walked over with their food. Demetrious

rubbed his hands together and said, "I don't know 'bout you, but I'm starving." Mimi watched Demetrious for a second to see if he separated his food like Tariff.

Demetrious looked up, "What are you staring at?"

Mimi laughed, "Oh nothing."

As they finished up, Demetrious had to lean back. He wanted to unbuckle his pants he was so stuffed.

"How was your lunch?" Mimi asked.

"It was good as always."

Demetrious pulled out his wallet.

"Boy, put that wallet away! Tariff wouldn't let me pay for our lunch last time, so I got this. You guys are just trying to spoil me."

"Well, if you insist. I would hate to get on your bad side."

Mimi laughed as she handed the waiter her credit card. Demetrious took his last sip of tea.

"Well let's get out of here," Demetrious said as he stood up and walked around and pulled out Mimi's chair.

She looked up, "You are such a gentleman." They walked out together and Mimi gave Demetrious a hug. "I'll call you in a couple of days to check in. Tell Tariff I said hello." Demetrious walked back to the shop as Mimi headed back to work.

*　　*　　*

Mike sat in his office still playing catch up when he decided to take a break and call Tyrell.

"May I speak to Tyrell?" Mike was trying to sound professional.

"What's up, Mike?" Tyrell knew who it was right away.

"Hey man, all is well. How are things on that end?"

"Man, everything is good here. I'm just trying to finish up some work," Tyrell said, as he pulled some documents from his in basket.

"I feel ya man, I got a stack of work here. I need to get to as well."

"So, how's my boy, Reese?"

"Oh he's fine, I talked to him not too long ago, he had just finished up with morning practice." Mike looked at his watch and continued. "He should be on his way to the gym. How is Chuck, is he doing better?"

"Actually, he's doing a lot better, he's here at work today."

"Should he be back at work so soon?"

"Well, he's on light duty. As long as he doesn't stay on his feet too long he will be okay. He's more determined now to make that money so he can get into the studio."

"I'll give it to him, that brutha's got determination," Mike said as he turned on his computer.

"Hold on Mike, my other line is ringing."

"Hello" Tyrell said to the caller on the other line. "Hello," Tyrell could hear the same heavy breathing that he heard on his phone at home. The line went dead and Tyrell shook his head and switched back over to Mike. Now Tyrell was annoyed, frustration evident in his voice. "Yeah man I'm back!"

"What's wrong, man, bad news or something? You sound agitated," Mike asked.

"Naw, man, someone keeps calling and breathing on the phone. It happened a couple of times at home and now it's happening here at work."

"Next time they call just breathe back," Mike joked. "Do you have any idea who it could be. Maybe an old boyfriend or something?"

"That's the same thing Chuck said. I don't think so because you know I haven't dated anyone in a while."

"Well, don't stress out over it."

"I'm trying not to. Mike hold on that's my other line again."

"Why even answer it?" Mike said as he leaned back in his chair.

"I'm expecting an important call from a client. Hold on."

"Hello, Tyrell speaking."

"Hey, man, what's up?" Chuck said as he took a sip of his water.

"Not much, hold on for a sec," Tyrell said as he switched back to Mike.

"Mike, that's Chuck. I'll hit you back later."

"Yeah, you do that. Tell him I said hello and we need to talk more about this phone thing."

"Cool. Later Mike." Tyrell went back to Chuck.

"Hey, you, how you feeling?" Tyrell said as he tried not to let Chuck know he was upset.

"I should be asking you that, you sounded a little upset when you answered your phone. Everything okay up there on the fifth floor?" Chuck asked.

"You remember the calls I got at home?"

"Well, now they've started to happen here at the office."

"What about them?"

"Man, I don't like this shit. I don't want to have to hurt somebody," Chuck snapped.

"Don't talk like that man, it's not that serious." Tyrell

tried to reassure Chuck and himself that it was nothing.

"I'm sorry, but ain't no one going to mess with my niggah like that," Chuck said as he sat down.

"I'll be alright," Tyrell reassured him. "And you didn't answer my question how are you feeling? You in any pain today?"

"No, I'm cool. Today is actually a light day for me."

"Good 'cause I would hate to have to come down there and hurt somebody," Tyrell teased. They both started to laugh.

"Well, baby, even though it's a light day, I still need to get back to work. So will I still see you tonight?" Chuck asked.

"Now what do you think?" Tyrell said, as a smile came across his face.

"Alright, I love you," Chuck said smiling through the phone.

"Love you too, man." Tyrell went back to the papers on his desk. He was still racking his brain trying to figure out who could be making the phone calls.

Chapter 13

At the gym, Jay and Daunte had just finished up their workout and were sitting at the snack bar having a protein shake.

"So Daunte, how are things with you and the better half?"

"Things couldn't be better," Daunte said, with a big smile on his face big enough to light up a room.

"What's up with that big ass grin on your face?" Jay asked as he took a drank of his protein drink.

"You would not believe what my girl did the other night."

"I'm sure you're about to tell me." Jay thought to himself *I really don't want to hear about this.*

"Man, just thinking about it makes my dick hard."

"Too much information man, so what did she do?" Jay asked.

"Man, it had been a long hard day at work. I got home and when I walked in the door all the lights were out. There was nothing but candles burning all around the room. So I put my shit down and walked around the apartment to see what Mia had going on. When I made my way toward the bedroom, the door was closed, with this note stuck to it."

"So what did the note say?" Jay asked as his curiosity got to him.

"It said *Come in with no clothes on!* So I took all my clothes off and put them in a pile outside of the door. You only have to tell me once!" Now Daunte was laughing then continued, "When I got in the room, there were even more candles burning in the bedroom."

"Okay she's really being romantic," Jay said.

Daunte was in full agreement with that. "So anyway, on the wall facing the door, there's this big poster board sign on the wall with an arrow pointing towards the master bathroom. So I follow the arrow into the bathroom and she has candles all around the bathtub. There she stood with her tits out and only a towel around her waist. The tub was full of bubbles and soft jazz was playing and shit. She held a brandy glass with some Hennessey in it for me. Man, I was feeling like a bitch."

"Man, you crazy," Jay said as he chuckled.

"I've never had that kind of treatment before. I've always been the one to do that kind of thing for her. Man, I climbed into that tub and instantly my body relaxed. Shit, man I think women should do stuff like that for their man all the time. Hell! That shit should be a requirement." Jay laughed with him on that one.

"Anyway, as I laid in the tub, she washed me up all over and when she finished she told me to stand up and she started to dry me off. That was such a turn on my dick was standing straight up. Then she led me into the bedroom and laid me down on the bed." Daunte was again smiling from ear to ear as the last event passed before his mind, "She started to nibble all over a brutha's body. Man, she found this spot I didn't even know turned me on. I was like DAMN GIRL! I went to reach for her and she told me not to touch her and keep my hands down by my sides."

"So what did you do?" Jay asked.

"Shit I put my hands down as I was told."

Jay shook his head and laughed. "So then what happened?"

"I'm laying there and my dick got harder than it was when I got out of the tub if that were even possible. Man, she sucked a brutha's dick like it was her last meal. I was in the room screaming, I was about to bust, but she knew exactly when to stop. Man, then she got on top of me and rode me like a wild stallion. I said to myself 'DAMN' all this is mine. Man, I was tapping that ass like a mad man." Jay was just in complete awe.

"After I bust a good nut, I passed the fuck out. The next morning I called out sick 'cause a brutha was drained and couldn't get out of bed."

All Jay could say was, "Damn, man."

Daunte laughed with this big smile on his face. "Man let's go hit these showers, a brutha needs to get home."

Later that evening, after getting in from the gym, Jay sat in his favorite little Lazy Boy chair, positioned right in front of his television nodding back and forth to sleep. His phone rang and, rather than just pick it up, he looked at the caller ID. He saw that it was Ricky.

"Hello you, what's up?" Jay answered as excitement immediately took over.

"Damn, are you physic?"

Laughing Jay said, "Naw man, its called caller ID. So how was your day?"

"The day is over and now I can relax," Ricky said.

"I was doing the same thing and watching some television-- or it was watching me."

"Well, I have some news for you. I will be up your way this weekend. I have an interview with this firm in Houston on Monday. So I figured I would come your way on Friday and spend the weekend."

"Man, that would be right on time," Jay said as he sat up

straight in his chair.

"I did a preliminary phone interview with this law firm after they looked over my resume. So they're flying me up for a face to face interview."

"Well, that's cool, and of course you're staying here at my crib!" Jay offered.

Ricky was really testing the waters when he asked, "You sure about that? I don't want to put you out."

"Come on now, it ain't a problem. How could you even ask that?"

"Alright, cool. Now I have another question, do you know of a good barber there in your area? I'm very particular about who I allow to shape up my hair." Jay laughed.

"Of course I know of someone, they cut hair all the time."

"So is he any good?"

"No doubt and you already know him."

"Who man?"

"Didn't you know, Demetrious is a barber?"

"No, actually I didn't. We didn't really get to talk much when we were in Miami. I was more focused on getting to know you." Jay began to blush.

"Man, he's the best in the area."

"Cool. That will work. Do they have a good gym too?"

"I belong to this gym not too far from the house. You can work out with me and my boy Daunte."

"Oh that will work. You just have all the hook ups," Ricky said as he lay across his bed.

"Come to think of it, I think my boy Daunte was looking for a good barber too. We could make a morning of it. Hit the gym, work out and then go to the barbershop." Ricky was really looking forward to his trip to Houston.

"Well, man, let me get going, I still have a few details to work out. I'll see you at the end of the week, but of course I will talk to you before then."

"Alright, man, I'll call Demetrious and set up our appointments for Saturday." They said their goodbyes. Jay dialed Demetrious' number to get things rolling.

"Yo! Talk to me!" Demetrious answered his phone like he was in the hood some where.

"What's up, D?" Jay sounded just as excited as he did when Ricky called.

"What's up Jay? You recoup from the trip yet?"

"Man, you know I'm ready to go back to Miami," Jay said as he thought about, Ricky and his first meeting.

"You right about that."

"You remember Ricky from Miami?"

Demetrious looked up at the ceiling and thought, *I know he didn't just ask me that.*

"Of course I remember him! How is your 'MAN' doing?" Demetrious broke out in laughter.

"He's not my man yet! But I do like the sound of that."

"Anyway, what's up with ya' boy Ricky?"

"Well, he'll be out here this weekend."

"What? Already?" *He don't waste time, do he!* Demetrious thought.

"Come on now, man, go 'head with that. Anyway Ricky, myself, and a buddy of mine want to come by the shop on Saturday to get a hair cut and a trim up."

"No problem I'll schedule you guys for 3:00. I'll make you my last appointments."

"That will work. See you then and tell Tariff I said hey. And I'll chat with him in the next day or so."

"Alright bruh. Peace out!"

*   *   *

Tyrell and Chuck pulled up at Tyrell's place. Tyrell stopped at his mailbox and then proceeded to the steps to pick up his newspaper which was delivered once again after he had already left for work.

"What the fuck is this?" Tyrell bent down to pick up the paper. The paper was covered in red paint and torn to shreds. Tyrell dropped it back on the steps and went to stick his key in the door when he noticed his door knob was painted red.

"Shit!" he said as he looked at the door knob.

"What's this shit?" Chuck said, as he looked at the paper and door knob.

Tyrell looked around, "Somebody wants to play games." As he was about to open the door, he saw Ms. Reed, his nosey neighbor. When Tyrell thought of her, he thought of Mrs. Kravitz, from the television show Bewitched. Ms. Reed would sit by her window in her rocking chair and watch everyone as they came and went. She gave a new meaning to the word nosey.

"Excuse me, Ms. Reed, did you see anyone over here on my porch?" Tyrell asked.

"No, I didn't. Oh wait, I did see the woman that delivers your paper. I saw her while I made my grandson some lunch. Why, is there something wrong?"

"No ma'am. Someone left something here and I thought you might have seen them."

"No, baby, but I'll check with my grandson when he

wakes up."

"Thank you Ms. Reed, I appreciate that," Tyrell said as he headed inside the house.

"Chuck followed behind him and headed straight to the trash can. As he threw the paper in the trash, he turned to Tyrell, "I'm staying here tonight."

"Come on now man, you know you can't do that, you have to check in. I can handle this, trust me," Tyrell said as he tried to reassure Chuck. Chuck was furious, he paced back and forth. Tyrell knew he needed to do something to get him to chill out. Tyrell walked over and kissed him on the cheek.

"Don't try and distract me Ty, I know what you're doing, man, and it ain't working."

"Let's just forget about it and eat." As Tyrell opened the refrigerator, his phone rang. Tyrell froze. Chuck looked at Tyrell and then at the phone. Tyrell walked over to answer it.

Chuck stopped him, "Let me get it for you." Tyrell stood there and watched Chuck, as he picked up the phone.

"Hello?" Chuck listened, the caller breathed on the other end. "Who the fuck is this?" Chuck yelled into the phone. Whoever it was hung up the phone. Chuck slammed the phone down into its cradle.

"So that was them again?" Tyrell asked as he plopped into the kitchen chair.

"Yes it was." Chuck was hot and even madder now than before. The thought of everything that was happening was starting to piss him off.

"I'll tell you what," Tyrell said as he looked at Chuck. Tomorrow while I'm at work, I'll just call the phone company and have them change my number."

"That would be cool Ty. But whoever this person is not only knows where you live, but they have your work number too."

"You know I never thought about that. Damn!" Tyrell said as he banged on the table.

Chapter 14

Tariff closed his office door, sat at his desk and had his Mocha Latte with a blueberry muffin. This was his morning routine. As he sipped on his coffee, he looked out his big office window. His office was on the first floor, so he could sit and watch people as they walked in and out of the building. The skies were gray with clouds, but he could see the sun peeking through a little. It was still quite muggy and wet from the rain last night. He watched the little old gray haired lady who had a vendor stand in front of the building. On her stands she had sunglasses that everybody bought for $5.00. The woman had books, scarves and other knicknacks.

As Tariff finished off his muffin and looked at his watch, he realized he had enough time to make a few calls before his next meeting. His first call was to Mike and Reese's house. The phone rang a few times and finally he heard a faint voice.

"Reese, is that you?"

"The one and only, is that you, Tariff?" he said as he sat up in the bed.

"Yeah, it's me. I'm sorry, man, I didn't mean to wake you. I can call back."

"It's cool man, I need to get up anyway. Mike was supposed to call and wake me up. Anyway, what's up, man?"

"They must be keeping you really busy at practice. I haven't talked to you since we got back from Miami."

"They are killing a brutha. All I can do is come home and crash. I barely have time for Mike," Reese said as he sat on the side of the bed.

"How is my boy?"

"You know, Mike, my baby's been great, man. He left out for work not too long ago. I'm trying to get him to quit 'cause I know he wants to go back to school."

"That would be good for him, especially since he's only a few credits short of his Masters."

"That's what I told him, but you know Mike, he has to prove to people that he can handle things."

"I know, and you know we're all looking forward to coming to see you play."

"And of course I'll have tickets for my boyz!" Reese said as he walked over to the mirror. *Damn, I need a haircut,* he thought.

"That will be right on time. Reese, let me run this by you."

"Sure, man, what's up?"

"Well, one of my clients came into my office yesterday. We got to talking and it turns out that he owns a recording studio. I told him about Chuck and, as a favor to me, he's willing to let Chuck lay down some tracks." Reese was shocked and excited about the possibility of Chuck recording.

"Are you for real? Man, that would be on time for him. A voice like that, he needs to hurry up and get started on that."

"Yeah, I was going to call Tyrell at his office and see what he thought about it."

"Man, I think Chuck would be crazy not to," Reese stated.

"Well, I'm going to give Tyrell a call now while I still have some time before my meeting."

"Alright man, I'll talk to you soon Tariff. Let me know how things turn out, and if there's anything I can do just let me know. There goes my other line, Tariff, it must be Mike calling me."

"Be good, man. Thanks again. I'll talk to you soon. Tell Mike hello." Tariff hung up and picked up the phone and pressed the number 7, Tyrell's speed dial number. Tyrell answered on the first ring.

"Hello, this is Tyrell, how can I help you?"

"'Sup man, how you doing?" Tariff asked.

"I'm cool. What's up with you?"

"Everything is good on this end as well. I'm actually calling about Chuck and his music."

"Oh yeah? What's up?" Tyrell asked as he got up to close his office door.

"A client of mine was in my office yesterday and we got to talking about our trip. I told him about the banging performance Chuck did in Miami. He mentioned he owned his own recording studio and, as a favor to me, he would let Chuck come in and lay down some tracks if he's interested."

"If he's interested?" Tyrell stood up, "Oh man, Chuck would love that. He's coming over tonight for dinner, so why don't you and Demetrious come over and you can tell him all about it yourself."

"That sounds good to me, especially since I won't have to cook." They both laughed.

"Hell, I wasn't cooking either. I was going to order some Chinese food. I'll just order enough for all of us. I know how you and D can eat. Y'all greedy asses..." Tyrell commented.

"Ok, man, I'll see you guys tonight. I have to get ready for my meeting," Tariff said, as he stood up and put on his suit jacket.

*   *   *

After work that evening, Tyrell was ready to bust at the seams trying not to tell Chuck about what Tariff had told him earlier. They got out of the car and, as usual, Tyrell picked up his mail and walked to his front door. The newspaper was delivered late again this morning. He picked up his paper and mumbled to himself as he opened his door.

"Those damn newspaper delivery people. I have called them three times already to cancel my subscription and complain about their delivery person. I don't know what I'm paying for. I don't get the paper at the time I asked for it to be delivered. The paper is ALWAYS late." Chuck just let him rant for a few minutes before saying anything.

"Well, if you cancel it, then you won't have to worry about things happening to it."

"Ain't that the truth," Tyrell said as he walked through the door.

"So, what's for dinner?"

"Well, Tariff and Demetrious are coming over so I thought I would order some Chinese food."

"That's cool. How are things with those two?" Chuck asked as he walked over to the refrigerator.

"I think they're finding their way. They're just taking it day by day."

Tyrell looked in the kitchen drawer for the Chinese menu.

"I'm going to run up stairs and jump into some other

clothes."

"Okay man," Tyrell said as he found the menu on top of the microwave. When he finished calling in the order, Chuck reappeared in the kitchen wearing a pair of grey sweat pants and a T-shirt. Tyrell took a long look at Chuck as he opened the refrigerator and grabbed some juice.

Damn, my man looks sexy in everything, Tyrell thought to himself. Chuck turned and saw Tyrell staring at him.

"Take a picture, man. It will last longer," Chuck said sarcastically.

Tyrell couldn't help but laugh at his sarcasm, "Now I'm going to go change." As Tyrell headed up the stairs, the phone rang.

"I got it," Chuck yelled.

"Hello. Hello!" Chuck took a deep breath and then spoke. "Since you don't want to say anything, I'm going to say this to you. If I find out who...no," Chuck corrected himself, "when I find out who you are, and I will find out, you are going to regret the day that you ever called this house." Chuck slammed down the phone poured out his glass of juice, and grabbed a beer out the refrigerator. *Fuck, Fuck* Chuck thought out loud.

The doorbell rang and Chuck yelled up to Tyrell, "I'll get it, baby!" He walked over to the door and opened it up to Tariff and Demetrious.

"What's up, fellas? How you guys doing?" Chuck said as stepped aside to let them in.

"What's up? Chuck you're looking a lot better," Tariff observed.

"I'm feeling a lot better. Tyrell is upstairs changing. He'll be down in a second."

"Good to hear you're better," Demetrious commented.

"Well, it's good to see you guys again. Would either of you like something to drink?"

"Sure, a beer would be good," Tariff quickly decided.

"Sounds good. I'll have one too," Demetrious seconded. Chuck walked over to the refrigerator and pulled out two beers. As he handed them to Tariff and Demetrious, Tyrell came down the stairs.

"Hey guys, what's up? I see Chuck was being ever the good host." Chuck just smiled.

"Here, baby." He handed Tyrell the beer he had in his hand. Chuck turned back to the fridge and took out another for himself.

"Let's go sit in the living room until the food gets here," Tyrell suggested as he took a drink of his beer. Making themselves comfortable, Tyrell looked over at Chuck and started smiling. Chuck winked and smiled back.

Tariff spoke up, "I called Tyrell earlier cause I wanted to come by and talk to you about something."

Chuck looked over at Tyrell and then back at Tariff, "Okay, what's up?" Chuck's heart began to race as he quickly thought they had found out he'd been locked up.

"Well, a client of mine came by yesterday and he owes me a favor. He and I were talking about the trip to Miami and I mentioned to him how you performed your ass off." Tariff's compliment brought a smile to Chuck's face as he continued, "He mentioned that he owns his own recording studio. So, as a favor to me, he is willing to allow you to lay down some tracks and help you with your demo."

Chuck breathed a sigh of relief and then jumped out of his seat, "Man, you shitting me!"

"Naw, man, this is on the real!" Tariff said with a big grin on his face.

"I don't know how to thank you, other than just thank you, thank you! This means so much to me." Chuck gave Tariff a big brotherly hug.

Then he turned to Tyrell, "Baby, you knew about this and didn't tell me?" Tyrell and Demetrious started laughing.

Tyrell gave him a big smile, "Yeah, I'm guilty. Tariff told me earlier today and I promised myself I'd let him tell you."

"Tariff, man, you don't know how much I appreciate this. No one has ever done anything like this for me. I owe you big time."

"You can pay me by going in that studio and doing a hell of a demo, and when you make your first CD, I want mine autographed." They all had to laugh at that.

"Man, you got it! You got it!" Chuck said as he shook his head from side to side.

"There is one more thing. This I didn't even mention to Tyrell, I wanted to surprise you both," Tariff said.

"Nothing can beat that," Chuck responded.

"Well, also turns out his uncle works for Virtu' Records and he's going to take your demo and let him listen to it." Chuck really jumped up out of his seat forgetting all about his mending wound, immediately he bent over and grabbed his side.

Tyrell quickly ran over to him, "You okay, man?"

"I'm fine. In all the excitement I forgot I'm still healing." Chuck sat back down in the chair. Tyrell walked over and gave Tariff a big hug.

"Thanks, man."

"Guys, I won't let you down. So when do we start?" Chuck asked.

Tariff grinned, "I took the liberty of telling him we would come by tomorrow. That is, if you're ready?"

"What? Hell yeah, I'm ready without a doubt, man."

Tariff had to ask, "What about your stomach? Will it affect your singing?"

"Man, don't worry. I feel much better than I did when I was in Miami. So you ain't heard nothing yet?"

"Well, I'll call him tomorrow at work and let him know and, if everything is a go, Tyrell can bring you over to the studio after work."

Looking disappointed, Tyrell said, "Oh man, I can't. I have a meeting at 4:30 and there's no telling when I may get out of there."

"Well, I tell you what, why don't I pick you up since I pass right by your office? Then I can take you to the studio," Tariff suggested.

"Works for me," Chuck said.

"Okay then, its settled. I will call you guys tomorrow with the details." The guys got interrupted by the doorbell.

"It must be the food. All this good news has made me hungry," Tyrell said.

"You can say that again." Demetrious chimed in.

Tariff was the first one to dig into the food after Tyrell had set everything up on the table. After filling their stomachs, the guys sat around and discussed Chuck's getting into the studio and making his CD. They were really enjoying their time with each other.

Demetrious looked at his watch and then at Tariff, "Man, we better get out of here. We all have to work tomorrow."

Tariff looked at his watch, "I didn't realize it was that late. Man, you're right. It is time to go." Tyrell and Chuck walked Tariff and Demetrious to the door.

"I can't thank you enough for what you've done for me." Chuck was gushing with his thanks to Tariff.

"You've got a great voice and I'm just glad that I'm able to help you."

Once the door closed behind Tariff and Demetrious, Chuck grabbed Tyrell and pulled him into his arms, "Baby, ever since I met you, everything good has been happening to me. You are my good luck charm."

"You are mine too, man. I have all the faith in you that you will go in there and make me proud. I love you, baby." They stood there at the door just kissing and embracing each other.

Tyrell was the first to break away, "Man, let me get my keys and get you back or we'll both be in trouble." Chuck gave Tyrell a huge smile and patted him on the ass as he walked to get his keys.

Chapter 15

The next morning, Tariff got to work early. He looked at the wall clock and immediately he picked up the phone to call Mr. Townson to set up the meeting with Chuck after work. After he finished his call, he speed dialed Tyrell.

"Good morning, this is Tyrell."

"Hey boy what's up?"

"Oh nothing man, just working on some spreadsheets," Tyrell said as he shuffled through his papers.

"I just wanted to let you know that D and I really enjoyed ourselves last night. Thanks for the Chinese food."

"Man, you don't have to thank me for that. I need to be thanking you for all you're doing for my boy."

"Well, he's one of us now. You know how we do, we look out for each other. Speaking of last night, I talked to my client this morning and we are all set for this evening. I'll be by there to pick Chuck up right after work."

"Thanks, man. I will let him know. Thanks again, Tariff. I'll call him now and get the ball in motion. Thanks again, man. I love ya, boy"

"Yeah man, I love you, too." Now get back to work and make that money," Tariff said laughing as he wrote on his daytimer.

Tyrell dialed Chuck's number, "Hey, man," Tyrell said as Chuck answered. Chuck immediately smiled.

"Hey you, what's up?"

"I just got off the phone with Tariff and you are all set for this evening."

"Wow, man I can't believe this," Chuck mentioned.

"I have to get ready for this meeting, so I may see you there. Good luck man."

"Thanks, man, I'll talk to you later," Chuck said as he grabbed his next printing job off the table. Chuck was so hyped it was hard for him to concentrate at work. The day seemed to move in slow motion. Every time he looked at the clock it seemed like it was only going minute by minute and time was standing still. Finally, the end of the day came. Before Chuck left, he called Tyrell.

"Hey, baby. How are things with you?"

"Everything's good, just finishing up some last minute things before my next meeting. Are you ready? Do you have your music together?" Tyrell asked.

"I'm set. I'm just a little nervous," Chuck said feeling it in his stomach.

"Don't be nervous, baby. You are going to blow them away just like you did in Miami."

"Yeah, but I would still feel better if you were with me."

"Well, if I finish this meeting early enough, maybe I'll come to the studio."

"Alright, baby. You know I was up most of the night trying to decide what songs I wanted to do."

"Did you decide?"

"Yes, I had written some songs while I was locked up and I decided to work on a couple of those."

"Wow, a man that is multi-talented! I didn't know you wrote lyrics too. I thought you just sang." Tyrell was amazed that Chuck had so many hidden talents.

"When you had as much time on your hands as I did, you learn to use that time constructively."

Now Tyrell was confused, "I thought you told me you

152

stopped singing?"

"I did. Instead I wrote a lot of songs. I wouldn't and did-n't sing them for anyone. That is until now." Tyrell was blushing. Chuck had a way of doing that to him.

"Well, good luck, baby, not that you need it."

"Thanks, baby. I should go. Tariff should be out front by now."

"Alright. Love you."

"Love you, too." Chuck hung up the phone, grabbed his stuff, and headed out front to where Tariff was already wait-ing for him. Chuck opened the door and slid in.

"Hey Tariff. I'm not late am I?"

"Naw man, I just drove up, so that was perfect timing. So are you ready?"

"I'm as ready as I'm going to get," Chuck said as he put on his seat belt.

"Man, you look like you a little nervous," Tariff said smiling.

"Can I be honest with you?" Tariff took a quick glance at Chuck.

"Sure. What's on your mind?"

"Man, I am shaking in my boots with nerves." Tariff just laughed.

"You will be fine. Look at it this way. You're in your ele-ment."

"I guess that's a good way to look at it," Chuck agreed.

Tariff could tell he was starting to relax, "See, there you go."

"Man, I really do appreciate you doing this for me. I mean really. I wish I had friends like you guys back in the day."

"Where are your friends now?" Tariff asked.

"Man, no telling where those guys are," Chuck said trying not to divulge too much information. "I had to let that group go. They aren't the type I should've been around in the first place. Hanging with them got me into a lot of trouble."

Tariff started to wonder if these guys had anything to do with Chuck being locked up. He did feel that Chuck was a very admirable person.

"Well, at least you were smart enough to know you had to let them go."

"Yeah, sometimes you have to hit rock bottom before you see things."

Tariff's instincts told him that these friends had to have something to do with Chuck's incarceration.

Tariff gave Chuck a friendly pat on the hand, "Man, sounds like you had a rough time of it, but don't worry, you got enough of us to keep you on the straight and narrow.

"No pun intended." They both shared a laugh.

Tariff changed the conversation back to music, "So, how long have you been singing?"

"Wow, man, I've been singing since I was a kid, but then I stopped."

"With your pipes, why did you stop?"

"I don't know. Things were really screwed up in my life at the time. I didn't have anything to sing about." Chuck began to smile, "Until now that is."

"Well, this looks like the place." Tariff pulled up to a small brick office building surrounded by a nicely trimmed lawn. A man in the parking lot walked around rolling a big garbage can around picking up trash as the meter maid walked from car to car looking to see who she would give a ticket to. Tariff found a open parking spot. He and Chuck got out and walked over to the meter. The meter had a half-hour left on it. Tariff pulled out a quarter adding another thirty minutes. By that time parking would be free. As they walked to the building, people were coming out and, by the looks of them, their day was over. Once inside the building, the security guard sat behind a desk with various monitors behind blinking to different locations in the building.

"Tight security system," Chuck commented as they stepped into an open elevator.

The elevator opened at the fourth floor. Tariff's client was standing at the water fountain.

"Tariff, I see you made it," the older black man said as he walked up. Tariff extended his hand.

"Mr. Townson, how are you today?"

"I'm fine, Tariff, and this must be our singer," Mr. Townson said with a raspy voice. Mr. Townson reached out to shake Chuck's hand, "So you're the new up and coming artist."

Chuck gave a nervous smile. "Hello sir, my name is Chuck Williams. Nice to meet you."

"Well, guys, let's get started," Mr. Townwson suggested as he ushered them into a studio just a few steps from the elevator. Tariff and Mr. Townson went into a room over-loaded with sound equipment. Then there was the big glass window across from a piano, different guitars, microphones and other equipment. Tariff was amazed. He had never been in a studio before.

Chuck saw the piano and asked Mr. Townson if it was okay to go in and warm up some.

"Sure, son, go right ahead," Mr. Townson said as he and Tariff continued to talk. The sounds of Chuck's piano play-ing echoed throughout the studio, interrupting their conversation.

Mr. Townson turned to Tariff, "He plays the piano too?" Tariff, just as amazed, shrugged his shoulders, "It looks that way."

"Damn, he's good too," Mr. Townson said, "I wonder if he sings as well as he plays."

"I'm just as surprised as you are. I knew he could sing, I heard that for myself."

Mr. Townson pushed a button on the panel and then said to Chuck on speaker, "You can start whenever you're ready."

"Okay, I'm ready," Chuck said and began to play. After a few bars, Chuck started to sing. Tariff and Mr. Townson watched and listened. Neither one wanted to move. They wanted to hear every note. Chuck had their attention. They couldn't believe how natural his voice was.

"Tariff, this man is good, I mean really good."

"I heard him sing in Miami and thought he was good, but this is beyond that." Tariff and Mr. Townson continued to listen as Chuck finished up his first track.

Mr. Townson pushed the button for the booth, "One second man." Tariff smiled at Chuck and continued to talk to Mr. Townson. Chuck watched them, trying to figure out what the two were saying.

Finally, Mr. Townson pushed the button, "I'm going to play your track back so you can hear what it sounds like." Mr. Townson walked over to the phone and called someone. Mr. Townson's call was rather short because five minutes later he was hanging up the phone and shaking Tariff's hand.

Mr. Townson pushed the button, "Chuck can you come out here for a second."

Chuck pushed himself back from the piano and went outside to the other part of the studio.

"Yes sir?" Chuck said not knowing what to expect.

"Man, did you know you have an incredible voice? I was blown away," Mr. Townson said.

"Thank you, sir," Chuck said with a big smile.

"Well, I made a call to my uncle who is in charge of our new talent. I played your track back and he liked what he heard and he would like to sign you right away."

"Are you for real?" Chuck asked.

"Man, I can't even believe you got it on the first track. Of course we need to clean it up a little, but that was like DAMN!"

"Thank you, Mr. Townson," Chuck said trying to hold in his excitement.

"Do you have a manager?"

Chuck didn't know what to think of what he was saying, "A manager?"

"Yeah a manager, someone that could help you handle things."

Chuck was so perplexed he didn't know what to do, so he looked over at Tariff. "All this is happening so fast. I don't know...Tariff could you be my manager?"

Tariff began the same nervous laughter that Chuck showed earlier, "Me, your manager? I don't know anything about being someone's manager."

Chuck was almost begging Tariff with his eyes, "I don't trust anybody else but Tyrell, besides you were the one that set this entire thing up." Tariff looked from Chuck to Mr. Townson, seriously thinking about it.

"Tariff, you can do it." Mr. Townson tried to persuade him.

"Just treat it as if you're supervising an employee at work. Those things you have a problem with I can help you.

It will be nothing for you, you can handle it."

Tariff looked back at Chuck, "You sure you don't want to think about this some more or discuss it with Tyrell?"

"I think Tyrell would be happy with this." Tariff turned toward the door and saw Tyrell coming toward them.

"Well, here he comes now and this couldn't be a better time." Chuck turned around and walked quickly to him. Tyrell came into the booth greeting everyone.

"Tyrell, guess what?" Chuck was all smiles as he looked at Tyrell.

"What's up, man?"

"They want to sign me up as their new talent to Virtu' Records."

Tyrell became all excited. "See, I knew you could do it."

"Not only that, but Tariff has agreed to be my manager."

Tyrell just smiled at Tariff, "Your manager? Wow! That would be a great idea."

"But Tyrell, this is out of my league," Tariff said.

"Tariff you can handle it. What you don't know we can all figure out together. I think you would be the right person to do it," Tyrell said as he walked over and put his hand on Tariff's shoulder. Tariff finally agreed.

"Well, Tariff, I will have my office put together a contract and we will overnight it to your home. The sooner we get started the better," Mr. Townson commented. They all shook hands and made arrangements to meet after Tariff and Chuck reviewed the contract.

"Once you guys read over the terms of the contract give me a call and we will get started. "

Tariff turned to Mr. Townson, "My client and I will definitely review the contract and then get back to you."

Tariff's expression was serious until he busted out in laughter.

* * *

A couple of days later, Tariff walked up the stairs to his house. He saw Demetrious' car in the driveway. Once inside the house, he caught sight of an overnight package laying on the dining room table. Immediately, he knew it had to be the contract for Chuck. As he sat down at the table, he could hear the shower running so he knew Demetrious had to be in the shower. Tariff searched for scissors to cut open the envelope when the phone rang.

"I see you made it home."

"Sure did. What's up Jay?" Tariff said as he sat down to open the envelope.

"I'm cool. I was trying to catch up with D. He didn't answer his cell phone and he's not at the shop."

"He's upstairs in the shower."

"The shower," Jay said laughing.

"What are you laughing at?" Tariff said as he pulled the documents out of the envelope.

"Oh nothing." Jay looked at this as a sign that their relationship was growing.

"Well, I know you didn't call to talk about me and D," Tariff said sarcastically.

"You definitely got that right. Anyway, can you let D know that Ricky couldn't make it in town this weekend? So it will be the following week that we will be by the shop."

"Everything's okay isn't it? Nothing serious I hope." Tariff asked out of concern, putting the contract down to give Jay his full attention.

"No, he's fine. They just rescheduled his interview."

"I know you're disappointed. I could tell you were looking forward to seeing him."

"I was, but it's only a few more days. So he will stay an extra few days while he's here. Tariff could hear the anticipation in Jay's voice.

"That's good. Well I just got Chuck's contract here so I need to read it over. I'll call you later and I will give Demetrious the message. A'ight boy."

"A'ight, man thanks. I will talk to you guys later. I have to give Tyrell and Chuck a call to give my congratulations." Tariff hung up the phone and decided to call Tyrell and Chuck. The phone rang a few times and Tyrell answered by yelling into the phone,

"Hello!"

Tariff held the phone back from his ear, "Dang man, why are you shouting?"

"Sorry about that, but I keep getting these prank calls. All they do is breathe on the phone never saying anything then they hang up or I hang up on them. So what's up?"

"I was calling because I got Chuck's contract today. I'm going to look over it tonight and I will come by and talk to you guys tomorrow."

"Sure that's fine. Chuck's upstairs taking a nap right now, but as soon as he wakes up I'll let him know."

"Is Chuck feeling okay?"

"Oh man, he's fine. I just think he needed to get some rest. He should be getting up any minute now anyway."

"Good. I'll see you guys around 7:00 p.m. tomorrow and it shouldn't take no more than a hour. All Chuck has to do is sign on the dotted line."

"Alright then. We'll see you then. Oh, by the way, where's my boy D?"

"He's upstairs. I think he just got out of the shower.

"Tell D, I said what's up."

"Sure thing." No sooner than they hung up Chuck came from upstairs and Tyrell filled him in.

* * *

The following evening Tariff was in his office taking one final look over the contract. His secretary walked in his office.

"Tariff, I have a Mr. Townson on line two."

"Oh, good. Thanks. Could you close my door please? Thanks."

"Mr. Townson, how you doing today?" Tariff asked as he started to put papers in his briefcase.

"I'm fine. Thank you for asking. I just called to see if you got the contract and if you had time to look it over."

"Actually, Mr. Townson, I got it yesterday evening and I looked at it last night," Tariff said as he yawned, "I just finished reading over it again. Everything looked pretty much in order. I am about to leave here and meet with Chuck."

"That's great," Mr. Townson said, "if you have any questions, just call me on my cell."

"I sure will. Thanks again, Mr. Townson." Tariff closed his briefcase, pulled the drapes in his office, and headed out to Tyrell's.

Tyrell and Chuck settled down at the table to eat dinner. They hadn't taken more than a few bites, when the doorbell rang.

Tyrell looked at Chuck, "That must be Tariff, he always did have bad timing," Tyrell said as he pushed back his chair from the table. He opened the door to Tariff standing there grinning.

"Hey man, I was just telling Chuck about your bad timing. We were just sitting down to dinner while we waited for you. Did you eat?"

"I did. I picked up a sandwich on the way over here," Tariff said as he walked in.

"Okay, well, come on in. Chuck and I were in the kitchen. Let me go get him and we can go into the living room." Tyrell didn't have to go far because just as he turned around, he bumped right into Chuck wiping his mouth with a napkin. Tyrell looked at Chuck and laughed. "Man, what did you do, gobble down that food?"

Dropping the napkin, "Naw I couldn't eat another bite, I'm too excited. What's up, Tariff?"

"Nothing man. Just working hard is all. Are you ready to look over this contract?"

"I sure am, let's do this!" Heading to the living room, Tariff and Chuck sat on the sofa. Tariff opened his briefcase and handed Chuck the contract.

"Here's the contract. I took a look at it last night and it's pretty straight forward. The record company will be paying for all your studio time. They will also handle all the promotions for your first single and the CD. Once you sign the contract, we'll get a check for $75,000 dollars. Then once the CD is done, you'll receive another check for $60,000. They go by the point system when it comes to CD sales. You will get a point or two for each one sold. I'm getting myself familiar with that part so I can fill you in on that later. This other part I think you'll like too, you get to keep all of your masters to your music. What that means is all the tracks you write and record belong to you."

All this is happening so fast. Chuck thought to himself. Chuck nodded his head once or twice, as he listened without saying a word. He was still trying to let all this sink in, but he trusted Tariff to keep everything in order.

"Now out of all of this, I will get 10 percent as part of my fees and services as your manager." Chuck was overwhelmed with what Tariff had just said.

"Man, it all sounds great to me," Chuck agreed.

"Well, it looks like if you really blow up, I may have to quit my job and make this a permanent gig." Tariff laughed.

"Man, I would definitely like that. I have absolute confidence that you will have both of our best interests at heart. What do you think, baby?" Chuck asked.

Tyrell rubbed his chin and looked at Tariff and then at Chuck, "I think it sounds good to me. I know my boy here won't steer you wrong. He is very detail oriented and I know that you can trust Tariff with your life." Tariff smiled at the confidence that his buddy had in him.

Tariff looked at Tyrell and smiled, "Thanks man. You know I got your back." Chuck moved over to where Tariff sat and picked up the pen on the table next to his briefcase.

"So where do I sign?" Chuck said, as he looked through the contract.

Tariff laid the contract on the table and started turning pages, "Sign here," he turned another page, "and here and here. Well, I think that should do it."

Chuck looked at Tariff and asked, "What do you think I should do about work?"

Tariff put the contract back in his briefcase as he turned

to Chuck, "Well, for now I think you should continue working, at least part time, especially since you will be spending a lot of time in the studio. But if things go like I think, you can probably kiss that job goodbye."

Tyrell got up from the loveseat and sat next to Chuck, "That's a good idea."

Chuck agreed, "I'll talk to my boss in the morning."

"Now let's seal the deal with a toast," Tyrell said as he pulled a bottle of champagne from behind the bar. Tyrell pulled out three champagne glasses and a corkscrew. As he pulled the cork out, the champagne started foaming out of the bottle.

"Whoa, I'm glad I put that contract away," Tariff said, looking at Tyrell like he'd lost his mind.

*　　*　　*

Mike had just finished dinner. Reese was running late from practice, as usual. He wrapped the plate with aluminum foil and set it on the stove. Since the season began, Reese had started eating lots of chicken breast and vegetables. As Mike wiped down the kitchen counter, he heard the key turn in the door. Quickly, he took the foil off and put Reese's plate in the microwave to make sure it was good and hot for him. Reese dropped his bag down right by the front door. He placed his keys on the key rack that he had mounted by the front door.

"I'm in here!" Reese heard Mike's voice come from the direction of the kitchen. Seeing his baby brought a smile to his face.

He walked up to Mike and kissed him on the back of his neck, "Hey, baby boy, how are you?" Baby boy was Reese's pet name for Mike. Mike couldn't help smiling.

"I'm fine and you? How was practice?"

"It was brutal, as usual, but at least it's over. Oh! Before I forget, here are the tickets for the guys for the preseason game this weekend," Reese said, as he washed his hands for the dinner Mike prepared.

"I am looking forward to going out there and watching you do your thing," Mike said as he poured Reese a glass of iced tea.

"Well, I plan to do my best. Oh yeah, baby boy, me and some of the guys are going out to dinner Friday after practice. It's a mini celebration for making the team. One of my boys, Keith ended up getting signed too."

"That's cool, just don't drink. You know how much that tires you out." Reese thought to himself, *my baby knows me so well.*

Then he made a little come hither motion with his finger, "Come over here for a second." Mike had been leaning on the edge of the counter, watching Reese gobble down his food.

He walked over to him and Reese put his arms around Mike's shoulders, "In case I haven't told you in a while, I want you to know that I love you. I know that lately it's been practice, eat, come home and go straight to bed. Always remember, I will never take you for granted. You are still, and you will always be, the best thing that ever happened in my life. If I forget to tell you sometimes, always remember that my heart is your home and I love you."

"Trust me baby, I know and I love you, too." Mike gave

Reese a long passionate kiss. Reese was the first to break the kiss.

"Good. As long as you're okay, then I'm okay," Reese said with a smile on his face.

"Have you found a house yet?" Reese asked.

"I looked at a couple, but I didn't see anything I liked," Mike said as he leaned against the counter once more, "I would like to be moved in before Christmas."

"If it weren't for these two-a-day practices, I would love to go with you and look."

"I know. I'm actually enjoying it," Mike said.

"Well as long as you're enjoying it, baby," Reese said as he threw him a quick wink.

"Oh yeah, I talked to Tariff today. It looks like Chuck may be a superstar. He's going into the studio on Friday to start work on his first single," Mike said, as he pulled out a chair to sit across from Reese.

"Sounds like things are going well for him."
Mike grabbed Reese's tea to take a sip. "Looks like they are. I think I'll give Tyrell, Jay, and Demetrious a call. Maybe we can all get together and hang out at Jay's house, since Tariff will be at the studio with Chuck and you'll be out with your teammates. Plus, I want to find out what's up with Jay."

"Why do you think something's wrong with Jay?" Reese asked as he rinsed off his plate.

"I called him today and he just sounded a little funny. It may be nothing, but can't hurt to see."

"Did you talk to Demetrious? Maybe he knows something. You know how tight those two are," Reese suggested.

"Hmm, that's a good idea. I'll give him a call," Mike said as he finished drinking Reese's tea.

"Are you ready for bed, baby boy?" Reese asked.

"I thought you were tired," Mike said as he gave Reese a quick smile.

"I got to take care of home. Never too tired for that."

Chapter 16

Early Friday evening, Tariff and Chuck arrived at the studio. Just inside the door a group of guys sat inside the booth. A skinny white guy walked up to Chuck and Tariff.

"Is one of you Tariff?" he asked.

"Yeah, that would be me," Tariff said as he extended his hand.

"My name is Taylor, but my friends call me Strings." Chuck couldn't help but wonder if it was because of his hair.

"Mr. Townson is running a little late, but he wanted a band to play for the new guy. That must be you?"

"That would be me, I guess. I'm Chuck," he said shaking Strings' hand.

"Well, are you guys ready to start?" Strings asked.

"We will be in a minute," Tariff said as he pulled Chuck aside, "let's go over here and have a seat and let me talk to you for a moment."

Chuck, unsure what was going on, whispered, "What's up, Tariff?"

"Sit down, Chuck."

"What's up, Tariff?" Chuck repeated as he took a seat on the sofa.

"We hope to release your single in the next month or two and then your CD by Christmas."

"Wow, that fast?" Chuck started to get excited.

"Well, when I say release, it won't be ready for purchase, it will be ready to be played on various radio stations. I guess you could call it the teaser for the CD."

"Tariff, I really have to thank you for everything."

Tariff just gave him a smile, "Man, I'm just doing my job. So do you have a song in mind for your single?"

"Actually I do. It's a song I wrote for Tyrell. He hasn't heard it yet."

"What's the name of the song?" Tariff asked.

"Then You Came Along."

"Catchy title. I like it," Tariff said, as he nodded his head in approval.

"I'm hoping he likes it."

Tariff looked at Chuck, "I am proud of you, man. You are a very special person and never let anyone tell you anything different. Let me give you a little advice, manager to client, friend to friend. Once your CD drops, if it goes the way I expect it to, your life is going to change drastically. Remember to stay humble and always treat people with respect. That will carry you a long way. Always stay focused. Now any questions before we get started?"

"No, and thank you for everything. I'll always remember what you just told me."

"Good. Now go in there and let me hear that song."

*   *   *

Reese was at the club hanging out with a couple guys from the team. This local hot spot was owned by an ex-football player, so a lot of athletes frequented the spot. Reese sat at the bar facing the crowd, his elbows resting on the bar top. If it weren't for the disco ball and the flashing lights, he would barely be able to see anyone's face, unless they were right up on him. All the booths were covered in leather, the same as the bar stools. He noticed the bouncer as he walked by, dressed all in black.

Damn, Reese thought, *We could use that brother on our defensive line as big as he is.* The music was loud, *Shake, Shake, Shake, Shake your Money Maker* blasted from the speakers. Reese could almost feel the vibrations. Most of the women on the dance floor were dancing with each other trying to be cute as they scanned the room looking for their next meal ticket. Most of the brothers were out with their homeboys, watching and waiting for the right time to go and get their mack on. Antonio and Keith were no different. Reese could only laugh when he watched them about to make their move.

"Check out the two honeys over there," Antonio said to Keith as he pointed in their direction. Reese looked too and thought *they looked like your run of the mill hoochies,* but Antonio and Keith didn't care. They were just pieces of ass for the night. Antonio finally waved the women over.

"'Sup ladies. My name is Antonio and this is my boy Keith."

"What's up beautiful ladies?" Keith said as he took a sip of his drink, not taking his eye off either one.

"Oh yeah ladies, this is our boy Reese."
Reese lifted his glass and feigned a seductive smile, "Ladies."

"Hi, my name is Tonya and this is my girl, Barbara." Tonya wore a skimpy outfit and her girl Barbara was dressed pretty much the same way.

"Nice to meet you, ladies. Can we buy you a drink?" Keith said deciding Barbara was the one he wanted. Antonio didn't care which one he wound up with. He just wanted to get his dick wet.

Barbara spoke for both of them, "We'll have apple martinis."

Tonya shook her head in agreement. Tonya liked Antonio 'cause he had the thuggish thing going on. *Shit, I hope he got some money,* Tonya thought.

Keith turned around to the bartender, "Let me get two apple martinis."

"Hi Reese," Barbara said, as she threw him a seductive smile.

Reese couldn't believe this girl was trying to flirt with him and his man, but, no matter what, Reese wanted to be polite and respectful. That's how he was brought up.

"Hello," Reese said forcing a smile. Reese was not feeling the circus act, so he finished up his juice. "I hate to be a party pooper, but I have an early day tomorrow. You ladies enjoy your night." Antonio and Keith were so wrapped up in the ladies, they didn't really care that it was early and Reese was leaving already.

Without even looking in Reese's direction Keith said, "Catch you later, Dawg."

"Later," Antonio chimed in. Reese headed toward the door and to what was waiting at home for him.

* * *

Demetrious, Mike, Tyrell, and Jay all hung out at Jay's house. Mike walked into the kitchen to refill his drink and as he poured, he noticed an invitation half torn in the garbage can. He picked it up and read it. It was an invitation to Jay's family reunion. Mike got his drink and then rejoined the guys in the living room. Mike walked into the living room with the piece of paper. "Are you planning to go, Jay?"

Jay stared and turned not saying a word.

"I guess not, but why?" Mike asked. "Why not?" Mike stared at Jay as he talked to him.

"You guys are my family. Besides, I heard my brothers are going to be there and I really don't want to deal with them. Since my brothers found out I am gay, they treat me like a stranger."

"I know how you feel." Mike thought back to the day his parents found out. "My mom found out about Reese when we came back from that Aruba trip he and I took a couple of years ago."

"I remember that trip," Demetrious said.

Mike continued, "My moms was at my house and I had left this picture of Reese and I on the table. Normally I'm good with putting that stuff away before she or my dad come over. Well, I guess she saw the picture. It was the one of us hugged up. I had run upstairs to get something and, when I came back down, she was ready to go. When I asked her why she was leaving she gave me some lame-ass story.

Oh man... Tyrell thought.

"A couple of days later, my dad called me and said "Michael I need to talk to you." I asked him what it was about. He just said he would tell me when I got there. I really didn't think any thing of it, but I knew it was important."

"How did you know?" Demetrious asked.

"Know what?" Mike asked.

"That it was important."

"Because whenever my parents are upset with me or

want to talk serious they don't call me Mike, they call me Michael. I just knew it couldn't be about my lifestyle. I had that under wraps, or at least that's what I thought.

Anyway, when I got there my mother was crying and just kept saying, 'We know, we know.' I said 'know what? She says, "We know that you're gay, Michael." I didn't know what to say, so I tried to play it off, 'Why would you guys say that?' My moms refreshed my memory about that day she left abruptly. She told me she saw the picture of me and some man embracing. Then she started blaming herself saying 'What did I do wrong?' My father just sat there as if to say, 'how could you do this to me and our family?' I finally came out and told her that yes, I am gay and that I was in love with the guy in the picture.

Mike laughed sarcastically, "Man they actually wanted me to get counseling, like I had some kind of illness or something. They even offered to pay for it. Moms also wanted me to see the pastor and talk with him, in hopes that he could cure me.

"Your moms really didn't say 'cure you' did she?" Jay asked as he rolled his eyes.

"Her exact words," Mike said, "the more she spoke, the madder I got. Finally I had had enough and told them there was nothing wrong with me. I told them I was just as healthy as the next person in mind, body and spirit. Whom I loved and what I felt had nothing to do with them. My father jumped up from his seat and started screaming and yelling about how he didn't raise no faggot and how I need-ed to leave his house and get myself cured. I stepped back. It took everything in me not to curse that man out. I had to remember this was my father. I used to sit on that man's lap and tell him how much I loved him and wanted to be like

him. This man used to be my role model.
My moms said she didn't know me, but she knew me. She just didn't want to face it."

"Mike, why didn't you ever tell us about this?" Tyrell asked as he shook his head.

"I don't know. But Reese was really great that day. You know what, as much as I was hurt, I would not allow myself to cry. It's been two years and I haven't spoken to my parents since. They haven't called me and every time I call and leave a message they don't return the call. I would give anything to pick up the phone one day and have it be my parents apologizing for everything. The way I see it, they owe me an apology and I don't owe them a damn thing. I am who I am and that's the way it's going to be."

All the guys were in their own worlds, thinking back to their own experiences of coming out and their families' reactions. Jay looked over at Mike with sadness in his eyes.

"I want to go home, but when I was told that my brothers would be there I changed my mind. I haven't talked to any of them in years. It seems they can't accept my lifestyle. A few years back when I was home, for the first time I was confronted with their true feelings. I felt like it was me against them." Jay's head moved side to side as he continued. "I remember like it was yesterday, I was hurting. My brothers broke my spirit. I didn't know what to do, so I called James. He was furious, he told me not to let my family break me and he reminded me that my 'chosen' brothers were waiting for me to get home." Jay looked up at his boyz and smiled. "James asked me if I wanted him and Tariff to come out to get me. All I had to do was ask. To this day, I haven't spoken another word to my brothers. I do miss them, but I look at it as their loss. Now they will never know what a good person I am."

Demetrious thought to himself, *This is why Jay holds us all so dear.*

All the guys thought about James and realized just how much they really missed him.

Chapter 17

Early in the morning Barbara's alarm clock went off. She had forgotten to turn it off the night before. As the alarm sounded, she slowly reached for it but couldn't find it. In the dark room the only bit of light was seeping from under the cranberry colored drapes. She finally found the clock and slapped it to shut it off. She pulled her comforter back over her head, ready to go back to sleep until the phone rang. "Damn, can a bitch get some sleep?" she grumbled out loud.

"Hello," she said irritated.

"Hey girl, let that bed go. Is that man still over there?" Tonya asked as she painted her nails.

"Girl, no. Keith left early this morning." Barbara turned over on to her right side cradling the phone between her ear and her shoulder.

"Antonio left earlier this morning too. Barbara, girl, he must have been on a dry spell because that niggah wore my walls out. I thought he was going to lose his mind."

Barbara laughed, "Keith was alright, I wouldn't say he was all that, but you know we got a plan right?" Barbara reminded her.

"If only they knew we were working them. Men can be so stupid. I'm surprised they didn't see us as we peeped them out. Of course they don't know that we know they're NFL players," Tonya replied as she started to count the dollars in her head.

"Girl, that is money in the making and I'm trying to get paid." By this time, Barbara had sat up in the bed.

"I tried to fuck that man all night," Tonya said. "I just need to get knocked by Antonio and I'll be set for life, or at least for the next 18 years," Tonya said with a wicked laugh.

Barbara couldn't help but laugh, "Yeah girl, I hear ya. So, how did you find out about that place anyway?"

"The ladies at the gym talk about it all the time." Barbara was grinning now, because she knew that Tonya was a true ear hustler. She could hear a rat stealing cheese if it meant she could get paid from it somehow.

"Girl, that place is a gold mine." Tonya was on a true hunting expedition. "Did you poke holes in the condoms like I told you to?"

"Just like you told me," Barbara said. "I took that needle and jabbed holes all in the middle of the pack over and over again. He was none the wiser."

"I remember this one brutha, I think he was suspicious of my ass, girl," Tonya replied as she sucked her teeth.

"How? What did he do?" Barbara was all ears.

Tonya started laughing thinking back, "He brought his own condoms and would only use those."

"Well, how did you get around that?" Barbara was now wide awake.

Tonya felt proud of herself. "On our way home to my place one night I told him that I didn't have any condoms and he didn't either. So we stopped at the mini-mart around the corner from the house. I bought a box like the one I already had at home. I made sure he saw the box I bought. As soon as we got to the house and his back was turned I switched boxes. Girl I'm a woman with a plan and ain't nothing more dangerous.

"Bitch, you are off the hook. Remind me not to get on your bad side," Barbara said as she started to lie back down.

"Well, girl I'm going to lie in this bed a little longer. I will see you this evening."

"Alright, girl, lata."

Barbara caught Tonya before she hung up, "Oh yeah girl, you won't believe who I thought I saw last night.

Tonya was clueless, "Who?"

"Chuck."

"Our Chuck? Girl you know he's in jail with Curtis and Carlton," Tonya spit out.

"I could have sworn it was him," Barbara said.

"Well, you know they say we all have a twin somewhere in this world. You probably just thought it was him. Anyway, girl, I'll call you later."

*   *   *

Demetrious woke up with Tariff on his mind. It had been a while since he woke up in his bed alone even though he and Tariff hadn't consummated their relationship yet. Both still enjoyed each other's company. Normally, Demetrious was either at Tariff's house or Tariff was at Demetrious' house. Since Tariff was in the studio with Chuck late last night and Demetrious was at Jay's with the guys, they both decided just to go to their own spots. Demetrious started thinking and wondered if Tariff would ever get past the loss of James and finally give into what they both were feeling for each other. Demetrious was falling in love with Tariff. Demetrious sighed and decided he just needed to continue to be a little patient. Demetrious picked up the phone and called Tariff.

"Hello," Tariff said, half asleep.

"Hey boo, you up?" Demetrious said.

"Lying here in bed. I'm about to get up. You know it felt funny waking up and you not being here in the bed next to me."

Demetrious smiled. "You must have E.S.P, I was just thinking the same thing. How did it go last night with Chuck?"

Tariff now sat on the edge of the bed, "He finished his first single. Man, it's really hot. He decided to use a song that he wrote for Tyrell. He blew everyone away with that song."

"So it's that good?"

"I'll say this, you thought he was good in Miami? He was ten times better than that."

Demetrious thought to himself, *I guess love will do that to you.*

"We were hungry and just went to grab a bite to eat." Tariff mentioned, changing the subject, "Jay will be by the shop today to get his hair cut. Don't forget about Reese's game tomorrow."

"Oh trust me, I wouldn't miss that for the world. Will I see you tonight?" Tariff questioned.

Demetrious started to smile at the thought of seeing Tariff, "Do you even have to ask?"

Now Tariff was smiling, "I guess that would be 'yes'."

"Your guess would be right. What did you want to do?" Demetrious didn't really care what they did as long as it gave him more time to spend with Tariff.

"Well, I got some tickets to that new Tyler Perry play."

"That's cool. I'll get out of the shop around 7:00," Demetrious said as he glanced at his watch.

"That's perfect, the show starts at 9:30."

"I'll need to rush home and grab something to wear," Demetrious said.

Tariff thought for a moment, "I have a light day today, I can go by your house and pick up something for you to wear. Then you can come straight here after work and change here." Demetrious smiled at how attentive Tariff was being to his needs.

"I see you got everything worked out."

"Don't I always?" Tariff said as he pulled out a pair of Demetrious' underwear mixed in with his.

"Oh yeah, don't forget I need some clean underwear," Demetrious reminded him.

Tariff chuckled to himself as he returned Demetrious' underwear to the drawer, "Don't worry, man, I got this."

Demetrious just laughed, "I guess we're all set then. I'll see you tonight, babe."

"Alright, man. Later."

*   *   *

Reese got out of bed and went into the bathroom to take a shower before going to practice. Mike woke up and turned on the TV to ESPN so he could watch some sports highlights. He heard the shower shut off and then Reese emerged from the bathroom drying himself off. As Reese dried off, Mike took notice of how much bigger and better Reese's body had become. Mike assumed all that working out and practice was paying off.

"Damn baby, the body is looking real good."

Reese gave Mike a little pose, "You think?"

Mike had to laugh at how playful Reese was, "Yeah, I think. So how did it go last night?"

"It was cool, but nothing big. The guys met these two hoochies and probably took them home last night. I left before they did and passed the hell out. I must have been more tired than I thought, because I didn't hear you when you came in."

"You looked so peaceful," Mike said. "I tried to be as quiet as possible; I didn't want to wake you."

"Thank you for being so considerate," Reese said as he finished drying off. "How are the guys doing? Did you find out what was up with Jay?"

"Yeah, I did. I was right. It had to do with his family. The evening was good, we all got a chance to get some things off our chests."

"So you guys kind of exhaled a bit," Reese said as he put on some deodorant.

Mike began to smile, "I guess you could say that. We were talking about families."

Reese slipped on a pair of underwear and walked over to Mike, "That had to be hard for you since you haven't talked to your family in a few years. Man, I feel really bad about that."

Mike took Reese's hand, "There's no need to feel like that. I love you. Maybe one day my family will come around, who knows, but until that happens, I have you and the boyz."

"Family can sometimes complicate one's life..." Reese's voice trailed off as he thought about his own family.
Mike brought Reese out of his thoughts, "By the way, I found a house."

Reese was surprised. "Man that was quick."

"The house is nice; the realtor's card is on the dresser. I told him that you may be calling him so you can go and take a look at it."

"Cool, I'll call him today after practice and go check it out."

Reese had finished dressing and was getting ready to leave, "You get yourself some sleep, I'm going to get out of here. I'll call you later this afternoon." Reese gave him a kiss and hug, then headed for the door.

Mike called out to him as he left, "I love you, man. Have a good practice."

Reese stuck his head in the bedroom and winked at Mike, "I love you too, baby boy."

*　　*　　*

Jay was just getting out of the shower after his workout. He couldn't believe he had worked out for almost two hours. He remembered he had an appointment with Demetrious to get his hair cut. Daunte was still out of town with his girl, so Jay worked out solo.

When Jay pulled up to the shop, Demetrious was standing out front with a couple of his clients, talking. Jay got out of the car and was walking over when he tripped over a small pole sticking up out of the side walk.

"Jay, you okay?" Demetrious asked.

"I'm good, but they need to fix that before someone gets hurt." Jay stared at the pole.

"I've complained several times about that shit. I've told

them they need to pull it up. Anyway, guys, this is my boy, Jay." Demetrious introduced him to the guys he had been talking to.

"What's up, fellas?" Jay threw the nod.

"I just finished cutting their hair so you're right on time."

"Yo, Demetrious, when you moving to the new shop?" the client inquired.

"I just talked to the owner this morning. I was supposed to be moving next week, but the building isn't quite ready yet. So it may be another couple of weeks. If anything changes, I'll hit you up on your celly," Demetrious said as he headed into the shop.

"Alright man, good looking out. See you next week!" the client yelled.

Jay was already sitting in the chair. "I see you're pretty busy today."

"Just a little bit. You doing okay today, knucklehead?" Demetrious asked.

"I'm cool. It was good to spend some time with you guys last night, it really helped."

"It's like we said last night, we're family. We look out for each other," Demetrious said as he shook the hair off the smock and put it around Jay's neck.

"I appreciate that man." Jay smiled.

"Are you ready for the game tomorrow?"

"Come on Jay, you know I am."

"I'm looking forward to it. Mike told me we have really good seats. You know we're all wearing Reese's jersey. Big number 22."

"Man, I already got my jersey ready." Demetrious said as he put his scissors down and grabbed his trimmer, he leaned Jay's head back. "So D, how did it go last night with

Chuck and Tariff at the studio?"

"I talked to Tariff this morning. He thinks that Chuck is going to blow up. You know I think he and Chuck are starting to become real good friends."

"Well, maybe we should get Chuck's autograph now." Jay chuckled.

"The way Tariff was sounding, he may quit his job and manage Chuck full-time."

"Man, you got to be shittin' me?" Jay commented.

"He's that confident that Chuck is going to be making some big money."

"Then you guys can buy a new house like Mike and Reese," Jay joked.

Demetrious stopped cutting Jay's hair to pop him in the back of his head. Jay just started to laugh.

"Mike mentioned last night that you went looking at houses with him."

"Yeah he found a real nice one. I think they want to move in before Christmas. By the way, how are things going with you and Tariff?"

"Things are going slowly, very slowly. We're going to see the new Tyler Perry play tonight. Tariff won some tickets on the radio."

"I've heard good things about that play," Demetrious said, as he began to trim Jay's goatee.

"What's up with you and Ricky?"

"Actually, I talked to him this morning and he will be in town this week." *That will give me a chance to interview him more,* Jay thought out loud.

"Well, in Miami he seemed like a good guy. I hope things work out for you. It's about time you settled down. I don't know if I really liked that last character you dated.

Will was his name, I think," Demetrious said. "Looks like I'm done man," Demetrious said as he handed Jay a mirror.

Ignoring Demetrious' last comment about Will, Jay inspected his haircut. He noticed a picture of Demetrious and a pretty looking girl. He didn't mention it to Demetrious, but he knew she had to be someone close to him.

"Looks good, as usual. I guess I'll be back on Friday, you know how fast my hair grows." Jay paid for his cut and gave Demetrious a tip.

"Who's the girl in the picture?" Jay asked.

"Oh that's a friend of mine and Tariff. Her name is Mimi."

She's a pretty girl, Jay thought. "You two look pretty intimate to me. If I didn't know any better..." Jay joked.

Demetrious leaned in close to Jay and whispered in his ear so the other barbers couldn't hear. "Well it's just to throw the guys in here off."

Jay just shook his head, "Fuck these muthafuckers in here."

"I feel you. But it's just until I move to the new shop. Then I won't play that game anymore."

"I understand. Just be careful. I'm outta here. I'll see you tomorrow. We're all meeting at Mike and Reese's crib right?"

"Right!"

"Tell Tariff I said hey and I'll see him tomorrow. Love you, man."

Jay put his arm around Demetrious and gave him that brotherly hug. Demetrious whispered in Jay's ear, "I love you too, man."

Jay stood back looked at Demetrious, shook his head,

"You need to get over that."

*   *   *

After the game, the guys all went back to Mike and Reese's house to celebrate the victory. The crisp fall air whipped past them as they entered the house.

"My boy was all over that field today," Mike said. "I was so nervous with each hit he took. I was so afraid he would get hurt. I don't know if I can do this every Sunday." Mike was a worry wart, and ever since Reese got hurt in college, seeing him play put Mike's nerves on edge.

"Come on, man, he will be fine," Jay said. "The man is built like a monster."

Jay was trying his best to reassure Mike that Reese could handle the NFL.

Reese walked in the door and the guys all cheered.

"That was some game. I was all over the place." Reese demonstrated the moves he used on the field. Mike gave Reese a look to let him know that his nerves were shot from watching him on the field.

"Are you okay, baby boy?"

"I'm fine." Reese walked over to Mike and opened his arms wide. Mike fell into his embrace like a terrified child needing a hug. "Come on baby boy, its okay."

Mike held on to Reese tightly, "You just be careful out there."

"Alright guys," Tariff spit out, "quit all that hugging and mushy stuff and hand your boyz some more drinks."

Chapter 18

Jay had decided to turn up the heater as he sat in the car. It was unusually cold. Sounds of horns came from every direction. Jay watched a policeman walk up to the cars telling people they had to move. *Everyone must be coming into town today,* Jay thought. Jay hated coming to the airport. It was always so congested. Jay saw the police officer coming in his direction. Jay started the car to drive around and come back. Just as the officer approached, a smile crept across Jay's face.

"Excuse me sir, but you can't park here," The officer said.

"I know, but I'm here to pick him up," Jay said quickly as he pointed to Ricky.

"Alright then you gentlemen have a good day," The officer said as he walked toward the next car.

Jay jumped out of the car grinning from ear to ear. Ricky and Jay embraced, neither wanting to let go of the other.

"So another man trying to beat my time," Ricky said softly as they broke their embrace.

"Well, men in uniform drive me crazy," Jay spat out. They broke out in laughter as Ricky put his luggage in the trunk.

"So how was your flight man?" Jay asked as they both got in the car.

"It was great. I'm just glad to finally be here," Ricky said as he grabbed Jay's free hand.

"It's so good to see you," Jay said flashing a kool aid smile.

"I missed you so much," Ricky said as he reached to put on his seatbelt. "I'll be here until Monday. Do you think you can put up with me that long?"

"I think I can manage." Jay's cell phone rang and he pushed the button on his hands-free to answer.

"Hey, Daunte, What's up?" Jay answered.

"Everything's good man. Are we still working out tomorrow?"

"Daunte, hold on a sec." Jay hit the mute button.

Jay turned to Ricky, "You feel like hitting the gym tomorrow?"

"I'm wit dat," Ricky said in a seductive tone, and giving Jay a quick wink.

Jay hit the mute button again back to Daunte, "Sounds like a plan. I'll see you tomorrow. Later."

"Is this the guy you were telling me about?" Ricky asked.

"You remember?"

"I don't forget much."

"Yeah, I see. So what did you want to do tonight?" Jay asked as he merged onto the highway.

"This is your city. I don't care if we spend a quiet evening in, or go out on the town. It doesn't matter to me as long as I'm with you."

"We can stay in and keep each other warm," Jay said quickly. "Oh yeah, the guys want to see you while you're here. Maybe we could get together with them tomorrow after the gym and our haircuts."

"It would be nice to see them too."

"Why don't we just rent a couple of movies and have a

quiet night?" Jay suggested.

"That sounds good to me."

After a quiet evening at home and a good nights sleep, Jay woke up before Ricky and watched him sleep. Jay loved his honey brown skin and his full sexy lips. To Jay, he looked like an angel. Jay started thinking to himself, *how can a man this fine be so sweet and available? Maybe I should grab him before he gets away.* Jay kissed Ricky's lips and Ricky felt like he had just been kissed by Prince Charming.

"Were you watching me while I slept? This is me at my worst," Ricky said giving Jay a sheepish smile.

"Well, if this is your worst, I would love to see you at your best!" Ricky and Jay became aroused by the playful banter.

Smiling a seductive smile, Ricky looked into Jay's eyes, "See what you did to me; now I need to take a cold shower."

"Shit look at me. Look what you did! Well, I'll use the shower in the hall and you can use the shower in here." Knowing now was not the time. They knew without words when the right time would be.

*　　*　　*

Jay, Ricky and Daunte finished their workout at the gym and were headed to the shop to get their hair cuts. Jay called ahead and told Demetrious to expect them in a few minutes. A short time later Demetrious had Daunte in his chair.

"Hey, Demetrious, where's your girl, Mimi? I haven't seen her around lately," one of the barbers asked.

"She's been busy. You know how that goes," Demetrious said.

Jay, playing around said, "Yeah, where is Mimi?" Even though Jay disagreed with what Demetrious was doing, he had to look out for his boy so he played the game.

"Can you see if I can meet her sister," the barber asked.

Daunte thought to himself. *Mia's sister called her Mimi. These niggahs can't be talking about my girl.* Demetrious turned the barber chair around with Daunte in it. As soon as the chair stopped, Daunte saw the picture of Mia and Demetrious hugged up. Daunte became furious and jumped up out of the chair. Demetrious moved back with the clippers in his hand.

Daunte pointed his finger, "What the fuck is my girl's picture doing on your stand? And what do you mean *your girl?* Oh I get it now! You're the muthafucker that Mia's been talking too. I'm about to kick your muthafuckin ass!"

Jay jumped up from where he was sitting and grabbed a hold of Daunte, "Man it's not what you think!"

"Then what the fuck is it?" Daunte said as he got into Jay's face.

Demetrious looked at Daunte, "Man, let's step outside so I can clear this up. It's a complete misunderstanding."

Daunte snatched the bib from around his neck and headed for the door, "Yeah let's step the fuck outside!"

Daunte walked to the door talking to himself, "I knew that bitch was cheating on me. I'm going to whip her ass right after I kick yours!"

Ricky stood there looking like a deer caught in headlights not knowing what was happening. With all the commotion going on, Ricky never saw the picture of Mia and never even made the connection. Demetrious, Daunte, Jay, and Ricky all stood outside the shop. The other barbers and customers stood in the doorway watching Daunte and Jay start to argue. Daunte had his back to Demetrious.

Daunte got right up in Jay's face, "You're supposed to be my got damn boy and you didn't tell me shit!" Ricky was about to step between the two. Demetrious moved Ricky back.

Jay tried to explain what the situation was, "I didn't know that was your girl. I knew your girl by Mia, and I never met her, Daunte."

"Save that shit man, you ain't shit!" Daunte yelled, not listening to Jay's explanation.

Demetrious grabbed Daunte's arm to turn him around so he could explain to him what was going on. Daunte spun around and punched blindly at whoever grabbed his arm.

The punch landed right in Demetrious' face, causing him to fall back. As he fell he tripped over the same pole Jay had tripped on the week before. Demetrious tried to brace his fall by putting his arms down. As he fell to the ground, his head hit the mirror of a car parked along the sidewalk. Demetrious hit the ground like a rag doll; his head slamming down hard on the concrete. Blood started to spurt from the gash.

Jay looked at Daunte and then rushed over to Demetrious calling his name, "Shit, Demetrious, Demetrious...somebody call 911!" For the second time Ricky was part of an unfolding drama. One of the barbers called 911. The other barbers prepared to rush out and jump Daunte and kick his ass, but were stopped by the shop manager.

Daunte began to pace and yell! As he held his head, "I didn't mean it! God--I didn't mean it!"

Jay turned and glared at Daunte, "Do you see what the fuck you just did?! For what? Some damn girl!" Jay turned back to Demetrious, "Come on, D wake up, wake up man…come on wake the fuck up!"

Ricky stood there muttering, "What the fuck?" The ambulance and the police pulled up to the scene at the same time. Two paramedics rushed out of the ambulance. The taller one pushed his dreads aside as he bent down to attend to Demetrious.

Daunte sat on the curb, tears running down his face as he tried to figure out what had just happened. Ricky and Jay watched the emergency team work.

One of the paramedics tried talking to Demetrious, "Sir, can you hear me?" The other checked his vitals.

Looking concerned, the taller paramedic said, "Keith his vitals are weak. We can't waste any time."

They loaded Demetrious into the ambulance, slammed the door shut, and took off. Jay now stood with Ricky, self-consciously hugging his shoulders. At this point, Jay didn't care what anyone said or thought. All he could think about was that another one of his best friends may not make it.

Ricky took Jay's keys out of his pocket, "Get in the car!" Jay stood, unable to move. "Jay get in the car! We need to get to the hospital; you know I don't know how to get there, c'mon."

With slow, wooden movements, Jay got into the car and closed the passenger side door. They drove off, leaving Daunte on the sidewalk talking to the police. They arrived at the hospital a good ten to fifteen minutes faster than the law usually allowed.

Ricky turned to Jay and said, "You need to call Tariff and let him know what has happened." Slowly and obediently, Jay took out his cell phone and tried to dial Tariff's number. Ricky, seeing that Jay was to upset, grabbed the phone, found the number and dialed.

"This is Tariff," he answered.

"Tariff, this is Ricky. Demetrious had an accident. Jay and I are here at the hospital with him now." Tariff started to panic when he heard Jay in the background.

"Is D okay?" Tariff asked shaking his head.

"I'm not sure. We just got here and we're about to run in."

"Jay is straight up trippin'. I really need for you to get here as quick as you can."

"I'm on my way. How is D?" Tariff asked again.

"I'm sorry man, but I just don't know yet," he said turning a worried eye at Jay.

"What hospital are you at?"

Ricky looked up at the emergency room sign, "Houston Memorial, we're at Houston Memorial."

"Okay, Ricky, I'll call the other guys and we'll be right there."

Ricky managed to get Jay out of the car and they headed to the emergency room. The nurse on duty directed them to seats in the waiting room. Jay sat down and leaned back in the chair.

Ricky comforted him, "It will be alright, man, it will be alright." Ricky cradled his head in his hands and thought, *I can't believe it's happening again.*

On the way to the hospital, all Tariff could think about was the day James died. He pulled into the parking lot, *God, I couldn't handle another death. Please make things alright,* he thought as he got out of the car. Tariff knew he had to pull himself together and be strong for the other guys. He slowed his pace and the one tear that rolled down his face, Tariff quickly wiped away. Tariff took a deep breath and walked through the doors only to see that he was the last one to arrive. Tariff felt a pang of fear in his stomach. Everything seemed to be moving in slow motion. To Tariff, it was as if his shoes were filled with lead. It seemed like it was taking forever to reach the guys. All he kept thinking was *I would rather be anywhere else but here.*

Reese held Mike in his arms. By their expressions he could tell that Ricky was filling them in. Tariff finally reached the guys. The sea of red eyes told Tariff that the news wasn't good. For a few seconds everyone stood without speaking. A voice broke the silence. Everyone afraid to ask, Chuck stepped up. "Excuse me Doctor, our brother Demetrious Wright, was just brought in. How is he?"

The doctor pulled the drawstring on his scrub pants, looked at his chart and then at Chuck. "Gentlemen, it looks like when Mr. Wright fell and hit his head, he fractured his skull. A skull fracture is a very serious injury. We have to operate right away to relieve the pressure on his brain. He's being prepped for surgery as we speak. As soon as we're done we will come out and let you know the prognosis."

Tariff could see the doctor's mouth move but didn't hear a word he was saying. "What are his chances, Doc?" Chuck asked.

The doctor took a deep sigh, "This is really a delicate surgery. He has a 50/50 chance here. I'm sorry I don't have better news," the doctor said with a sympathetic smile before he quickly turned and walked away. Tariff stumbled into a chair and put his head between his hands.

Tyrell sat next to him to try and comfort him, but because of his own pain, it didn't seem to help. The group waited quietly, for six hours, with no word. The guys took turns pacing the floor. Every time they saw the doors that led to the operating room open, they would all stare, hoping it would be news about Demetrious. They shuffled like zombies not knowing what to say to each other. Finally, a few hours later, the doctor came out. Immediately everyone walked right up. Jay was the first to ask, "How's Demetrious?"

"Well it was touch and go. We almost lost him. Mr. Wright is definitely a fighter. The next 24 hours are crucial. The sooner he wakes up the better. All we can do now is wait." The doctor looked at the group, "Does anyone have any questions?"

"Thank you, Doctor," the guys echoed.

"Can I sit with him?" Tariff asked the doctor with pleading eyes.

"Yes. I'll have someone come and get you when we move him to a private room. Sometimes it's good for a patient to hear a familiar voice. Talk to him and hold his hand. Sometimes it helps."

Tyrell turned to Chuck, "Aren't you supposed to be back at the halfway house at 10:00 pm?"

Chuck wiped a tear from Tyrell's eye. "I couldn't leave you and the guys hurting like this. I had to be here for y'all. Isn't that what friends and lovers do for each other? Besides, I called my probation officer and told him what happened. He cleared me. You're always worrying about me. How about you let me take care of you for a change?"

"This feels like a nightmare and I'm ready to wake up," Tyrell mumbled.

Chuck held Tyrell tighter, "I know baby, I know. Sit tight. I'll be right back." Chuck hugged him tightly and walked away. Chuck's heart was heavy with the love and pain he felt for Tyrell and the others. The guys had no idea how afraid Chuck was for Demetrious.

Chuck headed for the one place where he thought he could find resolution--the hospital chapel. He slowly opened the door and peeked inside. The room was dark. The only light came from the candles at the alter space. Eight rows of benches filled the worship space. It was so peaceful and quiet. When he saw that there was no one inside, he went in and sat down.

Chuck wasn't one to go to church every Sunday, but he did have a strong belief in God. Chuck collected his thoughts as he sat with his eyes closed. He didn't even hear Tariff walk in. Tariff moved to say something but stopped as Chuck began to pray: *"Heavenly father I come to you with a heavy heart. I'm not sure how I am supposed to talk to you. My friends need your strength. Lord, Tariff is a good man and he deserves all of the blessings that you have in store for him. I've only known him for a short time, but he has a good heart. They all have good hearts. Wrap them in your arms of comfort and serenity. Give them the strength to cope with whatever your will may be. I can only imagine the hurt and pain that they all are feeling right now. I know how I would feel if you were to take Tyrell from me. I don't think that I could go on. So dear Lord, let Demetrious come back to us for a while longer. We all love him and need him to be with us through this life's journey. In your name, amen."*

Chuck finished his prayer and as he sat in silence a smile came across his face.

Tariff, quietly left the chapel and went into a bathroom nearby. While Tariff was in the bathroom, Chuck made his way back to where he had left Tyrell sitting. He looked around for Tariff, but didn't see him.

"Where's Tariff?" Chuck asked.

"He went to sit with Demetrious."

Not one of the guys intended to leave the hospital before Demetrious opened his eyes. Mike looked up to see how Jay was doing. He didn't see him anywhere, nor did he see Ricky. He hadn't seen Jay and Ricky leave. Mike asked if anyone knew where Ricky and Jay went, but no one had a clue.

Jay sat out in the car. He was furious at Daunte for what he had done to Demetrious with his irrational behavior. Ricky sat next to Jay, not sure what to say. Jay started the car and drove off. Ricky wasn't sure were Jay was going until they pulled up in the police parking lot. Jay collected his thoughts and got out of the car and headed inside with Ricky close behind.

Ricky tried to talk Jay out of going in, once he figured out what Jay was about to do. "Are you sure you want to do this now? You're not really in any shape to do this. We should be back at the hospital waiting on Demetrious' progress."

"I know we should, but this is something I need to do right now." Jay didn't say anything else to Ricky. He just opened the door and went into the station with Ricky right on his heels.

Jay walked in and asked the officer at the front desk if it would be possible for him to see Daunte Ramsey. The officer looked at his log and then told Jay to have a seat. Jay sat down and Ricky sat right beside him. A few minutes later another officer appeared at the end of the hall.

"Who's here to see Daunte Ramsey?" the officer asked. Jay stood up and followed the officer into another hallway to where the holding cells were, leaving Ricky waiting. Ricky wanted to go with him, but Jay insisted that he needed to do this alone. Jay wasn't quite sure what he would say to his good friend of so many years.

Jay wrestled with his emotions. His mind was truly back at the hospital. Finally, Jay was in front of the cell where Daunte sat. Daunte looked at Jay as if he had just lost a good friend. The officer stepped away from Jay and informed him that he only had fifteen minutes. Jay thanked the officer then turned his attention back to the cell.

"Do you know what you have done? My best friend in the world is in the hospital fighting for his life because of you." Daunte tried to interrupt, but Jay put his hand up. This would be more of a 'Jay talks and you listen' conversation. Jay was too angry to let Daunte speak.

"You let your jealousy and irrational behavior take you to a place that you may not be able to come back from. Demetrious and I tried to explain to you what was really going on with your girl Mia, but you wouldn't give us a chance. The truth is, my boy Demetrious is gay and he is in love with my best friend Tariff. You have now managed to rip their worlds completely apart. Your girl was doing Demetrious a favor by coming by the shop pretending to be his girlfriend. Oh, by the way, I'm gay too!"

Daunte's jaw dropped open. "Yeah, that's right. I'm gay. I've never hated anybody as much as I hate you right now. You, my brutha, have taken me to a new height. All those times you talked about how much you hated gays and that WE were going to hell! The whole time your own best friend--I was gay and you had no idea. So I guess you hate me now that you know that I am 'ONE OF THEM' as you put it…But know this, you had better pray long and hard to

200

God Almighty that Demetrious makes it through and recovers completely, because if he doesn't, you can best believe what I say. *I will find you and kill you my damn self!* You can take that to the bank."

Jay didn't give Daunte a chance to respond. He stormed out the way he came in. When he came through the door, Ricky was standing next to a woman consoling her. Jay was already frazzled and nerves shot to hell. Now he had to figure what was going on with Ricky and this woman.

This was Ricky's first time in town, Jay thought, *He didn't know anyone other than me and the guys.* The closer Jay got, the more the woman's face started to look familiar. It was the woman he saw in the picture with D. It hit him, it was Mia!

Jay got to Ricky and demanded point blank, "How do you know her?" Ricky didn't even look at Jay. He looked down at the floor then at Mia, "This is my ex-wife, Mia."

Jay was still upset from seeing Daunte, now he had to deal with this, "What the fuck is this shit?" Jay was now drawing attention to them with his yelling.

"Why didn't you say something back at the shop? Is she the real reason why you came to Houston…to see her?"

"Jay, calm down, I didn't see the picture at the shop. When all of the commotion started with Demetrious and Daunte, I followed you guys right out. I didn't even know Mia lived here. I haven't talked to her since our divorce was final."

Jay looked at them both. "You expect me to believe that shit? She just happened to live here and now she's here all of a sudden." Jay pointed to the spot where they were standing.

Mia tried to explain to Jay, but didn't think it was getting through, "Jay, please calm down. Ricky didn't even know that I moved here. He's telling you the truth. When I moved here, I wanted a fresh start. So I haven't been in contact with him since our divorce. I am so, so sorry for what's happened to Demetrious."

Now Jay was pacing back and forth fuming, "You're sorry? You're sorry? This shit is your fault! Do you see now what secrets can do? I told Demetrious this could backfire. If you had been honest with Daunte this would never have happened."

Jay turned and walked away, talking to their backs, "I have to get out of here. I can't deal with this right now. I have to get back to the hospital to see how Demetrious is doing." Jay walked out the door, leaving Ricky and Mia in the station. Mia began to cry and her sobs echoed throughout the corridors. Ricky was torn at this point. He wanted to console Mia, the woman who he shared his past with, but at the same time he wanted to go after the man he wanted in his future.

He looked at Mia, "I'm sorry about everything. He's just a little upset right now. Are you going to be okay?"

"I'll be fine. Thanks Ricky."

"I need to go after him." Ricky didn't say another word to her. He left to go find Jay.

Mia composed herself and walked to the desk officer and asked to see Daunte. Ricky found Jay leaning against the car. Ricky moved to pull him into a hug, but Jay pushed him away.

"Come on, man, let me take you back to the hospital to check on Demetrious."

Ricky grabbed Jay who yelled, "I don't know what to do!" Slowly he let Ricky hug and comfort him.

Jay stepped back and said, "Let's go to the hospital."

Down in the holding area, Mia looked at Daunte, who couldn't yet see her. She called out his name and he turned to look at her. She could see in his eyes that he felt bad about what had happened. She walked closer to the cell, the bars separating them.

Daunte got off the cot and walked over to her, at the bars, "Mia, I am so sorry for overreacting and not trusting you. When I saw that picture of you with that guy, I just lost it."

Mia felt this was all her fault. *If only I had been honest with you,* she thought.

Mia took a deep breath and said, "It wasn't your fault Daunte, it wasn't your fault. I should have been completely honest with you and told you the whole story. I didn't because I knew how you felt about gay men."

Looking at Mia, Daunte said, "When Jay told me that he was gay, I didn't hate him. All I could see was the best friend that he'd always been. I'm not sure what's going to happen to our friendship from this point on."

"What happened?" Mia placed her hand on Daunte's hand that rested on the bars.

"Baby, I don't even know. All I know is, one moment I was arguing with Jay and the next moment Demetrious grabbed my arm. I just turned around and blindly punched him in the face. He tripped over something sticking up out of the sidewalk. As he fell, he hit his head. Baby, I didn't mean it…and now he could die because of me."

Mia began to rub his hand, "Daunte, he is going to be just fine. I'll go to the hospital and see how he's doing. I love you, baby," she said as she leaned closer to the bars.

"I love you, too." Daunte poked his lips through the bars

and kissed her on the forehead. She smiled at Daunte, turned, and left the way she came in.

*   *   *

Tariff went home long enough to change and freshen up. The guys had been taking shifts sitting by Demetrious' side. In twenty fours hours Demetrious had not opened his eyes. Tariff walked into his room where the nurse was checking his vitals. Demetrious lay there still, unmoving. The crown of his head was completely bandaged. Tariff was concerned seeing the IV lines in his arm. Once the nurse left, Tariff sat next to Demetrious' bed. He watched the line on the heart monitor. He grabbed hold of Demetrious' hand and watched him closely for any sign of a change.

Tariff remembered what the doctor told him about talking to Demetrious. Tariff began to talk to him, hoping the sound of his voice would wake him, "I know that you have been very patient with me and now I think that I'm ready to let our love grow. I need you in my life Demetrious. I didn't know how much until right now. I'm ready for us to start a fresh, new life together." Tariff started to cry as he laid his head on the bed. Demetrious' eyes slowly opened. His blurred vision quickly focused. He turned his head a little and saw Tariff's head on the bed. Oblivious to Tariff, Demetrious heard the words of love Tariff was speaking.

"I love you so much. I want us to spend the rest of our lives together. Please don't leave me," Tariff said. Demetrious lifted his hand and rubbed Tariff's head. Tariff slowly looked up into Demetrious' eyes. Demetrious smiled at him.

Demetrious whispered softly, "Remember what you just said." Tariff smiled and gingerly touched Demetrious' cheek with his fingers.

Tariff pushed the button for the nurse.

When she appeared inside the room, Tariff looked up, "Could you get the doctor please?"

She quickly closed the door and returned in what seemed like a matter of seconds with the doctor. Demetrious looked at the doctor as he walked toward him.

"How are you feeling, young man?" the doctor asked as he checked Demetrious' pulse. Demetrious didn't respond. The doctor checked the reaction of his pupils with a flashlight and then checked his extremities.

"Everything looks good," the doctor replied, "it's going to take some time, but with some physical therapy, he should recover nicely."

Tariff was now beaming with joy, "Thank you, Doctor, thank you so much." The doctor left the room and Tariff immediately sat down next Demetrious. Demetrious just stared at him with a crooked smile on his face. He tried to speak. Tariff couldn't hear him so he leaned over.

"How are the guys? They all okay?" Demetrious asked. He knew they would be worried. "Is Jay okay?"

"I'll call Tyrell and he can call the fellas." Tariff picked up the phone and dialed Tyrell. Demetrious could see how happy Tariff was as he relayed the news to Tyrell on the phone.

"The doctor wants him to get a little bit more rest and then you guys can see him later. Make sure you call Jay right away," Tariff added before he hung up. Tariff sat back down beside his bed. Demetrious reached out to Tariff.

Tariff took his hand and placed it on his cheeks.

"I was so afraid that I had lost you." A sole tear rolled down his face. Demetrious shook his head from side to side at him as if to say no tears, I'm okay. Tariff smiled, understanding.

"Get some sleep. I'll be here when you wake up." Tariff kissed him deeply. Demetrious' eyes drifted closed in a matter of seconds.

Tariff decided to go outside and get some fresh air while Demetrious slept. He took a seat on one of the benches. He was so tired that he didn't see Mia walk up.

"Tariff, how's Demetrious doing?"

"He's doing okay, he's sleeping right now."

"I came by yesterday, but I saw you with your friends and after my encounter with Jay, I didn't want to upset anyone. So I decided to come today instead."

Mia sat down on the bench next to him. "Tariff, I am so sorry for what happened."

Tariff replied, "I knew something likes this was going to happen. That's why I hate secrets."

"Can I see him?"

"Maybe in a day or two, but right now Demetrious needs all the rest that he can get."

"I understand. Would you give him my love? I know this is entirely my fault."

"I can't let you take all the blame. Demetrious was a willing participant in this charade. It's just sad that two people had to get hurt behind it--Demetrious and Daunte."

"I just came from seeing Daunte and he feels really bad about the whole thing."

Tariff blew out a deep sigh, "He should Mimi; violence is never the resolution to anything. It just makes matters worse."

"I met your friend Jay the other day. Who would have known that he and Daunte were best friends. He was really angry with Daunte."

"Talk about six degrees of separation."

"Yeah, I know what you mean."

"You know we are a close-knit group, so when someone hurts one of us, it's like they hurt one of our family. Jay is very protective. When it comes to his boyz, he can get a little crazy. I'll talk to him."

"Tariff, I just want you to know that I'm going to bail Daunte out."

"I wouldn't expect anything less, after all, he is your man." Tariff smiled and gave Mia a hug.

"Please don't forget to give Demetrious my love." Mia got up off the bench and walked back toward the parking lot.

Chapter 19

Months after Demetrious had his accident, Tariff decided he wanted Demetrious living with him. Chuck's single had been released and was doing well. It was the most requested R&B song on the radio. Tyrell still got the phone hang ups. He didn't tell Chuck, because he wanted him to focus and enjoy his newfound success. Reese and Mike were closing on their house at the end of the month, so they could move in time for Christmas. Ricky got the new job with the law firm and moved to Houston. Jay and Ricky's relationship was going strong. Daunte got out of jail on bail. His court date was scheduled for next month.

Thanksgiving morning, all the guys were coming to Tariff's house for dinner. Tariff was in the kitchen with his eyes watering from cutting onions. Demetrious sat with him, cutting green peppers.

"Run the onions under water while you're cutting them, that will cut down on the tears," Demetrious suggested.

"I see you know a little something," Tariff chuckled.

"Maybe a little."

"You look tired, why don't you go and rest a little before the guys get here. Don't forget, you're still recovering."

"Are you really concerned or are you just trying to kick me out the kitchen?" Demetrious laughed.

"Okay. I'm kicking you out the kitchen," Tariff said as he gave him a quick wink.

"I am kind of tired," Demetrious said as he got up to get a drink. He saw Chuck's sample CD cover on the counter.

"Have you talked to Chuck about his past yet?"

"No, I haven't. I'm not sure how to even bring it up, but I know I need too. I want to do what ever damage control I can before the CD drops.

"You know Christmas is next month. So you might want to get on it," Demetrious said as he was about to head upstairs.

"I will. I think I'll talk to him and Tyrell tomorrow or Sunday. Today is Thanksgiving and right now it's all about being thankful."

"Sounds like a car just pulled up," Demetrious said. "I'm going to go up and get at least an hour's nap. Is that okay?"

"Of course it is, babe." Tariff walked over to kiss Demetrious. "I'll let the guys know you're resting. I'm sure they'll understand."

"Alright." Demetrious left Tariff in the kitchen and headed upstairs. The doorbell rang and Tariff went to the door and looked through the curtain. Tyrell and Chuck stood there with Chuck holding the ham that Tyrell cooked the night before. Tariff opened the door.

"Happy Thanksgiving, guys!"

"Happy Thanksgiving to you too, Tariff!" they both said. They took off their coats and Tariff hung them in the foyer closet.

"You guys are the first ones here, so you get the honor of helping a brutha out with the cooking," Tariff said as he handed Tyrell a knife and Chuck a spoon.

Tyrell looked around. "Where's Demetrious?"

"He was a little tired so he went to lie down for a bit."

"How are therapy and recovery coming along?" Tyrell asked.

"It's going pretty good. He gets a little frustrated because he can't move as well as he used to. He just needs to be a little patient and he will be back to his old self."

Chuck stood there holding the spoon in his hand. Tyrell looked at Chuck and then Tariff.

"Tariff, take that spoon from him before he hurts somebody or himself." Chuck waved the spoon at Tariff.

"What can I do to help you?" Chuck asked.

"Chuck what do you know about a kitchen?" Tariff said as he pushed the bowl of cake mix in front of him.

"Just stir, baby, just stir," Tyrell said and winked.

"I don't know anything about a kitchen. I'm just happy that it's Thanksgiving and I'm spending it with good friends." Chuck stirred the mix that Tariff put in front of him.

Tyrell cut the vegetables for the salad. "So when is the rest of the crew going to get here?" he asked.

"They're on their way. Reese wants to get here so he can watch some of the football games."

When the guys arrived everyone sat down to eat. There was a feeling of family in the air as they got ready for a good meal. Lovers and friends shared the love of family. As they all sat around the table, they grabbed each other's hand and Tariff blessed the food: *Thank you, Heavenly Father, for the group that has gathered here today to break bread and enjoy a special bond. Let this food nourish our bodies and make us whole. Bless the hands that prepared it and bless the bodies that will receive it. Amen.*

The group said, "Amen" in unison. They wasted no time passing and serving the food.

"Damn man, you guys put your foot in this food," Reese said licking away the little bit of mashed potatoes he dropped on his hand.

Chuck looked at all the food on the table and continue to pile his plate, "Man, I ain't had food like this since I ate at my grandmother's house, years ago." Mike finished loading food on his plate and began to eat.

"So Ricky how do you like the job and the new firm?" Tariff asked.

"It's going pretty good. I've been assigned my first case. There's a gay couple who want to adopt, but some people from the state are fighting it."

Jay jumped in and asked, "Why are they fighting it?"

"Can you believe, they think that the couple will raise the kid to be gay. They don't think gay people should raise children!"

"You're joking right?" Demetrious asked shaking his head. "What is wrong with these people? I don't know about you guys, but both my parents were heterosexual and I grew up to be gay."

Tyrell said his piece, "They don't see it like that. If they paid attention to the majority of gay men and women they would know that we were brought up by heterosexual parents."

Reese cut back in, "We are positive working black men who are out here everyday earning an honest dollar.

"You are so right. We have our own homes and stability in our lives. We have so much love to give, but because we sleep with the same sex, we are considered a bad influence. I just don't get it. Can someone explain it to me?" Ricky asked.

"The bottom line is people are just afraid of what they don't know. I wish that there could be a reality show since that is the big thing now. I wish a straight man or woman who is filled with such hate could spend a week with anyone at this table. I bet that would change their mind about gay people," Tyrell commented.

Tariff looked at everyone around the table, *You don't choose this lifestyle it's a lifestyle that chooses you. If I could take a pill and change that...* Tariff thought for a second. "...I wouldn't. I am who I am, a man with a good heart.

Jay interjected again, "Now, you do have some people that may choose to participate and they decide they like it, but they can get out anytime they are ready. We can't because it's who we are."

Demetrious, who had been quiet for most of the conversation came in, "Maybe one day the world will be a little more compassionate when it comes to guys like us. Until that happens, I'm just glad we all got each other. And I'm thankful for that."

When dinner was over, the guys sat around for what felt like hours. It was getting late and Tyrell and Chuck headed to get their coats. Tariff walked Tyrell and Chuck to the door, "What are you guys doing tomorrow?"

Tyrell was the first to answer, "We both have to work. Why? What's up?"

"I just wanted to come by and clear up some things before Chuck's CD is released next month. I want to get a jump on things," Tariff explained.

"What about Saturday afternoon?" Chuck suggested.

"That works. I'll see you guys then," Tariff responded.

Mike and Reese decided it was time for them to go. Reese was getting a little tired. Tariff waited to walk them to the door as they said their good-byes to Demetrious, Ricky, and Jay. Tariff walked Mike and Reese to their car.

"You guys know Demetrious' birthday is next month?"

"I remember," Mike said, "Reese and I were thinking, since we're all going to have Christmas at our new house this year, why don't we give Demetrious a little party?"

"The last few months have been really hard, so I think that would be good for him. Plus, Mike is looking for a reason to throw a party at the new house any way," Reese said as he smiled fondly at Mike.

"That's a good idea," Tariff thought, "how 'bout I call you guys tomorrow and we can get started planning? You guys be careful going home," Tariff said as he hugged the guys good night. Tariff waved at the guys as he walked back up to the house.

Ricky and Jay were saying good night to Demetrious when Tariff walked back into the house.

"Tariff, we are out of here," Jay said as he gave Tariff a hug.

"Demetrious, I'll be by to see you tomorrow," Jay said as he left. Jay had been over almost everyday since Demetrious got out of the hospital.

It was a cool, quiet night. Mike thought as he rode looking out the window that the skeletal trees looked like props from an Alfred Hitchcock movie.

"That was a good dinner," Reese said.

"It was. All that food was off the hook. It's good to see Demetrious getting back to his old self. Tariff is taking good care of him."

"This has been a crazy year, first Chuck got hurt and then Demetrious. This is one year I will be glad to see go," Reese said as he merged onto the highway.

"It has been, but you know everybody is still here. Jay and Tyrell finally found someone. Tariff and Demetrious are together. Everything is good baby, every thing is good,"

Mike commented as he looked over at Reese, "By the way, do you have practice tomorrow?"

"No. Actually, I don't have to be back until Saturday." Mike got quiet, thinking about what he wanted to do when they got home. They got home and decided the best way to relax after a Thanksgiving meal was to take a hot bath before going to bed. As Mike filled up the tub and lit some candles the phone rang. When Reese answered the caller was babbling and Reese couldn't understand what they were saying.

"Okay, calm down and talk slower so I can understand what you're saying."

The voice on the other side of the phone became clearer to him. "Calm down, Mr. Green. I can get Mike for you. He's just in the bathroom…but...but, I do…you think you should? Okay I'll get Mike and we'll be on our way." Reese hung up the phone and took a deep breath before going into the bathroom. Mike bent over the tub swishing the water around to mix in the scented oil. He turned around and saw Reese as he stood there with a sad expression on his face.

"What's wrong, baby? Who was that on the phone?" Reese was fighting to find the words to tell him what Mr. Green had just said.

"It was your father. He's at the emergency room. Your mother was on her way home from a neighbor's house and was hit by a drunk driver. Your dad said that we should get there right away."

Mike was in shock. He lost control of his legs and slid down the side of the bathtub to the floor. He shook his head violently then put his hands over his ears as if to say *I didn't just hear that.* Reese went to pull Mike up from the floor, but Mike slapped his hands away. Reese, with his size, managed to pull him up off the floor and got him to realize they needed to go. They quickly dressed and rushed out. As they took the ten minute drive to the hospital, Reese gripped the steering wheel with one hand and Mike's hand with the other.

Mike just stared straight ahead, "Is this God's way of telling me that I should have put more effort into healing my relationship with my mother and my father? I mean my mom was never really the one to end contact with me." Mike's voice trailed off. Reese squeezed his hand to let him know he was there for him.

"Calm down, baby boy, we're almost there. I'll drop you off at the door and swing around to park." Mike barely let the car come to a stop before he bolted from the car. Storming through the emergency room doors, he could see his father pacing. He ran straight to him, almost knocking down a nurse that had crossed his path.

"Where's Mom? How is she?!!"

"The doctor said they'd come out and tell us something as soon as they're done working on her. Sit down somewhere. You're making a fool of yourself."

Mike's face was twisted with the pain he'd carried for years and the anger he was feeling for his father.

"You know you're pathetic. Even with the possibility of losing the love of your life looming in your face, you still have to put on an act. With all due respect, a real man would be worried sick about not knowing whether his wife was going to live or die. A woman he's been with for over 34 years." Mike's father turned and looked at his son with the color of disgust and anger in his face.

"Look here, you ungrateful excuse for a man. I love my

wife and I'm keeping it together and being strong the way she would want me to. Now sit down before we both say something we'll regret."

Mike turned away from his father and saw a nurse,

"Excuse me, nurse! I need to see the doctor that is treating my mother, Mrs. Green, right away." The nurse didn't answer him. She was preparing a syringe and needed to get back to the operating room. She quickly turned back and went through a set of glass doors. As she did, a gray haired doctor came through, headed straight toward Mike and his father. He stopped in front of them. He lowered his head and he sucked in a few quick breaths before he spoke.

"I'm Dr. Stephens. You must be Mr. Green and this must be your son? Mrs. Green sustained very grave injuries, and the impact to her internal organs was too great."

Mike looked at him like he was the devil, "What do you mean was?" Mike asked.

"I'm sorry, but she was hemorrhaging and we couldn't stop the bleeding. She had massive internal injuries. I'm sorry to say she didn't make it." Reese came through the emergency room doors just in time to see the doctor walk away from Mike and his father. Mike collapsed to the floor. Instead of helping his son to his feet or caring about what happened to him, Mr. Green stepped over him and followed the doctor to be at his wife's side.

Reese squatted down on the floor and pulled Mike to his chest. Mike's loud sobs filled the emergency ward.

"Oh, I'm so sorry. I'm here, baby boy." Reese pulled him to his feet and helped him into one of the cushioned chairs that was against the wall of the emergency ward.

"It's all my fault. I could've made things better with her. Now she'll never know how much I loved her. I can't ever

make things better." Reese helped Mike to his feet support-
ing most of his weight on his hip.

"Come on, baby. We need to get you home. Should I ask
your dad if he needs a ride?"

"No! Let's just get out of here. He's the reason I lost my
mom...long before this accident ever happened. Oh God!
This isn't happening." Mike straightened up and started
walking at a hurried pace away from Reese and out of the
emergency room. He walked out into the middle of the dark
parking lot.

Reese grabbed his hand, "The car is parked on the other
end of the lot. Let's go home." The ride home was in
silence. Their hands meshed in a bond that went beyond
anything physical; the silence was spiritual. They got back
to the house and Mike slowly walked to the front door.

Reese opened the door for him he walked in, heading
towards the stairs, "I'm going to bed. Maybe I'll wake up
and realize that this was just a bad dream..."

Reese stopped him and wiped away the tears that fell
down his face. His soft hand dried them away. Mike turned
away from him and went up the stairs to the bedroom.
Reese picked up the phone and called Tariff. His gasp was
mirrored by each of the other guys when they received the
news that night.

*　　*　　*

Mia and Daunte had just finished Thanksgiving dinner.
Mia was putting the food away and Daunte was cleaning off
the table and putting the dishes in the dishwasher. Daunte
pulled out a bottle of wine and the two went into the living

room to chill.

Mia had her feet in Daunte's lap. She always loved when he massaged her feet.

Mia looked at Daunte, "Did you enjoy your dinner?"

"It was a great. You put your foot in it as usual," Daunte said as they both laughed.

"Seems like your mind is somewhere else. Are you worried about the court hearing that's coming up?" Mia asked with concern.

"I am."

"It's going to be okay, but no matter what happens, I'll be by your side. Remember that. We can worry about that when the time comes. This was all my fault."

"No, it was just an unfortunate accident. I need to learn to control my temper," Daunte said, as he lowered his head.

"This incident with Demetrious has taught me a lesson about keeping secrets. I need to tell you this. With all the stuff that has been happening I wanted things to settle down first."

Daunte's eyebrows went up as he took a deep breath and thought to himself, *What am I about to hear now?*

"Okay, hit me with it."

"Do you remember Jay's friend, Ricky?" Mia asked.

"That's the guy that worked out with us that day. Yes, I remember him. What about him?" Daunte inquired.

Mia took in a deep breath, "He's my ex-husband."

Daunte dropped his empty glass on the carpet, "Your what?! Oh man."

"Wait, let me finish. I never told you why he and I divorced. Ricky came to me and told me he was gay. He had been fighting feelings for a long time and he couldn't fight it anymore. He never cheated on me, so the divorce just seemed like the best solution."

"So did you know that he was coming here?" Daunte asked.

"No. I actually left Charlotte because, as I told you, I wanted a fresh start. I never told him where I was going. I ran into him at the police station that day I came to see you. It appears he met Jay in Miami and then came here for a job interview."

"Oh man...you got to be kidding me. This whole situation is crazy."

Mia continued, "After talking to Demetrious it seems that he and Jay are a couple now."

"Well, I appreciate your telling me." Daunte motioned for her to come to the end of the sofa where he sat, "Come here. We will be okay."

Mia laid on his chest as he wrapped his arms around her. "Have you tried calling Jay to try and salvage your friendship?"

"Yeah, but he won't talk to me. He won't return any of my calls. I figured since Demetrious forgave me then he would too."

"Just give him some time. He'll change his mind," Mia said.

"I will, but I need to ask you something."

"Sure what?"

Daunte reached in his pocket and pulled out a small purple jewelry box. "First let me tell you that I have never been with a man, nor do I desire to be. I don't have and I've never had feelings that I'm battling with."

Mia didn't move from her spot on his chest.

"Well that's good to hear." They both chuckled.

Daunte brought the small box into Mia's view, "I want to

marry you. Will you marry me and be my wife?"

"Oh my god! NO! Daunte."

"What do you mean, no?"

Mia playfully slapped Daunte's arm, "You know I will marry you. I'd better marry you quick before you hurt some-body." Daunte laughed, as he slid the ring on her finger and they shared a long passionate kiss.

He broke off the kiss, "Let's take this bottle of wine and these two glasses and go into the bedroom and seal the deal."

"I'm right behind you."

Chapter 20

Mike solemnly dressed for his mother's funeral. He was still having a hard time coping with the fact that she was gone. While he was upstairs getting dressed, Reese let the guys in downstairs. The whole group was there to support Mike at his time of loss. Mike slowly came down the stairs to see the guys standing in the foyer. The site of his boyz standing there gave Mike an overwhelming feeling of warmth and brought a smile to his face. The guys looked up and saw Mike coming down the stairs. They all went over to him and offered big hugs to console him. They all stood in this embrace for some time, until Reese came into the foyer and to let them know that the limo was outside and it was time to go. Reese rented a limo so that all of the friends could ride together.

They piled up into the limo and headed over to Mike's parents' house. The ride over to the house was a solemn one; the pain and grief were palpable in the limo. Once they got to the house, they could see that they were the first ones there. As they got out of the limo and walked up to the door, Mike's dad slung the door open and stared at Mike as if he were an intruder and not his son. Mike looked at his father and saw the large dark circles and puffiness around his eyes and realized that his mother's death had taken quite a toll on him. Mike walked into the house behind his father, leaving the guys standing outside on the porch. In their grief they had forgotten to close the front door. Mike's father looked over Mike's shoulder and saw the guys out on the porch.

His father stopped walking and turned around to face Mike, "How could you disrespect your mother by showing up on this door step with those queers? You're pathetic! You know that, just pathetic!"

At this point his father was yelling and the guys could hear clearly everything that he was saying.

"You and your little queers can just get the hell away from my house." Outside Reese and Demetrious looked over at Jay who, at this point, was fuming. Jay was about to walk into the house until Reese grabbed him by the arm.

Reese looked at Jay, "Man, let it go. This is not the time nor place. Mike will be okay. Let him handle this."

Jay snatched his arm away and turned, leaping down the steps two at a time.

He walked to the limo and turned around to look at Reese, "How can a father treat his flesh and blood like that? And how can you let him treat our boy like that?" Demetrious took one step at a time and went to Jay.

He put his arms around him, "We have to stay strong for Mike, man." Jay got back into the limo and closed the door. Inside the house, Mike looked at his father, refusing to let him see the hurt and pain that he was still inflicting.

Mike turned away from his father and walked out of the house, slamming the door behind him. He walked down the steps and the guys followed behind. Once they were all back in the limo with Jay, Mike began to apologize for what his father had said about them.

Tariff spoke up, "Man, you don't have to apologize for him. He is grieving too. Give him some time and he will be okay."

Mike smiled, "What would I do without you guys?" They pulled off from his father's house and headed to the church. Once outside the church, the guys got out of the limo. As the guys walked through the church doors, friends of the family stopped Mike to give their condolences. Mike saw the family funeral car drive up, he watched his father as he got out alone. Mike waited for him and they walked into the church together. His father walked a few steps ahead, treating Mike as if he didn't see him. The guys had already gone inside and sat down. Reese lagged behind until he saw Mike and his father about to come in. He smiled at Mike and walked over and sat with the rest of the guys.

Mike and his father sat in the front row reserved for the family. Jay, Demetrious, Tyrell, Chuck, Ricky, Tariff, and Reese sat a row behind them. During the whole funeral procession, no embraces or intimate moments were shared between Mike and his father. As the funeral service ended, the guys left the sanctuary and waited for Mike to come out, all except for Reese who stayed right by Mike's side.

When Mike and Reese finally exited the church, Reese hugged Mike and whispered in his ear "You okay, baby boy?"

Those words sent Mike over the edge. All the emotions that he had bottled inside of him came pouring out. Reese held on to Mike as tight has he could.

"Go ahead, let it out, just let it out. I'm here, we're all here." Reese tried to be the rock that Mike needed, but his man's pain and grief cut him to the bone. He hated to see the man he loved more than anything in the world so broken. And there was nothing he could do to fix him.

*   *   *

One week later, early on a Saturday morning, Demetrious woke up and looked over at Tariff, "You're kind of quiet this morning. What's wrong?" Demetrious asked.

"I'm just trying to figure out the best way to approach Chuck about this jail thing."

"I thought you were going to talk to him the weekend of Thanksgiving," Demetrious asked.

"That was my intention, but when Mike's mom died, I thought that would be the wrong time. So I wanted to wait until things kind of mellowed out."

"Oh yeah, I guess you have a point."

"At this point, I have to. Christmas is about three weeks away."

"You and Chuck have bonded since you've been his manager and you've gotten to know him pretty well. Do you think whatever he says about his jail time could have an impact on you still managing him?"

"I don't see how. I can't even imagine Chuck as a criminal. You know I've never said anything to you or the guys about this not even Tyrell, but when you were in the hospital, I didn't know what was going to happen. I went to the hospital chapel to pray. Chuck was already there. He was saying a prayer for you, me, and the guys."

"So what did he say when you talked to him?"

"He didn't see me. I left out and went to the nearest bathroom."

"Since we all met Chuck, he was stabbed as he saved Mike and Reese. From what you said, he stayed by Tyrell's side when I was in the hospital and tried to be as supportive as he could for you and the guys. I can't even image him being an ex-con."

Tariff looked over at the clock. "It's getting late, man.

We need to get you to your therapy appointment."

"Thanks for reminding me, I will be glad when this therapy thing is over. I'm feeling much, much better,"
Demetrious said as he walked into the bathroom.

"You have gotten much better, only a couple more
months to go and then you will be done," Tariff said with
encouragement.

Tariff was dressed first and walked downstairs to fix him
and Demetrious some coffee. Just as Tariff fixed the cups
Demetrious walked down the stairs ready to go. Tariff
grabbed both cups and they headed out the door to the car.
The sun was shining but there was a chill in the air. Once
inside the car, Tariff handed Demetrious his cup.

This particular morning as they drove down Tariff's
street Demetrious noticed the nicely trimmed yards.

"One thing I can say is your neighbors do keep their
lawns looking good.

Tariff looked over at Demetrious with a big smile on this
face. "You mean our neighbors don't you."

"Aw, yeah I mean our neighbors," Demetrious said as he
shook his head in agreement. After about a fifteen minute
drive Tariff and Demetrious pulled up in front of the hospital.

"Good luck baby," Demetrious said as he opened his
door.

"Thanks, man. I'll let you know how it went when I pick
you up. Good luck on your therapy," Tariff said as he leaned
over and gave him a quick kiss.

"Well, let me get in here to this session." Tariff watched
Demetrious as he walked into the hospital.

Chuck pulled into Tyrell's driveway. Since he got his
advance, he was able to get himself a nice little ride to get

around in. As Chuck got out of his car, he noticed that Tyrell's car had a flat. Chuck walked up to the house and used his key to get in.

Walking through the house, Chuck called out to Tyrell, "Hey baby, where you at?"

"I'm upstairs. I'll be down in a minute."

"Okay. Did you know your tire was flat?"

"What? I can't hear you."

Chuck repeated himself this time a little louder, "Did you know your tire was flat?"

Tyrell came down the stairs, "It can't be flat. I just put new tires on that car." They walked outside and Chuck showed Tyrell the tire. Chuck walked around the car.

"Baby, you have two flat tires. Chuck bent down and took a closer look at the tire. Looks like someone stuck a knife or an ice pick in it. See, look at the size of the hole?" Chuck said as he ran his finger across the hole so Tyrell could see.

Tyrell stood up and rubbed his head, "Shit, who would do this?"

Chuck looked at Tyrell suspiciously, "Have you gotten any more hang ups here or at work?"

"You promise you won't get mad..." Tyrell said quickly and looked away.

"Don't bother answering, I already know. Why didn't you tell me?" Chuck snapped.

"You were working on your CD and then Demetrious got hurt I guess it slipped my mind."

Chuck started to raise his voice, "Man, I don't believe you! Let me tell you one damn thing, I don't care about anything else, but you. So if someone is harassing you, they're harassing me. I am never too busy when it comes to you.

You understand me?"

"I'm sorry okay! I'll go call the auto club. Tariff should be here in a few minutes."

"Okay." Tyrell and Chuck went back into the house. While they waited for Tariff and the auto club they sat down to eat a light lunch. Just as they sat down to the table, the doorbell rang. Tyrell sat his plate down on the table and went to get the door. He opened the door to Tariff as he stood there with a briefcase.

"What's up?"

"Not much, we were just sitting down to have some lunch." They walked into the kitchen where Chuck had just finished off his lunch in the short time that Tyrell went to open the door.

"What's up, Tariff?" Chuck smiled.

Tyrell offered him something to eat, "You want to join us?"

"Oh no, I'm good for now. When I pick Demetrious up we're going to have lunch. Oh yeah, speaking of Demetrious, you know his birthday is December 27th? I talked to Mike and Reese, on Thanksgiving Day, about having a little something for him along with the Christmas festivities, but you know after Mike's mom died, I thought it was just better to wait."

"I hope Mike is doing better. It's hard losing a parent," Chuck said as he thought back to the day when his mom died.

Tariff was now serious and ready to get down to business.

"Chuck, I hate to bring this up, but, as your manager, I need to be prepared if certain information hits the media," Tariff said as he looked straight at Chuck.

Chuck started to look worried. "I can tell I'm not going to like this Tariff."

Tyrell was curious, "Tariff, what's going on?"

"I guess the best place for me to start is at the beginning."

"Okay…" Chuck stuttered.

"Do you remember the night that Chuck performed at the club in Miami?" Tyrell and Chuck both answered in unison, "Yeah, what about it?"

"Well, Demetrious and I weren't standing to far from you two. Chuck we heard what you guys talked about." Tyrell and Chuck looked at each other neither one able to remember what they had said. "We never mentioned it because at the time it wasn't any of our business."

Tyrell looked right at Tariff, "Mention what, Tariff? Come on, spit it out."

"We heard Chuck say that he had been locked up." Chuck's head immediately dropped. He started to feel this pang in the pit of his stomach. "As I said, the only reason we didn't mention it was because it wasn't any of our business, but now that you're about to release your CD in a few weeks, I need to be prepared, as well as you, Chuck if the media get a hold of this information. In this industry your life, past and present, becomes everybody's business, unfortunately. Now, as far as your lifestyle, that shouldn't be hard to keep under wraps. I'm assuming that we're the only guys that know."

Tyrell looked over at Chuck and then at Tariff, "Don't worry about that, we can handle that part," Tyrell said.

Chuck just shook his head. "I don't understand why people can't just buy my music because they like it, and not use my sexuality as a reason not to."

Tariff put his hand on Chuck's shoulder, "Man, you've got some ignorant people out there. I pray to God that one day that will change."

Chuck sucked in a deep breath, "I understand."

"Chuck, as much as I hate to ask, I do need to know about the jail incident, and don't worry this will stay between just us. The other guys don't need to know."

"I've tried to put this behind me, but I understand. It was a couple of years ago. I was hanging out with some friends at a carwash. We were checking out this guy detailing his ride and commenting on how well he kept his car. One of the girls that was with us told us that the guy was gay. So the guys I was hanging with decided that they wanted to take this brutha's car. So me and my two friends followed this guy from the car wash, he stopped at a red light, and Curtis and Carlton, they were my two buddies, hopped out of the car while I stayed in the car we drove up in. One of my boys, Curtis, had a gun. The guy didn't resist or anything, he told my boy, Curtis, to just take the car. Just as my boy, Carlton, was about to get behind the wheel, I guess the guy's cell phone rang or something and when he reached for it Curtis shot him. I guess the sudden movement made Curtis nervous.

The whole time I just sat in the car and watched. The guy fell to the ground. Curtis started to panic and he and Carlton ran back to the car and then we drove off. I couldn't believe what had happened. This was the worst day of my life. So the next day, I went to the police station and turned myself in. I turned state's evidence on Curtis and Carlton. So I spent two years in prison, but got out on good behavior."

Tyrell looked over at Tariff as a tear rolled down the side

of his face. Tyrell looked at Chuck and asked, "Where did this happen?"

"Over on Elm, not to far from the car wash."

Tariff couldn't take listening any more, "How could you? Dammit Chuck...How could you?"

Chuck was completely confused at Tariff's reaction, "I know it was wrong and I've been trying to do right ever since I got out."

Tariff stood up and headed for the door, "I've got to get out of here."

Now Chuck was more confused than ever, "What... What...Tariff," Chuck called out to Tariff.

Tyrell grabbed Chuck by the arm, "Don't you understand?"

"Understand what?" Chuck asked.

"That you were there when your boy, shot and killed James, Tariff's first lover." Chuck fell to the floor. The realization that the man they killed was James hit him like a ton of bricks.

Chuck shouted as he put his hands on his head, "No...No...How could that be? Tyrell please tell me that it's not true." Tyrell's thoughts were off the charts. He paced back and forth. The man he had grown to love was partly responsible for the death of his best friend.

"God no...God no... what am I going to do now? This can't be true...it can't be," Chuck kept saying to himself.

Tyrell watched Chuck for sometime. He knew that deep in his heart, Chuck was going to need him, but his focus at the moment was on Tariff. Tyrell ran to the door to see if Tariff may have been sitting in the driveway, but he was gone. Tyrell leaned on the open door. Eventually, he slid down, sitting on the floor. Chuck got up and headed for the front door. As he watched Tyrell leaning on the door, he knew that what he did two years ago has now cost him everything. Chuck grabbed for Tyrell, but Tyrell pushed his hands away. Tyrell was truly torn apart and didn't know what to do.

"Goodbye, Tyrell," Chuck said as he headed out the door.

Minutes later Tyrell got up walked to the phone and tried to call Tariff at home and on his cell, but didn't get an answer. The auto club hadn't gotten there yet so he couldn't drive his car to go and look for him. Tyrell knew that the other guys weren't ready for this kind of news yet. He didn't know who else he could call. Tyrell hung up the phone, and out of the corner of his eye he saw the hat that Chuck had been wearing was on the floor. Tyrell picked it up and put it to his nose to inhale Chuck's manly scent. Damn!

*   *   *

Demetrious had finished his therapy session and stood outside waiting for Tariff to pick him up. It wasn't like Tariff to be late. Being the worry wart that he was, Demetrious called Tariff's cell phone and got no answer. So he decided to call Tyrell.

"Hey, Tyrell, is Tariff still there?" Demetrious could hear the pain in Tyrell's voice.

"I don't know where he is," Tyrell said sadly.

"What do you mean you don't know where he is? What happened?" Demetrious questioned.

"He drove off!"

"You're not making any sense Tyrell...never mind he's here now, but what happened?"

"Talk to Tariff and I'll talk to you later." Demetrious closed his cell phone and walked over to the car. Tariff was staring straight ahead.

"Baby, what's wrong? What happened? Tariff look at me." When Tariff looked at Demetrious, he could see that he had been crying. Demetrious slowly got out of the car and walked around the front of the car to the driver's side. He opened the car door and Tariff got out and leaned into Demetrious' chest.

Demetrious wrapped his arms around him, "Man, you're starting to scare me. What's wrong? What happened at Tyrell's? Talk to me, Tariff."

Tariff finally pulled himself together and said, "Okay let's park the car and go over there." Tariff pointed at a small park bench from where they were. Tariff got in the car and Demetrious walked over to a bench and waited for Tariff. Tariff took his time. He finally made it over to Demetrious and sat down next to him.

"Okay, baby, what's up?" Demetrious asked anxiously.

"Well, I went over to Tyrell's to talk to Chuck about being locked up. I wasn't quite prepared for what he told me."

"Okay...Well what did he tell you, Tariff?"

Tariff looked down at his feet and then into Demetrious' eyes, "Baby he was with the guys that shot James."

"What!" Tariff started to cry harder than he had before. Demetrious hugged Tariff.

"So was he the one that actually shot James? I thought those guys had been arrested."

"It turns out that Chuck was in the car that followed

James, but he never got out. The next day, after it happened, he turned himself in and turned state's evidence on the shooter and the other one."

Demetrious started to get a little upset, "So you mean to tell me that all this time, Tyrell knew and didn't say a word to any of us?"

"Come on baby, you know Tyrell better than that. Neither he nor Chuck made the connection."

"Oh my God! I bet Tyrell is just falling apart right now. Should we go and check on him?" Demetrious suggested.

"No, I think we all need some time for this to sink in. We'll give him some time for all of this to register. Do you think we should tell the other guys about this?"

"No, for right now I don't think they should know. We need to just keep it between the four of us."

"What should I do?" Tariff had now directed the question toward himself.

Demetrious just held him tightly, "I don't know baby…I just don't know. Let's go home."

*   *   *

Later that night, Tariff and Demetrious were at home when the doorbell rang. Demetrious opened the door to find Tyrell standing there.

"Hey man!" Tyrell looked like he'd been slammed against a wall.

Demetrious grabbed Tyrell and hugged him hard, "Are you okay?"

"No, not really. Where's Tariff?"

235

"He's in the living room. We were just about to come see you." They walked into the living room and Tariff looked up and saw Tyrell standing there. He stood up and he and Tyrell just embraced each other for a good five minutes, one trying to comfort the other.

Tyrell stepped away from Tariff, "I can't believe that this happened. Tariff, Demetrious, I want you both to know I had no idea Chuck was involved."

"We know that, but what are you going to do about it?" Demetrious asked.

"To be honest, I really don't know. Ever since Chuck and I met, he has been completely honest with me. He never wanted to be judged by his past. He made me happier than I had ever been." Tyrell flopped into a near by chair and put his head in his hands. "I just don't know."

"I don't know how I feel right now either. Tyrell, you know I walked in on Chuck at the chapel in the hospital as he prayed for me, Demetrious, and all you guys?"
"Really! See that's what I mean? Chuck has a really good heart. I know I just got here, but I need to get out, I have some deep soul searching to do. What about you Tariff? Are you still going to manage him?" Tyrell asked.

"Oh, damn man, I completely forgot about that," Tariff said as he put his hand on his forehead.

"That is something that you really need to consider, baby. I think you both need to sit down and think about what your next steps are going to be," Demetrious suggested.

"Tyrell, right now Demetrious and I think it would be best if we just kept this between the four of us. There's no need for the other guys to get involved."

"That would be a good idea. I really hadn't thought about

them and how they'd react, especially Jay," Tyrell said as he stood up and walked to the door.

"Well, I'm going to say good night. I'll talk to you guys tomorrow."

*   *   *

A week later, Tyrell, Tariff, and Demetrious sat in the living room talking.

"Have you heard from Chuck?" Tariff asked as he took a drink from his glass.

"No, I haven't and he hasn't been at work either."

"Mr. Townson from the studio called me and asked if I had seen him. He hasn't been able to contact him. I just told him that I would see what I could do. Honestly, I don't know what to do," Tariff replied.

Demetrious stepped in, "Can I say something to both of you?"

"Please do." Tyrell and Tariff answered at the same time.

"What Chuck did two years ago affected all of our lives. Especially yours, baby, but look at what he has done for us all since we met him."

Demetrious looked at Tyrell, "He has been honest with you about his past from day one. He has never lied to you about anything. You said yourself he has made you the happiest you've ever been. He put his life on the line for Mike and Reese and almost got himself killed because of his bravery. When I was in the hospital, not knowing if I was going to live or die, he went to the chapel and prayed for not only me and Tariff, but for all of us. Tyrell he was there to comfort you."

Demetrious looked at Tariff, "Don't get me wrong, it's not going to be easy, but I heard this saying a long time ago and I always try to live by it, as we all should. *He who cannot forgive cannot cross the bridge he himself must cross.* So the two of you must make a decision and whatever your decisions are, I will stand behind both of you."

Tyrell just rubbed his chin and then his head.

"That was some food for thought and, on that note, I'm going to get out of here and get myself together. I love you guys and I will talk to you tomorrow." Tyrell grabbed his coat and headed out.

"We love you too, man."

Tyrell left and as he drove home listening to the radio and wondering where Chuck was, Chuck's single came on the radio. Tyrell got caught up in the lyrics of the song and could almost feel what Chuck was feeling when he sang the song. Tyrell had been singing along with the song and so deep in his thoughts that, before he knew it, he was in his driveway. He sat in his car trying to gather his thoughts. Tyrell walked up the steps and saw a large envelope on the porch. Tyrell picked it up and carried it into the house. He opened the envelope and inside were his house keys and a note from Chuck. He began to read it;

Dear Tyrell,

I didn't know love existed in this world until I met you. You've made these months the best. I have never been this happy in all my life. I took a walk today and I couldn't get you out of my head. I tried not to think about you and the times that we have spent together, but as the saying goes, YOUR HEART DOES WHAT IT WANTS TO DO. I'm sorry that I caused you pain. Without you in my life, there's no reason for me to sing. Your being with me, by my side, gave me the confidence to do anything and now I'm lost. I should have known things were going too well for them to last. Who could have known that one dreadful day two years ago could come between us? Tyrell, I just want you to know that I was completely honest with you from day one. I really didn't know that the man that Curtis shot was James. Had I known, I most definitely would have told you. If there is one thing that I did right in my life, it was to be completely honest with you about my past. I just hope that one day you can forgive me. I end this letter with a solemn goodbye. I will always have a special place in my heart for you.

With all my heart, soul and love,
Chuck

Tyrell let the letter fall to the floor like a feather as he sat in a chair and just stared ahead talking out loud, as though Chuck could hear him, "Chuck I have to find you. Baby, I love you so much. I need you in my life and I have already forgiven you." Tyrell sat in the same spot for hours.

*   *   *

Tariff sat at the kitchen table with a tank top and boxers on, drinking his morning coffee when Demetrious walked in.

"Good morning, sexy." He bent down and gave Tariff a kiss.

"Good morning to you, too. How are you?"

"I'm okay baby. I'm going to go check and see if the morning paper is here yet." Demetrious said as he walked to the front door. He unfolded the newspaper as he headed back into the kitchen, an envelope fell out onto the floor. Demetrious picked it up and looked at the writing and saw it had Tariff's name on it.

"This was in the paper and it's addressed to you." Demetrious handed him the envelope.

"Baby, it's from Chuck," Tariff said.

"What does it say?" Demetrious asked.

Dear Tariff,

I am so sorry that I have caused you so much pain. The day that I witnessed James getting shot plays over and over again in my head. I will have to live with what happened that day for the rest of my life. I started to call you the other day to ask you for your forgiveness, but how could I when I haven't forgiven myself? You're a good man and a great friend, Tariff. Hell, you all are.. Tyrell loves you guys so much he is going to really need you. Please take care of him for me. I don't want to come between you and his friendship. It would kill me to be the cause of your special bond being broken.

I know that you couldn't find yourself managing me any-more and frankly, I don't know if I even want to sing any-more. Tyrell was the lifeline for my voice. I'm going to go now and always remember how much I appreciated you and the guys taking me into your circle and making me feel loved. I will never forget that.

Chuck

Both Tariff and Demetrious put their heads down, not knowing what to think of Chuck's note.

The phone rang and Demetrious walked over to answer it.

"What's up Jay?" Demetrious asked as he looked at the caller ID box.

"I'm not sure. Have you talked to Tyrell lately?"

"Last night."

"Is he okay?" Jay questioned.

"Why do you ask?" Demetrious gave Tariff a look of *what should I say?*

"When I called over there, he sounded like he had been crying and he's not at work."

"Tariff and I are just getting ready to leave. We'll stop by there and check."

"Is Chuck there with him?" Demetrious was being evasive and Jay was getting suspicious.

"Jay, we'll call you back."

"Demetrious, if you don't call me back and let me know something I WILL go over there myself." Demetrious forced out a nervous laugh.

"Man, what are you laughing at?" Jay asked.

"The fact that you're so protective."

"You know I love you guys, besides, that's just how I am." Demetrious hung up from Jay and turned to look at Tariff.

"That was Jay, it sounds like Tyrell is really going through it. Maybe we should go over there."

"We should. Let me get dressed."

As Tariff got dressed, the phone rang again. Demetrious answered, "Hello."

"Hi, can I speak to Tariff?"

"Who's calling?" Demetrious asked with a puzzled look on his face.

"I am a friend of Chuck's at the halfway house. I'm calling about Chuck."

"What about Chuck?"

"Well, he's been drinking pretty heavily and I'm afraid he may do something crazy. He's passed out in his room, so I grabbed his cell phone and it only had a few numbers in it. Yours, a Mr. Townsend, his probation officer, and some guy named Tyrell. I called Tyrell's number first, but didn't get an answer. So I called you, but somebody needs to come and check on him. He's still on probation, I don't want his probation officer to come by and see him like this. Chuck had turned his life around, but something is wrong. I can feel it."

"What's the address?"

"We're on 5th street across from the Continental Motel."

"Thanks. I know exactly where that is, we'll be right there." Demetrious hung up from the caller.

"Who was that on the phone?" Tariff asked as he walked down the stairs.

"That was the halfway house where Chuck has been staying. It looks like he's been doing some drinking and has passed out. One of the guys that lives there felt that someone should come and check on him. We need to go see what's going on."

"Well, let's go," Tariff agreed.

242

"You sure you want to do this?"

"I'm sure. We can call Tyrell from the car."

Demetrious and Tariff called Tyrell from the car, but there was no answer so they went straight to the halfway house.

They parked the car to go inside, and as soon as they walked in, this short heavy set man with his pants hanging walked up. "Are you Tariff?"

"I am. Where is Chuck?" The man turned around and started walking down a long hall that resembled a dormitory hallway. When they got to Chuck's room and opened the door, all they could see were bottles all over the place. The room reeked of alcohol as though it were being occupied by a drunk. Chuck was slumped over in a chair, passed out. Demetrious and Tariff went over to him and tried to wake him up. He came to for a short time, but he was so drunk, he passed right back out.

"Let's get him in the shower." Demetrious bent down and lifted Chuck up out of the chair.

Tariff got on the other side of Chuck, "Demetrious, you're not supposed to be doing any strenuous lifting."

"Baby, I'm okay. Come on." Demetrious looked at the guy that showed them to Chucks' room.

"Where's the shower?" The shower was only three doors down so Demetrious and Tariff didn't have far to go. They took off his clothes and put him in the shower and turned on the cold water, waking him up rather quickly. Chuck tried to get out, but they managed to keep him in for another few minutes.

Demetrious inhaled a whiff of Chuck's breath, "Oh my God, his breath is kicking! Let's get him out and put him in some clean clothes." They maneuvered his naked body back to his room and laid him down on the bed where he passed out again. Tariff started looking through his dresser drawers and found some clothes to put on him. Tariff got Chuck dressed while the guy and Demetrious cleaned up the room. They got rid of all the empty bottles and the ones that Chuck still had left unopened. They also cleaned the room and made the bed.

Demetrious looked at Tariff, "I think we should take him to the house, so we can keep an eye on him. That way his probation officer won't see him like this."

"Good idea. You go get the car." Tariff turned to the guy that had been helping them. "Sir, can you help me get him to the car?" The man nodded his head. Demetrious brought the car around and jumped out to hold the backdoor open so Tariff and the guy could put Chuck in the back seat.

Tariff thanked the guy for calling them, pulled out his wallet, and gave him twenty dollars.

"You will keep this to yourself won't you."

"Man, I like Chuck. He is good people. I won't tell a soul. You guys just take good care of him."

"We will," Tariff said as he got into the car. Demetrious and Tariff got Chuck back to the house and put him in the spare bedroom to let him sleep off the alcohol. Once they got him settled in, Tariff and Demetrious headed downstairs. They sat down on the sofa and Demetrious began to rub Tariff's' shoulders.

"Baby, I know this hasn't been easy for you," Demetrious said as he continued to rub Tariff's shoulders.

"You know, in spite of everything, Chuck is still a good man that got caught up in a bad situation. You were right when you talked about forgiveness. I can forgive him. You know I forgave the other guys a long time ago, but I can

244

never forget the act." Demetrious stopped rubbing Tariff's shoulders and hugged him around the neck.

"See that's the man I fell in love with."

Tariff smiled, "All this time, I thought you just wanted me for my body and my mind." They both started to laugh; something they hadn't done in a while.

"I think we need to try and get a hold of Tyrell."

"I'll give him a call again." Tariff picked up the phone and called Tyrell. The phone rang eventually going to voice mail.

"He's still not answering his phone? Leave him a message." Tariff agreed.

A few hours later, Chuck finally woke up. He was unfamiliar with his surroundings, not sure where he was. He tried to get up, but he fell back on the bed and held onto his head. Demetrious came into the room just as he fell back on the bed.

"I think you better stay there. Don't try to get up." Chuck was feeling groggy and really hung over.

"Demetrious, man, what are you doing here? Where am I?"

Demetrious let out a chuckle, "I live here. You're in our spare bedroom. Let me get you something for your headache."

Demetrious walked down the hall to the bathroom and got a bottle of aspirin and a glass of water. When Demetrious came back, Chuck was trying to sit up again.

"What do you mean 'our'? You mean I'm in yours and Tariff's house?"

"Yeah, keep still and take these two aspirin." Chuck took the aspirin and the glass of water.

"Thanks. I feel like I've been hit by a truck."

"You were."

"I was?"

"Yeah, it's called Hennessy." Demetrious gave Chuck a sly smile, "Now lie down and get some sleep. We'll be up later to check on you."

"Thanks D. I'm sorry for being so much trouble."

"Just get some rest. It's been a rough few months for everybody." Chuck put the glass of water on the nightstand and then went back to sleep. Demetrious went back downstairs, where he left Tariff sitting on the sofa.

"Is he up yet?"

"He was for a minute, I gave him a couple of aspirin and he went back to sleep. Did Tyrell call?"

"He called while you were upstairs and he's on his way over. He was actually out looking for Chuck."

"Did you tell him he was here?"

"No, I didn't. I thought it would be best to wait until he got here."

"Good idea, baby," Demetrious said shooting Tariff a wink.

The doorbell rang right on cue.

"Speak of the devil." Tariff got up off the sofa and went to the door. Tariff opened the door smiling.

"What's up, man?" Tyrell hugged Tariff as he came into the door.

They walked into the living room where Demetrious was sitting.

"What's up, Tyrell? How are things with you?"

"I'm okay D. Thanks for asking."

"Well Demetrious and I need to tell you something."

"Shoot, you got my attention."

"It's about Chuck."

Tyrell had a look of panic on his face, "What about Chuck? Is he okay? Oh God tell me he's okay!"

Demetrious got up and went to sit next to Tyrell and put his arm around his shoulder, "Calm down, Tyrell. He's okay. He's upstairs asleep."

"Upstairs asleep? What's going on?" Tyrell looked over at Tariff. "Guys what is going on?" Tyrell asked even more confused.

Demetrious started to explain, "Well, it seemed Chuck went on a drinking binge. One of the guys at the halfway house called us. He didn't want him to get into trouble with his probation officer, so we decided to bring him here to make sure of that. Apparently, he called you first, but he didn't get an answer."

"Tyrell, Chuck left me this letter." Tariff handed the letter to Tyrell. Tyrell took the letter and started reading it. Tyrell finished the letter and shook his head.

"Can I go up and talk to him?"

"I think that would be a good idea. He may be asleep." I checked on him a few minutes ago.

Tyrell walked over to Demetrious and hugged him. "You know I love you so much. Thank you for everything." Then he walked over to Tariff and hugged him tightly.

Tariff pushed Tyrell away, "I love you too, Tyrell. You're family. All I want is for you to be happy and Chuck makes you happy. So go upstairs and work things out. Go get your man."

Tyrell gave them a giant smile, "I'm on my way." Tyrell went up the stairs two at a time, but when he reached the top he slowly walked to the spare bedroom door. He stood outside the door and took a deep breath, then he opened the door. Chuck was sleeping so peacefully that Tyrell didn't

247

want to wake him. As he got closer to the bed, Chuck opened his eyes and turned in Tyrell's direction.

"Tyrell, what are you doing here?"

"I'm here to see you."

"See me?" Chuck thought he was dreaming or maybe he was still drunk. Tyrell gave him a smile and sat down on the bed next to him.

"I told you before, you can't handle your liquor very well." Tyrell laughed.

"I guess you were right."

"Chuck, you lied to me."

"About what? Baby, I would never lie to you, I promise."

"You told me that you would always be with me and look after me."

"I thought that after what happened…" Chuck's voice trailed off.

"I know it's been hard since all this came out, but thank God it came out now rather than later."

"Chuck, I have not been happy in so long. I almost forgot what it felt like. When I'm with you I feel so free; love takes control of everything and I don't want to lose that."

"Baby, I don't want to lose you either, but what about Tariff?"

"Tariff will be fine."

"Are you sure?"

"Tariff will be fine," Tariff said as he stood in the door. Both Chuck and Tyrell turned to look at Tariff.

"Tyrell, can I talk to Chuck for a moment?"

"Sure. I'll be back, baby." Tyrell kissed him and walked out. Tariff sat on the bed where Tyrell previously sat.

"Chuck, the last couple of weeks have been really difficult not only for me, but for you and Tyrell as well. Since I've known you, you have been straightforward and honest. You've made my boy happier than he's been in years. You know that day Demetrious got hurt? I heard you in the hospital chapel as you prayed."

"You were there?" Chuck looked surprised.

"I was going to pray myself and saw you and heard what you said. I'm not going to lie to you, I was angry as hell when I found out what you did. I can't say that things are going to be easy. It's hard to forget what happened to James. You tried to make it right by doing what you did and that tells me a lot. I had forgiven you guys a long time ago, but, as I said to Demetrious earlier, it's hard forgetting the act."

Chuck looked down at the end of the bed, "I understand man."

"I'd like for us to put this behind us, not for my sake, but for Tyrell's. So why don't we start over?"

"I would like that," Chuck said. Tariff got off the bed and stood up next to the bed and stuck out his hand.

"Hi, my name is Tariff."

Puzzled, Chuck stuck out his hand and then smiled, "Hi my name is Chuck, nice to meet you."

"I heard you're a singer and you're looking for a manager." Tariff smiled.

"Yes sir, I am, do you know of anyone?" Chuck asked.

"I'm new at it, but if you hire me, I promise I'll do my best. So how about you get up out of that bed and come downstairs and let us hear if you can sing or not."

Chuck smiled and slowly raised himself out of bed. "Can you do me a favor first Tariff?"

"Sure what's that?"

"Can you hold this damn room still? It's spinning like

crazy!" All they could do was laugh.

Chapter 21

It was early Christmas morning and Jay and Ricky were just waking up.

Ricky wrapped his arms around Jay, "Merry Christmas, baby."

"Merry Christmas to you too," Jay said as he stretched. Jay was just like a child. He hopped out of the bed, ready to go downstairs and open his presents.

"Hold up before you go," Ricky said as he patted the bed, "come sit down here for a second." He reached in the night stand and pulled a nicely wrapped box the size of an 8 by 11 inch picture frame.

Now what can this be? Jay thought.

"This box signifies new beginnings and the contents mean a lot to me. I guess you can call me a sentimental old fool, but you'll understand once you open it up."

Jay opened the box slowly and saw it contained a picture frame. Inside the frame was a photo of Jay and Ricky when they were in South Beach. Below a wrinkled piece of paper with a phone number handwritten on it. "I don't understand." Jay was confused.

"The first time I met you back in South Beach, you gave me this sheet of paper with you're your cell number on it. The photograph was the first picture we ever took together. It was the beginning of something new for me. So I framed this for us, to remind us both of that wonderful day." Jay now understood just how special Ricky really was.

"Who would have known that something as small as this

could turn out to be something so special?" Jay leaned over and kissed Ricky.

Ricky pulled back, "Now let's go downstairs and open the rest of the gifts."

Jay started kissing Ricky and rubbing his thigh, "How 'bout we open the gifts later? All this sentimental talk has gotten me feeling sexy," Jay said.

Ricky lay back down, "Baby, you'll get no argument from me."

*   *   *

Tariff was in the kitchen with the music playing. He was listening to R&B Christmas songs while grabbing pots and pans, getting ready to cook. He decided to surprise Demetrious with Christmas breakfast in bed. Demetrious sneaked into the kitchen. Tariff didn't see him because his back was turned. Tariff stood there at the stove singing a song he was listening to on the radio. Demetrious stood there and watched him for a minute. Demetrious was always turned on by Tariff's body. Demetrious couldn't help but stare at Tariff in his tight fitting boxers. Finally, Demetrious walked over to Tariff and patted him on the ass and then put his arms around him.

He whispered in Tariff's ear, "Merry Christmas, Sweetheart."

Tariff just smiled, "Merry Christmas to you too, boo. I was trying to surprise you and fix you breakfast in bed."

Demetrious gave Tariff a sexy smile, "I can go back and get in bed and pretend I don't know."

Tariff thought for a moment, "The thought is nice, but that's okay."

They both broke out laughing, "You need any help, baby?" Demetrious offered.

"You can grab a couple of the coffee cups out the cabinet." Demetrious walked over to the cabinet. As Demetrious grabbed the cups, he noticed that the sterling silver frame with James' picture in it had been moved. In its place was a picture of him and Tariff, one they had taken in Miami. Demetrious, distracted, dropped a coffee cup. Tariff turned around quickly.

"Baby, you okay?"

"I'm fine." He was not sure how to ask about the picture.

Tariff walked over to him and grabbed his arm, "Lets sit down. I need to talk to you about something."

"Sure, what's up?"

Tariff took a deep breath. "I sold James' car."

"You did what?" Demetrious was shocked.

"I sold James' car."

"But why, baby?" Demetrious asked.

"I needed to let go of the past. I guess keeping it was my way of keeping James alive. I know I could never drive that car after what happened in it, so I thought it was best. I also took James picture and put it with the rest of the guys and put ours in its place. I need to start living in the present and prepare myself for my future with you. I love James and I will never forget him, just as I know you won't. Before James died, he told me to love again, something I thought I could never do."

Demetrious smiled and looked up, "Thank you, God. I owe you." As he did, he thought back to the night before they went to Miami and he remembered the prayer he said that night.

Tariff looked at Demetrious, "You owe who one?"

"I owe God for answering my prayer as I knew he would." They both looked at each other, smiled, and embraced.

Tariff whispered in his ear, "To new beginnings."

They both heard *Merry Christmas Baby* playing on the radio and Tariff grabbed Demetrious' hand saying, "Dance with me, baby." They embraced and got so caught up that they danced right through to the next song until the phone rang distracting them.

"I got it," Tariff said.

As he walked away, Demetrious smacked him on the ass again.

Tariff looked back, "I thought you got enough of that last night."

Demetrious replied, "I could never get enough of that." Demetrious winked. Tariff bumped into the table and chuckled as he picked up the phone.

"Merry Christmas, Tariff," Mia said from the other end.

"Merry Christmas, Mimi! Are you okay? You sound a little upset?"

"I'm okay. I'm about to go visit Daunte. He was sentenced a few days ago. Thank Demetrious for the letter he wrote to the judge. The judge gave Daunte three years and he suspended most of that. So all he has to do is six months. He has to complete an anger management class while he is incarcerated."

Tariff offered his apologies, "I'm so sorry."

"Thanks, but I'm fine. I just miss him already."

Cradling the phone gently, Tariff looked at Demetrious as he spoke tender words of encouragement to Mia, "We love you and anything you need, please call us."

"I love you both so much. I'll talk to you guys later."

Demetrious looked at Tariff, "You know, this is my fault."

"If I had dealt with my insecurities about who and what I am earlier, this would have never happened."

"The whole situation was so unfortunate, but Daunte also has to learn how to control that temper. That's what really got him into this position," Tariff said walking toward Demetrious. The phone rang again. It was Tyrell.

"Merry Christmas, buddy!" Tyrell's voice boomed through the phone.

"Merry Christmas to you and yours."

"Thank you, my friend. Chuck and I were wondering if we could catch a ride to Mike and Reese's house with you guys?"

"Sure, man, that's no problem. What's wrong with your cars?"

"Well, Chuck's car is parked in front of mine and all of my tires are totally flat. So we can't move it."

"We can, but what's up with you and your tires? Didn't someone flatten your tires once before?"

"Sure did."

"And they flattened the tires this time too?" Tariff questioned.

"It appears that way."

"What the hell is going on, Tyrell?"

"Well man, someone has been calling here and on the job and hanging up. They've flattened my tires twice."

"Do you know who's doing this?" Tariff questioned anxiously looking at Demetrious.

"Naw man, I have no idea, but lets not talk about that

today. It's Christmas--save it for later," Tyrell snapped.

Tyrell's abrasive tone caught Tariff off guard. Tariff knew then to back off. "I won't push it right now, but we will talk about it later. We'll see you guys in a few hours. Love you."

"Love you too."

Tariff got off the phone turned and shot Demetrious a playful seductive look, "So where were we?"

Demetrious smiled and said, "To hell with where we were, hello to what we 'bout to do."

$$* \quad * \quad *$$

Smiling from ear to ear, Demetrious beamed remembering the passion they just shared. As they rode to Tyrell's house, Tariff smiled at the thought of Demetrious' considerable gifts and talents.

Demetrious stroked Tariff's thigh and asked playfully, "How was it baby."

Tariff winked and said, "Ask me after the sequel."

As they pulled into Tyrell's driveway, Demetrious cast a worried glance at Tyrell's car. "They're definitely flat," Demetrious commented as Tariff rang the bell.

"Merry Christmas, guys. Come on in!" Tyrell shouted.

"Merry Christmas! Yeah, we need to talk about your slasher thing tomorrow," Demetrious said with a smirk on his face. "Where's Chuck?"

"He's in the living room, Grinch," Tyrell said.

They all walked in and Demetrious and Tariff gave Chuck a hug, "Merry Christmas guys," Chuck said with a big smile on his face. "Could you guys sit down for a minute? I have something that I want to give you," Chuck said.

Tariff put his hand on his chest, "You have something for us?"

Demetrious spoke up, "Give it to me, I love opening gifts." Chuck handed him the small packaged gift. Demetrious opened it up, smiled then handed it to Tariff.

"It's a copy of my CD cover. Read the dedication, all of you," Chuck said beaming and grinning.

Tariff read the dedication out loud, *"This CD is dedicated to James Wright. Someone who left this world too early and will always hold a special place in the hearts of those he left behind. God Bless."*

"Oh my God, Chuck! You did this?" Tariff said with a smile on his face.

"I know it doesn't come close to what I have done, but I owe this to him and to you, his friends. I needed to do it for me as well."

Tyrell hugged Chuck around the waist, "See, that's why I love this man so much."

"Go head man!" Chuck smiled.

Demetrious looked at the CD and read the dedication again.

"This is really nice of you to do. Thanks a lot."

Tariff looked at Chuck fondly, amazed at how much had been taken away, and yet how much Chuck was giving.

Tyrell spoke up, "We better get out of here and get to Mike and Reese's before they kill us."

*　　*　　*

Mike wanted everything right for when the guys came by. He stood in the foyer and took one final look. The staircase was covered with white lights and blue garland. Mike walked pass the two poinsettias they sat elegantly atop of white pedestals placed on opposite sides of the living room door. What a beautiful tree, he thought gazing at the seven foot white fir. Every blue and silver ornament was complimented by white lights. At the top of the tree sat a beautiful black angel dressed in lace and holding a lit candle. Mike turned off the lights, leaving only the glow from the tree and the fireplace. Only the crackling wood at the hearth spoke. The room was radiant; the tree was perfect with so many wrapped presents beneath it. Mike started to feel warm inside.

"Baby boy, looks like we're all ready," Reese said as he walked up behind Mike.

"I think we are. I can't wait for the guys to get here to see what we have done."

"You mean what you've done." They both stood mesmerized by the tree.

"It's getting close to the time for your gift," Reese said as he looked at Mike cradling his waist with one arm.

"Where is it?" Mike smiled holding out his hand with his eyes closed.

"Sounds like it's driving up right now."

"Driving up? Say what?" Mike said opening his eyes.

"You'll see." The door bell rang. "Answer that. Merry Christmas!"

"Okay, but who is it?" Mike asked as he walked over to the door and opened it.

Reese crossed his arm across his chest, "Would you just

open the door, boy?"

Mike obeyed. He was flabbergasted. He felt a flood of anger, surprise, confusion, joy, and happiness. Mike said nothing, he merely stepped aside and ushered his father in. "What…are you doing here?" Mike finally asked.

"Can't a father visit his only son?" Mike just stood there, in silence.

"Come in, Mr. Green," Reese said as he looked at Mike and closed the door.

"Nice to see you again. Thanks again for inviting me over," Mr. Green said as he shook Reese's hand.

Mr. Green walked over and gave Mike a hug, but he didn't hug him back.

Feeling his son's apprehension, he took a step back and looked at him, "Son, I am so sorry. I hope you can forgive an old fool." Mike was numb. "Do you mind if I sit down, my arthritis is acting up today?" Mr. Green asked.

"Sure, Mr. Green, excuse our manners. Come in and have a seat," Reese offered.

"Thank you, son," he said as he looked at Reese.

"You're welcome, sir," Reese said as he walked over and grabbed Mike's arm.

"Mr. Green, excuse us for a second," Reese said as he tugged Mike as he led him to the kitchen. "Baby, if you want, I can ask your father to come back another time or you can go in there and see if you and your father can fix your relationship."

"I don't know what to do, Reese. I am so damn mad at that man in there," Mike said, hitting the counter.

"I know, baby boy, but he is your father. Do you want your father to leave here and God forbid something happens? Can you live with that? I wish I had gotten a second

chance. Talk to you father, baby boy. Talk to him."
Mike desperately wanted to be any place but there, but he knew Reese was right.

"Okay, I will! I will!" Mike agreed reluctantly and leisurely paced into the living room.

"Hold up, baby." Reese put his arms around Mike and gave him a tight hug and kissed him on the cheek. "Don't worry I will be right here if you need me."

Mike took a deep breath and walked into the living room. His father sat staring into the fireplace. Mr. Green turned to find his son standing beside him. Mike looked in his father's face and could see how much his father had aged. His father had a sadness in his eyes that Mike didn't recognize.

"Son," he said as he walked slowly over to the sofa to sit back down. Mike walked over and sat next to his father.

"I know this has to be hard for you, son, but can you find it in your heart to forgive me?" Mr. Green turned his head to the floor as he spoke, "You know losing your mother was very hard for me. She was my world son, my heart, my everything. I don't think that I will ever get over losing her. I miss her so much. I know she wouldn't want us to live the rest of our lives not speaking and not being father and son."

That's exactly how Moms was. Mike smiled as he thought out loud.

Mr. Green turned his gaze back to Mike, "I want us to be father and son again. That is, if you can forgive an old fool like me. I would like to start today if you will let me. When your friend Reese called to invite me, I wasn't sure if I should come. I thought you might still hate me. The one thing that made me come was your friend telling me that this would be a perfect time for healing. I only have one son and being apart from you has been almost as bad as losing your mother."

Mike turned and looked at his father, then quickly turned away and looked back at him again. Mike's water filled eyes were a dictionary of emotions. This was the day that Mike had finally hoped for and he was at a lost for words.

"Son, I'm ready if you are." His father reached into his pocket.

"I want to give you this. Your mom and I picked it out a few days before she died. We had decided we were going to come and see you that weekend and ask for your forgiveness." Mr. Green extended his hand to give him the box. Mike just stared at the box and then at his farther. He took the box and held it for a second. Looking back at his father, Mike slowly unwrapped the box. In side the box was a diamond pendant that read *Number One Son*. Mike sat motionless staring at the pendant. He looked up at his father.

"I'm ready, Pop," Mike said embracing his father.

"I love you, son and I have missed you so much. I'm so sorry."

"I love you too, Pop." Reese came out of the kitchen, figuring he had given Mike and his father enough time to work things out. Mike looked up and saw Reese as he stood in the doorway. He walked away from his father and over to Reese.

"This is the best gift you could have ever given me."

"Merry Christmas, baby boy! Merry Christmas!"

Mike grabbed Reese by the hand and formally introduced him to his father.

"Dad, this is my man," Mike said, as he looked at Reese with a big smile. "Reese, this is my Pops."

"Mike needs you in his life sir, he needs his father."

"Thank you, son. You're a good man."

As Reese and Mr. Green embraced warmly the doorbell suddenly rang. Mike walked in with the guys close behind. They all came in embracing each other. Mike's father watched from the sofa seeing and truly understanding the love the guys share. He felt embarrassed by the way he had treated Mike and his friends the day at his wife's service. Jay walked from the group to greet Mr. Green with a warm smile.

"Hi, Mr. Green. I'm Jay," he said with a big smile on his face. Jay introduced all the guys one by one each one gave Mr. Green a hug.

Jay turned to Mr. Green, "We were hoping that you would come. Reese filled us in. We're all glad you're here, now you can get to know your eight sons, here to look out for you."

Mike's dad began to smile, "Wow, eight sons. --What do you mean?"

"See Dad, these are all my brothers," Mike said. Mr. Green now got the meaning. All of the men before him had become one family. Looking at them warmed his heart.

Mike looked at Reese and then at his father, "Dad, Reese, that's MY MAN." Reese waved smiling once again. "And these are MY BOYZ."

Read the First Chapter for The Sequel:

My Man, My Boyz
(Our Future)

COMING SOON

Chapter 1

The guys were at Tyrell's house the night before toasting the New Year happily with champagne. The past year had been filled with sorrow and happiness. Everyone was glad to see it go. Chuck woke with a taste of alcohol in his mouth, as if he had been up drinking all night. Beep! Beep! Beep! The sound of the horn blowing outside wouldn't allow him to go back to sleep.

I should have eaten something before drinking, he thought. He moaned all the way to the bathroom, his head spinning as he bent to turn the knob for the shower. My God, this water feels good. I could stay in here all day, he thought. Finally stepping out of the shower, he quickly grabbed for the bottle of aspirin that sat on the counter. The scent of Tyrell's bacon crept into the bathroom. Lazily, Chuck brushed his teeth then walked back into the bedroom.

Chuck looked around the bedroom and thought how glad he was that he finally moved out of the halfway house and in with Tyrell. No bathroom to share with a bunch of guys. No worries about the noises from the other guys that lived in the adjoining rooms. Chuck finally made his way downstairs.

"Happy New Year, baby," Tyrell said as he saw Chuck's crooked smile.

"Happy New Year to you, too," Chuck managed to get out.

"Are you feeling okay," Tyrell asked.

"Slightly hung over but I'll live. I should have eaten something."

"Was it not I who told you to eat something?" Tyrell said.

"Yeah, baby, you did and I should have listened," Chuck said as he sat slowly.

"Let me fix you a cup of coffee," Tyrell offered.

"Oh baby, thank you, thank you and I'll have a few slices of that bacon," Chuck said holding his head, "How did you sleep last night?"

"Slept like a baby," Tyrell said as he walked over and sat a plate of bacon and cup of coffee in front of Chuck."

Tyrell Smiled, "So what did you want to do today?"

"How 'bout we catch a movie" Chuck suggested as he sipped his coffee.

"Do you feel well enough to catch a movie?"

"I'll be fine. I took a couple of aspirin upstairs and the shower helped."

"What is there to see?" Tyrell asked as he sat down across from Chuck.

"We can check the paper," Chuck said as he got up and headed to the front door.

Tyrell watched Chuck walk away and thought to himself, *my baby looks good in the sweats I bought him for Christmas.*

Chuck opened the door and was greeted by the cold wind. He grabbed the newspaper and quickly closed the door.

"It's chilly out there, ain't it?" Tyrell yelled from the kitchen.

Chuck headed toward the kitchen and immediately stopped in his tracks. A puzzled look crossed his face when he noticed the only part of the paper delivered was the obituary section. *What the fuck?* Chuck thought.

Tyrell called out to Chuck, but got no answer. Entering the living room Tyrell noticed Chuck had plopped down on the sofa.

2

"What's up man? Chuck, do you hear me talking to you?" Tyrell said as he sat next to Chuck on the sofa. Chuck tried to hide the newspaper from Tyrell.

"What's in the paper that got you so quiet all of a sudden?" Tyrell asked as he grabbed for it. "Baby, these are the obituaries, what did you do with the rest of it?"

The look on Chuck's face told him all he needed to know. Tyrell tried not to show his fear. The last thing he needed was for Chuck to do something stupid.

"This shit has got to stop," Chuck said as he jumped up.

"Do you want some more coffee?" Tyrell headed back to the kitchen with Chuck right on his heels.

"Don't try to distract me, Tyrell. That shit ain't going to work this time. We need to find out who the hell is doing this," Chuck said shaking the paper in his hand.

Tyrell looked down at the floor deep in thought. Then he looked at Chuck. Tyrell snapped his finger.

"Baby, I have an idea!"

"Alright what's up?" Chuck asked impatiently.

"Give me one second…" Tyrell replied. Tyrell walked over to the telephone and dialed Reese and Mike's number. The phone rang eventually going to voice mail.

"Hey guys it's me, Tyrell, I'd hoped to catch you at home. I wanted to know if I could borrow your camcorder. Give me a call on my cell. Chuck and I may already be out."

"What you need a camcorder for?" Chuck asked. "You want to tell me what's going on in that head of yours?"

"I can get Reese's and Mike's camcorder. We can set it up somewhere in the front of the house and maybe catch whoever is doing this on film."

"Damn baby!" Chuck spit out, "Let me find out a brutha going CSI on me and shit."

Tyrell laughed, "I just know I need to take care of this quick, before you lose your mind and hurt somebody."

3

"Man, I will go straight hood on anybody that tries to hurt my niggah. The police better get this muthafucker before I do," Chuck said as he stormed out of the room.

Tyrell watched him leave and thought, *Lord, let the police get this person before he does.*

Chuck and Tyrell were making the bed when the phone rang.

Tyrell answered, "Hello." The look on Tyrell's face told Chuck who it was.

Tyrell, now past irritated hissed, "I know who you are and if its games you want to play, it games that you're going to get." Tyrell slammed the phone on the cradle without turning. Feeling Chuck's eyes on his back he gathered his composure and turned around to face Chuck.

"So you know who it is?" Chuck joked.
Tyrell could only laugh, "Naw, but the caller doesn't know that." Tyrell was glad that Chuck had calmed down a little even though he knew Chuck did it to help him relax.

"Baby, let me ask you..." Chuck paused in mid thought. "We know that whoever is calling you has your work and home number and that they know where you live."

"Right, so what are you getting at?" Tyrell asked as he leaned up against the wall.

Chuck now in detective mode asked, "When you changed your home number, you only got the calls at work. Now they have started back up here at the house. So who do you remember giving your number to?"

Tyrell stared through Chuck as he made a mental list. "I gave it to all the guys of course and to Ms. Reed my next door neighbor."

"Well," Chuck replied, "we know it ain't none of the guys."
Tyrell chuckled, "Well, we know it can't be Ms. Reed."
"And why can't it be?" Chuck asked tilting his head.
"Come on, baby, why would that little old lady do that. Plus I've know her for years."

4

"Yeah, but do you really ever know your neighbors?" As far as I'm concerned she's at the top of the list. Who else did you give your number too?"

"Coworkers and that's it."

"Ty, the camcorder idea is a good one, but we don't know when we might hear back from Reese and Mike. So why don't we stop by that electronic shop across town and pick up a spy cam. We can wrap it in the wreath on the door. Plus, I think that would be easier to hide."

"That's a good idea man," Tyrell said with assurance.

∗   ∗   ∗

Early the next morning, Mike and Reese lay in the bed watching the Lifetime network. Mike lay on his side with Reese spooned up behind him. Reese looked over at the answering machine and saw the blinking light.

"Did you hear the phone ring this morning, baby boy?" Reese asked.

"No, I didn't, but check the message. It may be important," Mike suggested.

Reese got out of the bed, and walked toward the answering machine scratching the top of his curly head. As he pushed the button he let out a yarn and stretched. The message on the machine was from Tyrell, from the day before. Mike, turned over in the bed and looked over at Reese.

"Why does Tyrell need the camcorder."

"Maybe he and Chuck want to make movies," Reese replied in a loud laugh.

Reese ran over and jumped in the bed on top of Mike, kissing him playfully. "Maybe we can make a movie of our own one day to look back on."

5

"Hmm. How 'bout we do a dry run right now and then if you ever try to leave me, I can use that against you." Mike laughed amused with himself.

"On second thought, maybe we better skip the camera." They both broke out in laughter. Reese reached over and started to tickle Mike.

"You're going to do what? You're going to do what?"

"Stop baby! Stop baby!" Mike managed to get out between laughs. "I was joking, I was joking."

"Who's your daddy? Tell me, who's your daddy?" Reese asked.

"You baby! You baby! Stop tickling me!"

Reese stopped and looked Mike in the eyes. "Baby, I really love you and, I don't know where I would be without you."

Mike rubbed his fingers through Reese's curly hair, "I love you too, man and you need a hair cut." Mike kissed him softly and playfully bit Reese's lip. "Now get your heavy butt off me." Mike said.

"I'm not that heavy," Reese said as he rolled over, "but you're right, I do need a haircut. I need to get up, baby, and take a shower. I need to go and hit the gym. I'll grab the camcorder and drop it off to Tyrell's."

"It's New Year's Day, don't they give you a day off?" Mike asked.

"Nope. The NFL never rests, but the season is almost over."

"Well, I'll be right here in bed waiting for you when you get back," Mike said.

"You promise?" Reese asked as he through Mike a seductive wink.

"I promise."

Reese finally dressed. "Baby, I'm going to run downstairs and fix something quick to eat. Are you hungry?"

"A little. Whatever you make for yourself make for me, too."

Reese came back up stairs with a sandwich for Mike. "Here

you go, baby."

"Thanks, what is it?" Mike asked.

"It's your favorite."

"My favorite?" Mike asked

"It's a bacon sandwich," Reese said taking a bite, "Well Baby, I got to run." Reese gobbled down his sandwich.

"Okay, see you later and don't forget to get the camcorder out the other room," Mike reminded him.

"I won't."

Reese grabbed his coat from the closet and headed to his car. Sitting in the car, he rubbed his hands together to keep them warm.

Turning the knob on the radio he thought, "Why does my baby keep changing my CD's?" Reese decided to drive over to Tyrell's house before going to the gym. He didn't want to take the chance of leaving the camcorder in the car while he was working out.

After a 15 minute drive, Reese pulled up to Tyrell's house and saw the cars in the driveway. He grabbed his cell phone, dialed Tyrell but it went straight to voice mail.

Reese headed for the door to ring the bell. He noticed some movement on Tyrell's porch as he got closer. It was someone he didn't recognize. Quickly he walked toward the stranger.

"Hey man, you need some help?" Reese shouted. Turning at the sound of Reese's voice the stranger dropped a can of paint, spilling it all over the porch.

"What are you doing with that paint, man?" Reese asked.

The stranger came at Reese. Reese dropped the camcorder then quickly grabbed the stranger's arm. The stranger swung. Reese pushed the small framed guy to the ground. He jumped up and swung again at Reese. Reese ducked, and punched him in the face.

One of the neighbors saw the scuffle going on and called the police. Minutes later a squad car pulled up. The stranger tried to

7

run, but Reese caught him by the leg. Two officers jumped out the car. The officer from the passenger side pulled his weapon.

"Freeze or I'll shoot!" he ordered.

Reese let go of the stranger and raised his hands. The stranger followed suit. The other officer handcuffed them both. He immediately put the stranger into the squad car. The officer had called for another car for Reese.

The officers walked into the precinct with Reese and the stranger in handcuffs. "You guys have a seat...and behave."

Reese sat across from the stranger. Reese looked at him, shaking his head.

"What the fuck is your problem brutha?!" Reese spat out.

"You the one with the problem, man."

"Both you guys need to shut your mouth," the officer said, "before I lock you both up."

Reese looked at the officer, "Can I make my phone call please?"

"You'll get your phone call, man. Don't worry."

Mike was worried. He looked at his watch again. It was late in the evening and he hadn't heard from Reese. He walked over to the phone and called Reese's cell but got no answer. He must be over at Tyrell's house and I bet they are in the basement, where you can't get any service. Mike hung up the phone and dialed Tyrell's home number.

"Hello?" Tyrell said half sleep.

"'Sup Ty, sounds like you sleep."

"Chuck and I took it easy today, watched some movies and chilled. What's up with you?" Tyrell asked.

"Have you seen Reese today? He was supposed to come over and drop the camcorder over to you."

"Oh damn, man, I forgot I called you guys about that, but no, I haven't seen Reese nor have I heard from him. Chuck and I were upstairs in the bedroom, so he could have come by without us hearing him ring the doorbell or knock."

8

"Okay, but I'm a little worried. It's not like Reese not to call. Hold on for a second. My phone is beeping"

"Hello," Mike said."

"Hey baby, it's me."

"You had me worried. Where are you?" Mike said, feeling relieved.

"I've been arrested."

"Arrested! What do you mean?"

"I went to drop the camcorder over at Tyrell's house and some guy was on his porch and shredding his paper. I tried to see what was going on. The guy started a fight. I guess someone called the police. Now they have arrested me, 'cause the guy said that I attacked him for no reason."

"Baby, I got Tyrell on the line and we are on our way. I love you."

"I love you too, man. Hurry and get me out of here please. Oh yeah, let Tyrell know the camcorder is in his yard. After all the confusion, I forgot about it."

Mike disconnected the call. "Hello, Tyrell. That was Reese."

"Good. Is he okay?"

"No he's in jail."

"In jail? What do you mean?"

"He told me the camcorder is in your yard. He came by to drop it off." He saw some guy on your porch and he said something about a shredded paper on your porch."

Tyrell walked toward the front door, opened it, and saw the shredded newspaper. A few feet away, he saw the camcorder lying on its side."

"Mike, I see the camcorder and newspaper. Chuck and I will meet you at the station." As Mike and Tyrell ended the call, Mike ran upstairs grabbed his coat and check book.   While Mike looked for his checkbook, his cell phone rang again.

"Hello," Mike said, frazzled.

"Hey, Mike this is Jay. What's up?"

"I can't talk right, now."

"What's wrong?" Jay detected the concern in Mike's voice.

"I'll have to fill you in later." Jay, insisted that Mike tell him now.

"Jay, I can't talk, Reese has been arrested and I'm on my way to the station.

"I'll meet you there," Jay said. "Are the guys going to be there?"

"Chuck and Tyrell will meet me there," Mike explained.

"So will I," Jay added.

"Okay. I'll see you there."

Jay pulled into the parking lot of the police station. He dashed inside the jail to find out what was going on with his boy. Frantically, he walked up to the desk. He saw Reese sitting on a bench, handcuffed. Jay made a u-turn to where Reese sat.

"Reese, what happened?"

The police officer stepped in, "Excuse me sir, but you will have to wait. This defendant has to be questioned."

"Questioned for what?" Jay asked. Jay's protective mode kicked in. "Who's in charge here? I need to talk to someone in charge." Seconds, later Mike walked in and saw Reese handcuffed and Jay at the front desk.

Mike walked toward Reese. "Excuse me," the police officer said, "but you can't talk to him right now. We have to finish processing him." A few feet away, Reese noticed a distinguished gentleman with glasses hanging halfway off his nose. The gentleman watched the scene with curious attention.

"Excuse me sir," the gentleman said to Reese, "You're Reese Rogers, you play for the Houston Bullets?" Reese shook his head.

"My name is Dirk Parks and I work with the Houston Chronicle."

Shit, Reese thought. Meanwhile Mike and Jay were off in a corner getting cleared on the details.

Jay was furious, "So who is this niggah that fucked with my boy?"

Chuck and Tyrell walked in the door, with Tariff and Demetrious.

"Where's Reese?" Tariff asked.

"They have him handcuffed over there like a common criminal."

Mike looked at Demetrious. "Can you calm Jay down, while I try to figure this nightmare out?"

"Sure, man. I got it," Demetrious responded. Demetrious immediately walked over and tapped Jay. "Let's go get these guys a soda or something," Demetrious said, that being the first thing to come to his mind.

Jay, with his keen intuition, immediately yelled, "You guys trying to get rid of me?"

"Naw, man they got this," Tariff said. Jay hesitated for a second then went willingly.

"Hey guys, we will be back, I mean right back," Jay said firmly.

Chuck and Tyrell started to explain to the officer the problems that Tyrell had been having. Mike listened. The police officer finally spoke, "I understand what you're saying sir, but right now it's your buddy's word against his. We don't know who to believe."

"Officer, can we at least talk to Reese before you take him back?" Mike asked.

Chuck, Tyrell, Mike and Tariff listened to Reese as he filled them in.

"Guys, you got to get me out of here. If the press gets a hold of this I could be ruined."

Chuck looked at the guys, "Listen. I got a hunch. I got to run out, but I will be right back." Tyrell looked at Reese and shrugged his shoulders.

The officer brought the stranger out to finish his processing.

11

Reese nodded toward him to clue the guys in. Demetrious and Jay walked back into the area where the guys were. Demetrious and Jay noticed that all the guys were looking at the stranger.

"What's going on?" Jay asked.

"That's the guy Reese got into a fight with," Mike said.   Jay started to walk toward the guy and Demetrious grabbed Jay's arm.

"Chill out, man. Chill out. We don't need to be trying to get you out of here too," Demetrious said.

Mike looked at Tyrell. "Do you know that guy?"

Tyrell shrugged his shoulders, "He doesn't mean anything to me."

"Do you think Chuck might know him? Tariff asked.

Tyrell responded, "I don't know."

Tariff noticed Mr. Parks glance toward their direction as he sat writing feverishly in a note pad. After twenty minutes or so Chuck walked in. He looked at Tyrell then walked over to the officer. He handed the officer the spy cam that he and Tyrell had stuck inside the wreath.

"Officer, I think if you look at this, it will clear all this mess up," Chuck explained.

Tyrell motioned for Chuck.

"Hey baby," Tyrell whispered in his ear, "that's the guy that was ripping my paper. Does he look familiar to you?"

Chuck took a look. He didn't recognize him either.

Tyrell turned to hear a familiar voice calling his name. As Tyrell turned he saw Ms. Reed.

"Ms. Reed," Tyrell addressed her, "what are you doing here?"

"My grandson has got into some trouble and called me."

"Your grandson?" Tyrell responded.

"I'm on a fixed income and he has been staying with me to help me out with bills, but I couldn't tell anyone 'cause if the state found out, they would cut my check."

Tyrell and Chuck looked at each other in amazement. "Ms.

Reed," Tyrell asked as he pointed, "is that your grandson over there?"

Ms. Reed turned to look, "That's him. That's him right there."

"Ms Reed, your grandson was arrested for fighting my best friend here."

"There's got to be some mistake. Why would my grandson be fighting him?"

By this time the officer came over and uncuffed Reese.

"Sir, you're free to go, sorry about all the confusion."

"What about my grandson?" Ms. Reed asked with much concern.

The police officer lifted up the microchip.

"This film shows your grandson shredding this man's paper and throwing paint. It also shows him initiating a fight with this gentleman as well," the officer said as he pointed to Reese.

The other police officer grabbed the defendant and took him to the back.

Ms. Reed looked at her grandson, "Why would you do this to this man?"

"Grandma, they're gay, they're all gay. I saw them through the window kissing."

Jay stepped up, "So what the hell does that have to do with you?"

"You guys are sick, you're all sick. You disgust me." the grandson said through clinched teeth.

Tyrell looked down and then looked at him. "How did you get my phone numbers?"

The grandson looked at the guys with anger, "I got it off the piece of paper on my grandmother's refrigerator."

"Take him back," the officer said, "take this piece of trash back and book him."

With downcast eyes, Ms. Reed apologized to everyone, "I am so sorry for the trouble he has caused." She looked at her grandson, shook her head, and walked out.

Reese stood up, massaging his wrist to ease the discomfort he felt from the handcuffs and watched Mr. Park as he rushed out of the police station. Mike looked at Reese. "Let's go home and put this all behind us."

Reese stared in the direction of the door and shook his head, "Baby boy this is not over. It's just beginning."